The
DISASSEMBLY
of
DOREEN DURAND

The
DISASSEMBLY
of
DOREEN DURAND

RYAN COLLETT

SANDSTONE PRESS

First published in Great Britain in 2021 by
Sandstone Press Ltd
PO Box 41
Muir of Ord
IV6 7YX
Scotland

www.sandstonepress.com

ISBN: 978-1-913207-39-7
ISBNe: 978-1-913207-40-3

Sandstone Press is committed to a sustainable future. This book
is made from Forest Stewardship Council ® certified paper.

FSC
MIX
Paper from
responsible sources
FSC® C018072

Cover design by Nathan Burton
Typeset by Iolaire, Newtonmore
Printed and bound in Great Britain by Clays Ltd, Elcograf S.p.A

For Mom

For Mum

PART ONE

PORTLAND

CHAPTER 1

A bird was trying to build a nest on top of the light outside Doreen's apartment. It had been trying for the past two days. On the second day, she went to see what was making that tapping and scuttling sound at her door. It was a swishing sound like wind, with little knocks up along the wall like trilling fingernails. She swung open the door but there was nothing there, just a few pieces of straw and dirt on the ground.

A metal lampshade covered the porch light on the wall. A bird would have a difficult time building a nest on its rounded top even without a human coming outside and interrupting its work. This particular bird watched from across the parking lot as Doreen looked around, puzzled, squinting up at the sun – the sun which was refusing to move from the center of the sky even this late in the afternoon. Two children in the parking lot stopped on their scooters to watch the bird and watch Doreen. They looked back and forth, from Doreen to the bird, as if this were the most authentic wildlife they'd get to see all day. They were boys, three and seven. Neither of them wore shoes or helmets and only one had on a shirt – the uniform for a hot, seemingly endless summer afternoon.

Doreen gave the boys a look, as if they had been the ones making the noises at her door. One of them smiled and waved at her as if he knew her, but she had already turned around and gone inside in a huff.

The kids were too far away to be the culprits. Her apartment was one floor up from the parking lot and there were a set of stairs and a wrap-around balcony the boys would have had to sprint up and down in order to play a prank on her, but she lobbed the accusation at them anyway since kids were made for that sort of thing. Doorbell ditching – that's what they were doing. The old standard. Even though there were easier, more satisfying ways for kids to pick on a neighbor these days if they really wanted to.

The bird made a second attempt right when Doreen was back inside. *Swish*, it went across the parking lot, diving through the still air. It already had more building material stuffed in its beak – perfect curls of dried grass. It wasn't the brightest bird that had ever lived, but it was one of the more determined. Biologically-speaking, it was operating on a dysfunctional calendar and if a potential mate bothered to stop by this late in the season, and if they had low enough standards to be impressed by a precarious nest on top of a wall lamp at an old apartment complex, then they would surely be turned off by the bird's blatant desperation.

'Careful, that's a commitment for life,' a friend at work had said to Doreen that morning. Not an actual friend, per se, but a person who was friendly with Doreen. But you wouldn't say that would you – a person who was friendly with Doreen, as if Doreen was not someone to be friendly with.

'If it's a dove, it'll come back to that same place and build a nest there every single year. Is it a dove?'

'It's probably a pigeon.'

'Pigeons are just less glamorous doves.'

'I think it's just the neighborhood kids throwing shit at my door,' said Doreen – neighborhood being synonymous here with apartment complex.

'Well, if it's a dove, you gotta act fast.'

So Doreen acted fast. The bird swooped in for its second

attempt and immediately when she heard the rushing and tapping sounds, she flung open the door. Again, there was nothing there. No one. And on the cement floor: more dried grass, more dirt, a bottle cap. The two boys were still down in the parking lot, gawking up at her.

'Stop throwing stuff at my door!' she yelled down at them.

The boys froze. The older one pointed over to the mailbox on the corner of the lot.

'It's the bird!' the boy said.

And there it was. The bird was perched there like a third brother in this little trio, its head tilted and twitching impatiently.

'He's trying to build a nest!'

Doreen threw up her hands. Bird, human child, whatever, she thought. She had had enough of both. She kicked away the debris on the ground and looked up at the porch light on the wall. A small cake of dried grass was stacked on top of it: the precarious beginnings of a home.

She reached up and twisted the lampshade. The barely-there nest fell off in a clump of dirt and broke apart when it hit the ground. She continued twisting the lamp all the way upside down so now the round metal top was on the bottom and the glass, circular hole was on top. Anything the bird tried to put there now would fall into the glass cup to the light bulb and be unreachable.

Everyone watching this little scene felt a kind of defeatist thump around their shoulders when Doreen enacted this easy solution. Even she, who went back inside and slammed the door again, empathized with the heartbreak that was abundant but inevitable in the animal kingdom. If it wasn't this, it was a confused whale washing up on a beach, a lion killing its own cub, a battered baby seal, that sort of thing.

* * *

5

The arrival of the bird was yet another home improvement battle joining the litany of things that had gone wrong in Doreen Durand's apartment since her roommate, Whitney, had disappeared. There was the chronically clogging toilet, the moldy smell in the washing machine, the strange rust forming in the bathtub, and the series of explicit prank phone calls, all of them haunting her, sometimes simultaneously, ruining her days. Whitney had up and left and all of these things had cropped up in the two months since, as if she had been the one holding them at bay.

'I mean, I'm sorry, but what do you want me to do? Not get a job and be successful?' Whitney had said cruelly, but in a tone that could be defended as satirical if it cut too deep. She had packed her bags one whole hour after telling Doreen she would be leaving for California the next day. Doreen had stood against the wall and watched as her roommate deconstructed the apartment in a matter of minutes, filling three suitcases with what had been their shared home for almost a year.

'It's just an internship though, right?' asked Doreen. 'You'll be back?'

'It's an internship, part-time-to-full-time, half-job type of thing, you know? It's not a Job-job, but it's the starting point for one. They call it an internship on paper. It's creative. Not structured. Everything's like that now. Come on, you know how it is. These things move fast. What were you expecting?'

'So you'll be back?' Doreen asked again.

'I mean. I dunno. Probably not. No.' Whitney shot this out, looking down at something, anything, on her phone, while Doreen stood there puzzled and shocked.

Whitney was a friend (and not just a person-who-was-friendly-with-Doreen), but more importantly, she was the leaseholder. Doreen had moved in with her nearly halfway into a two-year lease agreement, so her name was listed on nothing, it was all Whitney's. Even Doreen's parking spot was registered and listed under Whitney's name.

Whitney assured her that she would keep up her portion of the rent until the lease was up in four months, then after that, Doreen could renew it herself in her name, or do something else, or 'I don't know. Move? Go somewhere else? I mean, you don't really want to stay here another year do you? Does Mario's pay you enough to handle the full rent?'

Doreen retreated to her room.

To her own financial detriment, she hadn't said much else to Whitney in those last few hours of having her in the apartment – and she should have because by the next morning, nearly everything in the apartment was gone. The photos on the fridge, the coffee table books, the Nutriblender, the TV, the trendy chrome lamp that had hung in the living room, even a candle, all of it was gone.

Had a moving van come in the middle of the night? Doreen wondered. She hadn't heard anything. She couldn't remember getting a full night's sleep but somehow she had woken up and everything had disappeared. The things had all been Whitney's things, for sure, but Doreen had not been prepared for what their sudden absence would look like. Ownership aside, this was her home too, but now the rug in the living room was gone, even the shower curtain was gone. Everything in Whitney's bedroom, understandably, was gone, only a bare mattress was left. The closets were empty. The hair drier, the spider plant, the make-up mirror were gone. All of the kitchen gadgets were gone. There were no plates, spoons, or forks.

'That makes sense. I remember those days, internship-hopping.' This was what the person at work who was friendly with Doreen had said, practically unsolicited. 'When an opportunity comes, you just have to go for it. You have to establish yourself, then worry about who you're spending your time with. I wouldn't say she's necessarily cutting you out of her life, maybe just moving up.'

'I didn't say she was cutting me out of her life,' Doreen said with an air of annoyance. 'The real issue here is how I'm going to cover the rent on my own.'

'I thought you said she was going to keep paying her half until the lease was up?'

'I – you're right, I did. Sorry. Yeah, the rent isn't an issue then.'

Doreen was flustered. What was the issue?

There wasn't one, she reassured herself over the coming weeks. It was just the way people – people too friendly at work – prodded her with small talk and how it seemed to pry her open too easily, revealing nothing tender and normal, nothing she could easily mask with a funny anecdote about her roommate, about a trip they had once taken together, spur of the moment, about how that was just how her roommate was, how she was bound to run off to California at some point and leave her on her own. But nothing Doreen said sounded normal now. She was twenty-seven years old and without the subject of a roommate to deflect to, small talk only seemed to yield bigger and bigger questions. Throwing an easy 'Not bad' to someone asking about her weekend required a level of compartmentalization Doreen found that she increasingly did not have. There had been a sudden erasure of a counterbalance. Something was off, and maybe it always had been.

In a more tangible way, the full weight of Whitney's absence was manifest in unforeseen water and utility bills that Doreen now had to pay by herself. It was true that Whitney had agreed to pay her half the rent until the end of the lease, but it was understandable for her to no longer pay any of the other bills as she was no longer there. Still, it was an annoyance for Doreen to see this full cost hit her credit card without warning. She thought of texting Whitney something passive-aggressive: 'Hey, just got the full water bill. Anything else I should expect?' but thought better of it.

She's gone, the bills are mine to pay. These are obvious things, Doreen thought.

Instead of passive-aggression, she deferred to compassion – that would be something normal to do. She decided to ask Whitney how she was doing, if she had found a new apartment in the far-off sunny place she had disappeared to, if she was liking the new internship. She took out her phone to send a text but struggled to word a sentence. She scrolled up and read their last set of exchanged messages – a simple back-and-forth figuring out what time the other would be home. Texting 'How are you doing?' felt suddenly out-of-character. She scrolled further up but found only more mundane texts: asking if the other was home and could check on something, sharing flight details of visiting family members, asking if they were out of milk, tea, bananas, if a package had arrived. Not once had either of the women asked each other a personal question. If one of them ever had – and Doreen couldn't remember a time now – they certainly had never done so via text.

Ultimately, it wasn't that Doreen missed Whitney – she really didn't – but she was curious to see the gains she had made in Figuring It Out. This sudden Advancement. Achievement. Whitney had vaporized off into this nameless, ambiguous way ahead like it was something she had squirreled away for herself, only telling Doreen about it at the last minute as if there were the risk she would snatch it out from under her. This was the primary source of Doreen's curiosity.

She gave up on the text and turned to the post-communication methods at her disposal on the internet, but saw only what Whitney had always carefully curated: inspirational quotes, photos of her face, and one new photo of a cityscape with a vague caption about new beginnings; nothing about where she was working, how much money she was making, who she was living with, where she saw herself in five years. Doreen turned it all off.

The first weekend after Whitney left, a man showed up at the apartment unannounced. He knocked on the door too many times in a row, then rang the doorbell. Doreen ignored it at first – slightly scared, but also sleepily negligent – but when he drilled one more ungodly time on the doorbell, she pushed her hair around into something not haphazard, slipped on a pair of sweatpants, and answered it.

'Whitney, right?' said an older, grizzled man. He wore a stained t-shirt that wrapped too-tight around his globe of a gut and extended a callused hand in greeting. 'I'm Jack.'

'Sorry, no,' said Doreen, not saying her name and not taking his hand.

'I'm here for the couch.'

'The couch? What?'

'You must be the roommate. Whitney gave me the address. I'm here for the couch you girls were selling.'

Doreen looked over her shoulder at the sofa in the living room, one of the few things Whitney had left. There was the sofa, a coffee table, an empty TV stand, and not much else. 'I didn't know she was selling it,' Doreen said to the sofa. Jack craned his neck to try to see around her.

'I'm sorry, I don't want to cause a fuss,' he said. 'She posted an ad for the couch the other day. I said I was interested and we made a deal over email. I already sent her a hundred bucks

– pretty good deal for a couch that nice. She said this morning would be a good time to pick it up. She said you might be the only one here, but it was fine to stop by.'

'Right,' said Doreen. She picked at nothing behind her ear and squinted at the man. 'I guess, yeah, you have to take it. Sure.'

Jack called down to a younger man who had been waiting in a pickup truck in the parking lot and the two of them came inside, thudding across the living room carpet in heavy, dusty boots, Saturday-sweaty. They lifted the long sofa, but struggled to shimmy it out the front door. The apartment was built in the seventies – Whitney said she had had to sign a waiver about lead paint or something – and its age showed whenever furniture was moved around like this. The floor creaked, the walls were too easily scuffed. The wood around the doorframe might as well have been made of fabric and seemed to stretch around the sofa squeezing through.

'That's it. There we go,' said Jack. They marched it down to the pickup and threw it in the back. After they had it secured, Jack turned and nodded a mannish goodbye up at Doreen on the balcony, who shrugged and went back inside.

A brighter rectangle of carpet remained where the couch had been. Whitney had bought it, so she had sold it. That was it. Logic, running its course around Doreen like a river running dry.

What else had she bought? Doreen paced around and took inventory of all the things in her life that were not her own and could also vanish without warning. It was true, she hadn't bought any of the furniture in the apartment – Whitney had been living there for almost a year before she came along – but the sudden removal was still jarring. For a minute, it felt like her life was being uprooted without her, but that was followed quickly by the realization that these roots were never hers to begin with.

This scene repeated itself all weekend and the following weekend as well. With no warning, strangers showed up at the apartment asking for Whitney, explaining the transaction they had made and requesting entry. One after the other, the coffee table, the TV stand, the kitchen table and chairs, the decorative poufs, a mirror – all disappeared, taken away by strangers – men and women of varying ages and degrees of inclination towards small talk, like ants touring the shell of some dead animal, taking what they needed.

After the second weekend of this, Doreen still hadn't communicated with Whitney. An aggressive-aggressive text message would have been more than appropriate to send by now, but she didn't.

It wasn't that she was actively refusing to communicate – the idea of reaching out, of snidely asking if anyone else would be coming by, just wasn't there to be had. She sat on the carpet in the empty living room alone and did nothing while the dwelling around her disappeared. The trappings of life flew away. Sounds reverberated differently in the emptiness. She had no idea what to do with herself.

She started letting things go. Nothing extraordinary, but little things like letting the few dishes that were left pile up in the sink, leaving wrappers and pop cans on the floor, letting the long black tails of chargers for different electronics dangle out across the living room. It wasn't depression, she thought, it was simply a letting go. A closing. She felt a valve in her mind turn off, and another turn on, leading somewhere else, with some other function entirely. There was a miraculousness to it. She felt weightless. She had read once, in some quasi-self-help, tip-ridden pop-up article, about the importance of letting go – a more dressed-up version of spring cleaning, sponsored by a cleaning company – and how it could clean the mind, reformat the authenticity of life.

Doreen wasn't sure this was what was happening to her, but whatever was happening she allowed it.

She lost track of time. She started to forget things, like turning the lights off in the kitchen or in the living room before bed, leaving them on all night. Other times, she'd spend a whole day forgetting to turn them on, dwelling in the dark. She would run the air conditioner at arctic levels or not at all. She started sleeping at odd times throughout the day, napping all the time. She went to work, then came home and disrobed right in the living room, leaving her clothes on the floor. She dragged Whitney's bare mattress into the living room and fashioned it into a couch, which became a multi-purpose nest as the clutter gathered, until another stranger came and took that away, so then she dragged her own mattress out and never slept in her bedroom again.

After nearly two months of this, like an amoeba left to morph and transform (some might say break down), new household problems cropped up. That strange smell from the laundry machine – maybe it wasn't mold, maybe there was a dead rat behind it, Doreen wondered but did nothing about it – then the rust forming in the tub. The toilet and the kitchen sink continually clogging. These combined dangerously with her new listlessness – outliers that threatened to taint the overall image of her well-being as not one of letting go and living lightly, but one of neglect and mental illness. Objectively speaking, anyone stepping foot in that apartment would see more than a few reasons for concern, but after the strangers stopped coming to take her things away, she was left alone.

The only person who saw the inside of Doreen's apartment now was a delivery boy named Tyler, who caught glimpses of the chaos behind her when she opened the door for her dinner. She had stopped grocery shopping entirely and had taken to ordering in expensive meals every night when she came home from work. Money was another thing she felt herself letting go and she let it fly, ordering the best meals from the best places.

'Sorry, I know it's probably not my place to ask, but are you OK?' Tyler finally asked one evening. He had just dropped off a platter of sushi.

'What do you mean?' said Doreen. She leaned out. Her long hair draped like a privacy curtain between him and the scene behind her. He craned his neck to see past her. He shrugged.

'You're ordering food every night, tipping me way too much money, and – I don't want to be rude – but your apartment looks kind of messed up.'

'Messed up?' Doreen adjusted her jacket. She was still wearing her work clothes on this occasion. She looked professional, with a blue blouse with a high collar, a dark skirt, and a freshly dry-cleaned white jacket. Behind her though, was a nest of blankets, empty take-out boxes covered in crumbs, unopened mail, cords for electronics, silverware, mugs. Also, all of the lights were off and the blinds were closed. Doreen and Tyler were standing in almost total darkness.

'Not messed up,' said Tyler. 'It's just that it doesn't seem healthy to still have your take-out boxes from yesterday and the day before all thrown around back there. It looks like you've just let the trash stay there. And the lights are always off. Did they cut your power or something? Do you have any furniture?'

'How would I have charged my phone and used it to order dinner if I didn't have power?' said Doreen without missing a beat.

Tyler fumbled over himself.

'I'm sorry, I was just saying—'

Doreen leaned back into the living room and turned on the light, the mess behind her lit up in all its glory, then she stepped outside and stood next to Tyler, closing the door behind her. The two of them faced each other, illuminated by the orange glow through the window. Shadows cut across Doreen's diamond-shaped face.

'Is that better?' she asked. 'Now that you can't see it?

'I just wanted to make sure everything was OK,' said Tyler. 'I'm sorry, I shouldn't have said anything.'

'No, you shouldn't have.'

The next evening, when Tyler came back with a bacon cheeseburger, two orders of sweet potato fries, and a strawberry shake from a hip new gastropub, Doreen was standing outside the front door already, waiting for him. The porch light was on this time and the door was closed behind her. She accepted the food, thanked Tyler and stayed standing there until he left. He got on his motorcycle, consulted his phone for his next delivery, and drove off. Once he was out of the complex and Doreen could no longer hear his motorcycle bumbling off into the night, she finally went inside and closed the door. Nothing had appeared out of the ordinary this time except for a small pile of dead grass, dirt, and a bottle cap on the ground, and the porch light itself, which had been twisted upside down.

CHAPTER 2

Doreen was running out of money. The utility bills she now had to pay by herself, not to mention the expensive food she insisted on ordering every night, were beginning to take their toll. In two months, the apartment lease would be up for renewal. If she wanted to stay, she'd have to renew it in her own name and pay each month's rent all by herself, in full, unless she found another roommate, which she didn't want. She didn't know what she wanted, but she knew what she *didn't* want: a roommate, groceries, to sleep in her bedroom instead of the living room, a bird outside her front door.

Whitney had asked if Mario's paid enough for her to cover the rent on her own. It did, technically, but Doreen hadn't made any adjustments in her spending, even as she watched the number in her bank account shave itself down every day. In fact, she had increased her spending, what with the expensive meals delivered every night.

There had to be another way of doing things. There had to be another model. She thought she was onto something, she just needed more time, more leeway. Never had the act of digging oneself into a hole felt more like an act of discovery, excavation, not burial.

Doreen had the potential to be financially stable if she was thrifty enough. Despite the name, Mario's wasn't an Italian restaurant or an auto repair shop or even a high-priced clothing boutique, but a faceless technology company specializing in wireless sensors, and what they paid her for her entry-level position wasn't abysmal. Mario's was the company behind other companies, licensing out their naked technology to larger, more name-recognizable brands. Their wireless sensors were at the forefront of the connected internet – devices that wouldn't normally need to be connected to the internet but were anyway because why not. It was the Internet of Things (a phrase that made Doreen's stomach turn), or at least that was what they called it at the conferences Doreen attended, sitting in the back of the room and sneering. (She hadn't intended to be a sneerer when she first got the job, but no one ever does.) Companies from far and wide called on Mario's to cram wireless connectivity into everything from a hairbrush to a jet engine because it was neat and a thing that seemed to be the next most reasonable course of evolution, at least, for the sake of shareholders. Who wouldn't want a hairbrush that could exist somehow on the internet?

Doreen worked at a Mario's operations hub in a name-less business park in Beaverton, Oregon, spitefully outside Portland. She was one of three hundred people who processed and transmitted orders from buyers to Mario's's blight-of-the-world manufacturing plant in Shenzhen, China. She often spent the day speaking only in numbers. Sometimes, when she was really sick of things, she would type 'Mario's's's's's' in her company emails, amusing no one.

It was the kind of job that made a person want to pull their mattress out into the living room and build a nest.

Doreen detected something sinister in her job. What humanitarian atrocity was she complicit in when she pushed these invisible orders around? What teenager in China was she aiding in the exploitation of? What amount of carbon dioxide was she pouring into the air with every click of her mouse? These were the questions she and her colleagues often joked about when they were away from their desks – only

17

joking because saying anything with a degree of sincerity threatened to lead to true existential trauma and lunch was only thirty minutes.

She often thought of doing something radical – she had majored in political science in college, after all. She daydreamed of making some kind of statement: rallying her coworkers together and sabotaging the order for a defense contractor, hindering the production of a jet or a rocket by just a few days sure, but maybe far down the chain, saving someone's life in Yemen or Iraq or Sudan or wherever. Or maybe she'd just steal a bunch of money. She knew how she would do it, which company account she'd use, how she'd set up a fake bank account and charge a bogus invoice to it, connect that with her own bank account – just a couple of thousand dollars, nothing huge, nothing noticeable to these behemoths – and it would be for the greater good, namely, herself.

But she was also sensible and knew when a situation wasn't working. She knew she had to get out. In fact, the day Whitney told her she was leaving was the day Doreen had drafted up her two weeks' notice. She hadn't sent it to her manager yet, but she had written it out and she had told a few people about her plan: she was going to quit, get a menial part-time job, and volunteer at a nonprofit or a newspaper or a community theater or do a nomadic, citizen-of-the-world type thing until she chipped out enough experience to get hired to do something basically like those things but with money. Maybe the Humane Society. Maybe the Peace Corps. Or maybe she would sell out, use the Mario's name and get a job at any of the myriad companies they did business with. It wouldn't be quite as fulfilling as something for the greater good, but she'd rather work for a wireless hairbrush company than for a blatant tech demon. She'd stop thinking about Yemen or Iraq or Sudan at least.

But Whitney had been one step ahead of her this whole time and had evaporated right there in the kitchen.

Doreen couldn't afford to quit now. Increasingly, this had become a problem.

'Found a new job yet?' the person at work who was friendly with Doreen asked her.

'No,' said Doreen, voice slightly trembling. She had slacked off lately, letting calls roll over, messing up invoices, sometimes intentionally. She was filled with a word that needed to exist that described resentful corporate disembodiment.

'You should take some time off while you look. Take a break.'

'Actually, I think I'm going to stay here a bit longer,' she said, trying to convince herself in real-time as she spoke, trying not to look surprised when a wave of nervous nausea hit her. She said the word 'actually' very forcefully, all four syllables planted on the ground like the legs of a dog. 'Yeah. I think once I hit two years, I'll have that under my belt and that'll give me better leverage.'

Leverage? That wasn't a word she used.

She left work early and went home. She curled into her nest in the living room and slept. When she woke up a few hours later, in the late afternoon, she pulled up her dinner options on her phone and the cycle continued. She would be even more reckless, she decided. She would maybe even invite Tyler inside to have dinner with her and laugh at his unease at having to sit on her unmade mattress and her tangled sheets. She was one confirmation page away from queuing up a one-hundred-dollar meal when she heard the goddamn bird again.

Swish. The sound fluttered across the door. A brief staccato of taps on the other side of the wall, then silence.

Doreen groaned and sat up, still shaking sleep from her

head. Her elbows popped awake and she rolled her neck around. A shadow flew across the blinds over the living room window. She got up and crept towards it, using her fingers to peer between the blinds and watch the bird.

It was on the other side of the parking lot now, gathering materials from a patch of dead grass over by the mailbox. Also in the grass were two brightly colored helmets, lying there like jellybeans. Sunlight glittered off their warped plastic shells. She shuffled to the side of the window and pushed her face closer to get a better view of the lamp on the wall outside, careful not to disturb the blinds too much.

The bird flew back to the apartment and hovered in the air, carefully applying the grass in its beak. The lamp's cylinder covering was still twisted upside down and, just like Doreen had planned, everything the bird put there only fell down inside the long cup – but this hadn't deterred it. There was already a ring of debris, two inches deep, forming around the lightbulb at the bottom.

'What is your deal, bird?' Doreen said out loud. The bird could have built its own bird-sized mansion with the energy it was spending on this. She went to the door and was about to throw it open and shoo the bird away when there was a scream.

It was loud and high-pitched and lasted a few seconds too long.

She dashed back to the window and looked through the blinds again. It was the two little boys. Shirtless and shoeless, the parking lot rats. One of them was on a scooter this time, the other was dancing on the asphalt, playing on a cell phone, jumping around to dodge his brother zooming past him on the scooter, laughing and screaming.

Doreen breathed a sigh of relief. The scream had made her stomach turn. She stayed and watched them through the blinds, forgetting the bird for a moment. Her breath fogged up the window and when the fog cleared, the boys were standing together. The older one was trying to convince the younger one to let him on the scooter, to share the scooter together, they were giggling. And then there was – no – yes – she saw it – there was a car flying through them.

A speeding car appears and flies through them.

There's a blind corner in the parking lot. The kind of corner that funnels cars through it like marbles, tricking them into thinking that the quicker they speed through it, the less chance they'll have of hitting something – another car, a stray dog, two children. It's a white SUV, a big, metal and fiberglass marble that peels around the corner and rams right into the boys.

Several times, the boys' mother has come outside and yelled at them about this – giving them an embarrassing, public scolding about playing in the street. Doreen's mind goes to this, unfathomably, as if what is playing out right now is the logical conclusion: If children in street, then car on children. There is an explanation for this, surely, this sudden smudging of flesh and metal.

The car doesn't slow down. It doesn't even stop. And the children make no impact. In a way, it's as if nothing happens. A deer could dent the bumper or break the windshield if it's big enough. A large dog might make the tires bounce unpleasantly up and down. But the two boys do nothing – or, better said, the car does nothing and the boys do *everything*. Their bodies do everything possible to remain in the place where they had been standing half a second ago. Their limbs shrink and stretch diagonally, their faces twist, their eyes stay open, even their blood flies, in a soaring display, out of their bodies and over the car to land back on the asphalt next to the scooter.

If the boys had been wearing them, their helmets would have shattered – the styrofoam would have split right down the middle and crumbled into a million pieces, rubbed into the ground – but they aren't.

The SUV speeds up, continuing its sweep through the parking lot, out onto the main road, driving away, disappearing.

Doreen's fingers shake. They are rattling the blinds. She pulls her hand away and the blinds snap shut. Only a thin line of light runs across her eyes. She stays there, staring at it, frozen in silence.

She doesn't move.

The silence was the strangest part. The car had ripped a hole in this little universe and yet it had disappeared, leaving nothing but air. Where there could have been a vacuum, there was a staleness, a fuzziness that weighed heavy on the ground.

The children had been screaming and laughing. In fact, their noise was probably what had woken Doreen up from her nap. But now there was nothing. Less than nothing. Like a negative space had been created by some brainiac miscalculation. A void.

Then, there was a rustling sound, something outside. Doreen thought for a moment it was one of the children, still alive, maybe trying to stand up on a broken limb. But the sound was smaller than that.

Swish.

The bird's shadow fluttered around the window, breaking the lines of light between the blinds. Silence again when it flew away.

Swish.

Doreen knelt on the floor.

She thought she stayed kneeling there for a minute, but

looking back on it later, it was possible she stayed there for an hour. An hour in silence. Maybe, if she dared think about it – really thought hard about the sequence of events – she had stayed there even longer.

The lines of light through the blinds shifted their anti-shadow from the floor to the far wall, suggesting a passage of time. Her knees began to hurt so she shifted to a cross-legged position. The old floor played a requiem of creaks.

Silence.

Outside, the last dribbles of consciousness inside the little boys waited for someone, anyone.

There was the sound of a car approaching, coming to a stop. Tires feeling their way over asphalt. Brakes playing a sharp note. A door opened and closed. There was a scream and a gasp. A woman and a man saying, 'Oh my god,' and shoes running around. Clip clop, clip clop – nice shoes, shoes coming home from work. Shoes dropping decorum and rushing to the mess on the ground.

There was another slam, but further away. The slam of a wooden door on the other side of the parking lot, and then the worst kind of scream. A scream with the strength to change the seasons.

'NOOOO!'

Doreen felt sick.

The scream summoned a cacophony of noise. It was almost a relief – the sounds weren't isolated any more. They blended now into one solid, incoherent wave. Crying, screaming, yelling, and thrashing about, all bundled together. More cars came, more shoes. Oddly strung words. An idiot honked a horn. Doors opened. A whole chorus sounded. Surely the bird wasn't still building its nest in the middle of all this, Doreen thought. With only audacity left to power her, she thought for a moment of peering through the blinds again, just to see if the bird was back at its project, but her legs were locked and wouldn't move.

Sirens came, pouring over the chorus of screaming and yelling like hot butter over carnival food. Sirens ad nauseum. Curse words. Someone blowing their nose as if they were allergic to horror. Doreen tried her legs again. They worked – they had always worked – and she stood up. She peeked through the blinds. It was night. How? She couldn't see anything. There was only red and blue. Red and blue, red and blue, red and blue, and red and blue. The children were gone. They had been packaged up into metal and plastic and carted off. An ambulance door was slammed shut and its siren did that little stutter 'Wha-wha, wha,' before turning off into silence and driving away. There were four police cars, two ambulances, and one long firetruck that hadn't been able to fit all the way in the parking lot and was stuck out by the entrance, causing a traffic jam on the main road. They were like opera singers – seven grand dames of the stage coming to drown out the anonymous crowd of weepers that had formed at the scene in front of Doreen's apartment.

She backed away from the window as the crowd grew. She felt ashamed, as if she had been excluded, when in reality, she had disinvited herself. Such a strange thing, she thought. She wandered her living room, tripping over her things, marveling at this clerical error of the universe. Two children. Huh. She opened her phone and cancelled her delivery order and swiped away a missed call from a blocked number.

She fell asleep.

She dreamed she had fallen asleep standing up like a horse out in the middle of a dark, empty field. Tall grass surrounded her and she felt it around her legs. She became conscious of the fact that she was dreaming and was afraid, worried she had actually fallen asleep standing up in real life in her living room. She looked down and couldn't see her feet, only coyotes, nipping at her ankles, and the ground was jagged and sharp and she couldn't move for hours.

She woke up. She was lying on the floor, curled up against the window. Her hips and her back were sore, but she was alive and fine.

It was pitch black now. Red and blue still flashed in through the blinds.

Doreen willed herself back to reality. She went to the bathroom. Washed her hands. Went to the kitchen and drank a glass of water. She looked at the time on her phone – it was three in the morning – and there was another missed call from a blocked number and a text message this time, too.

'No dinner tonight?' it read.

She laughed at this different version of reality reaching out to her, a reality where the only bad news was that a delivery boy had somehow gotten hold of her number from a food delivery app and was texting her, not that two children had been ploughed across the ground right in front of her eyes. It was a reality that couldn't match with what she had seen. The image of their bodies – it couldn't be right. She couldn't be remembering it correctly. It was absurd, the way their bodies had moved.

She thought about the mother, whose scream had throttled the passage of time into a stupor but couldn't reverse it, couldn't change what had happened, couldn't scoop up the blood and ripped flesh and toss them back over the hood of the car like a do-over, repairing what had been ruined.

Doreen deleted the text and turned off her phone.

CHAPTER 3

Gravity, time, weather – the constants – they didn't care. Nothing stopped. And the things that did stop – the things that had been broken and sprinkled around – were worked back into motion like ingredients worked into dough. Night ended not with a blink but with an unnerving, fading stare. Morning ran forward without mercy. Sleep, if anyone had managed to catch it, finished its anemone suck and awakened the sleeper. There was a new date on the calendar, but to many it was only the next number in a sequence, nothing worth noting.

Early in the morning, on the new day, two police officers came to Doreen's apartment and knocked on the door: Officer Palmer and Officer Solloway. They wore badges that said as much. They had had quite a night – or Solloway had, at least. Palmer had managed to go home for just three hours and sleep, but Solloway had been the one who had stayed up all night at the station, trying to fix this mess before it became ensnared in a local news narrative. The case was making him itchy.

They had been unable to track down the white SUV. That was the main crisis at hand. Technology had failed: they had no plates, they had no face, they had nothing. They needed witnesses, actual people, maybe even someone with a good vantage point who had watched it all happen and had been able to write down something, anything, not even half the license plate or the exact make or model of the car but something. Instead, all they had was blurry Bigfoot footage from one security camera. A white whoosh. There were other cameras at the complex, but they were pointed away from the parking lot.

'But what about car robberies? That's not a problem here? You never thought you'd need more than one camera pointed at the parking lot?' Officer Solloway was demanding an answer from the property manager. He was frustrated and sleep deprived and the manager was too meek to be efficient. All they needed was a clear shot of the SUV and this would all be over with. What they had instead were white blurs in the bottom corner of the frame, not even a shot of the driver let alone the license plate.

The property manager, an elderly man, was inundated with guilt: his voice shook and his eyes were red. He too had gone without sleep. He explained to the police how he was used to apartment dramatics – spouts of domestic violence, drunk drivers, the works, but never a flat out tragedy like this. Two children dead.

'I see your point now, Officer, I really do,' he said. 'When the guys came and set up those cameras, gosh, we were mostly trying to protect the buildings – we had been having a string of break-ins a few years ago. I hadn't thought about cars, I really hadn't. I'll see if our maintenance guy can go twist some of them around. Don't know why we never thought of that.'

Officer Solloway was pacing the floor of the leasing office. His partner, Officer Palmer, the one who had gone home to sleep, sat in the windowsill, slightly crushing the spindly arms of an office plant.

Solloway was mad about everything. These injustices of the world that were making his day worse. He pointed out the window at the parking lot. 'And the mailbox over there, how many apartments use that mailbox?'

'Twenty-five units use that one, sir.'

'So you decided to put a giant mailbox right on a blind corner in a busy parking lot, making the corner even more blind. A mailbox for twenty-five people, who have to go there at least once a day, crossing that blind corner to get their mail. Have you ever thought about how careless that is? Am I being unreasonable?'

The manager wiped away tears. He fiddled with something on his desk, as if he would find an answer under a stray piece of paper or behind a mug of pens.

Solloway told him to consider moving the mailbox and at the very least put up a Caution Children Playing sign. 'If there are any children left,' added Officer Palmer, who had been completely silent otherwise.

They left the office and visited the block of apartments closest to the crime scene. They knocked on Doreen's door first. Solloway knocked four times and waited.

'You didn't need to say that back there,' he said to Palmer over his shoulder. 'About the children. That was too dark.'

'Yeah, I know,' said Palmer, and nothing more. His back was turned to Solloway. He was looking out over the porch onto the parking lot, leaning against the rickety metal banister. Flimsy yellow tape encircled the area below without much reason – there wasn't anything left to cordon off. Children were easy to clean up after. The tape was already coming loose.

In Solloway's experience, hit-and-runs had a way of sorting themselves out within twenty-four hours. Drivers usually turned themselves in once their fight-or-flight instinct wore off and they came to their remorseful, forever-damned senses before things threatened to turn into a citywide witch-hunt. But when children were involved, that energy was feverish and contagious. Already the local five o'clock morning news had mentioned the story as a footnote and Solloway could feel the tide of hysteria drawing out, gathering momentum. There was a news van parked outside the leasing office, some reporter camping out, getting ready to shoot footage for a whole segment. Solloway could count the hours with his fingers before everyone had details on the children, the mother, and screenshots of the white blur spearing its way across the parking lot like a jousting pony gone berserk.

'Go on! You can go through it, you're all right! Do the limbo!'

Palmer was shouting down at a jogger who had nearly run through the caution tape as if it were a marathon finish line. The jogger stopped with a lurch and hobbled up the curb, dodging the line as if it was cursed land. Palmer laughed.

'Let's move along,' said Solloway. The door remained unanswered.

They moved down the porch to the next apartment. A man answered the door with a granola bar stuffed in his mouth and a half-buttoned shirt. No, he said, he hadn't seen anything, he hadn't come home until late last night. 'I had to park by the leasing office because of all the cars.'

'Oh we're *so sorry* for having inconvenienced you,' said Palmer.

The next apartment was vacant. The three apartments on the ground floor were occupied, respectively, by a rambling elderly man who spoke in circles and saw nothing, another harried professional who had been gone at the time of the incident, and another person who did not come to the door but had a minefield of lawn ornaments and potted plants surrounding their walkway and wouldn't have been able to see anything.

The officers went back upstairs and knocked one last time on Doreen's door, this time ringing the doorbell as well.

'Of course the one person with the clearest view isn't home,' said Solloway. He rang the doorbell again and waited. He looked over at Palmer, who was silent now and not moving, not spewing another dry retort or cynical one-liner. He was fixated on something.

'What is it?' asked Solloway.

Palmer stayed silent but pointed at the porch light on the wall. It had been turned upside down and inside, protected by a cylinder of glass, was a tiny bird, sitting on top of a compact nest of twigs and dirt, completely covering the lightbulb as if it were a translucent, unfertilized egg.

Solloway stepped towards it, putting his face right up to the glass, and the bird didn't so much as flinch. It remained perfectly still, save for its little heart which could be seen thumping rapidly beneath its feathers on its chest. It trusted too much in the protection of the glass.

Both officers stared at it for a moment as if it would offer up some vital information about what it had seen. When no answer was given, they tried to peek through the living room windows, but the blinds had been drawn shut and, if the bird and its elaborate nest was any indication, the whole place seemed vacant.

CHAPTER 4

Doreen was in shock.

Yes, I'm in shock, that's what this is, she said to herself. That was her reasoning. That's why I didn't do anything; that's why I didn't say anything. It was shock.

She had seen a child fly up in the air like the arc of a rainbow and she had seen another child press right into the ground like a boot into packed, squeaking snow. Had it been that vivid? Had she been able to hear it? If she thought about it for too long, she began to shake and produce a reaction in her face that was the opposite of tears, like a lightning strike of dryness, a suction behind her eyeballs that she could feel pulsing at the base of her brain. It was physiological, truly, this adamant inaction. She paced around in the dark, tripping over shoes and blankets and books and trash.

The temperature inside the apartment rose in tandem with the sun outside. As the morning turned to the afternoon, the moldy smell from the laundry machine took on the smell of roasted wet cardboard. The place was unbearable and was made even more so by the closed blinds, which were practically sealed shut. She felt as if she were deep inside the stomach of a whale, unable to leave, unable to move, strangled with blankets, half digested.

There was another round of knocks at the door.

She froze in the middle of the living room. She couldn't even breathe. This was the second round of knocks. The first round had woken her up – freezing her in place just the same, riddled with fear. She listened to the voices on the other side of the cheap, thin door and it was the same guys, the policemen. This is it, she thought. They're going to bust down the door. She saw their shadows huddle around the door, crouching low in front of the window. Maybe they'll burst right through the window, guns drawn.

Why had she done nothing? They were children and she had just watched.

Shhh. None of that. No need for that right now.

She waited. Mind empty.

They finally went away and she exhaled.

Once she was sure they were gone, she distracted herself by finally summoning the will to clean up the place, pulling her mind away from the worst things she had seen. She pushed some piles of trash around. She detangled her phone charger from a coat hanger. She picked at a piece of seaweed left over from sushi that had embedded itself in the carpet. The stink eased up a bit. She found an old can of hairspray Whitney had left behind and sprayed it around the room, not necessarily freshening the air, but at least disrupting its stagnation.

The horrible smell made it easier to pretend something was wrong with her when she called in sick to work. Indeed, there *was* something wrong with Doreen, in a broad, abstract but very real sense, but being physically ill was more sensibly status-quo and was easier to fake over the phone with a cloud of garbage hovering in the air. Her manager was reasonable and wished her well, but curt... not exactly friendly, or believing.

'Is everything OK?' the manager asked. He said the word 'OK' extra pointedly like two open palms turning counter-clockwise, ready to catch whatever revealed itself.

Why was he suspicious?

Doreen felt her pale-green cheeks flush red. She parted

the blinds and looked out of the window, half-expecting to see those two police officers still out there waiting for her to show herself. Why had she done nothing? Why had they knocked so many times at the door? Why was her manager asking if she was OK? *Why had she done nothing?*

'Yeah, I'm fine. Well, I'm sick. Just a stomach bug, nothing huge,' she said. She ended the conversation as quickly as she could, dashing off a string of flulike symptoms and hanging up, maybe even too abruptly, maybe she had ended it mid-sentence, maybe she hadn't even said goodbye, she couldn't quite pay attention right now. Her head pulsed with fear.

She hadn't watched the news or read anything online. The full weight of seeing 'Hit and Run Leaves Two Children Dead' written in bold, black letters didn't sink in because she never saw it. But she felt something horrendous happening around her and now inside of her. It was as if everyone had moved on to the next level in dealing with the tragedy but she had stayed behind, with the shadow of it still watching her through the blinds. The smell of hairspray clung to the inside of her nose, a permanent sourness no matter where she sniffed.

One kid had gone under the wheel, the other had gone over the hood – had flown up and over, had flopped, almost comedically, over the car. One under and one over. Yes, a comedy routine. Both of them had just vanished into the earth. Doreen replayed the accident in her mind, backwards and forwards – no, it wasn't an accident, she thought. An accident was breaking a plate or bumping into a stranger or dropping sushi on the carpet, not this. There was no coming back from something like this. She tried to picture the driver, if she had seen him. She assumed it was a man, men were always doing this sort of thing. She tried to remember a watch, a ring, a hairstyle – anything that could be a helpful signifier, but all she saw was herself, floating in the reflection of the car window, watching from her apartment, a peeping Tom.

It was almost a relief, not remembering the car or the driver, it absolved her of having to be involved. And yet. And yet.

'I *would* have done something. I *would* have called 9-1-1. But I was in shock. I couldn't move.' Doreen said this out loud to no one. 'Anyway, it was only a few minutes until someone else came and found them there.' She knew this wasn't true – a considerable, even criminal amount of time had passed from the time the boys were hit to the time they were discovered, but thinking through the timeline and counting the number of minutes she had let pass by was out of the question at the moment. She still couldn't bring herself to open the blinds. She was trapped. And yet, the smell of the garbage and mold was almost pushing her out, hedging her up against the wall, on the very edge of her refuge. And yet. And yet.

She pounded her head with her fists and emitted a kind of growl. She turned and grabbed her keys, her wallet, her phone, and her shoes in one armful and banged open the front door. Sunlight startled her like the ding of a bell. She stumbled down the stairs into the parking lot. Her car was closest to the crime scene tape so she left it there, refusing to look at all in that direction, and walked on. She walked with a business-as-usual expression on her face, passing the already hallowed ground where It with a capital I had happened, past a makeshift memorial God himself had already beamed down from heaven, with anonymous flowers, cards, crosses, a sickly-sweet teddy bear. She stepped over and around these things.

The shrouded sense of death that had hung over the morning was already stretching out into the afternoon and

Doreen could do nothing but walk through it. The maintenance crew and gardeners were huddled together, murmuring amongst themselves. The property manager was making the rounds, visiting with people. Residents were hovering around, checking out the memorial, checking their mail. The news crew was still there, decamped and ready for the midday specials, top story, B-roll, all of it, and surely in every shot, there would be Doreen's apartment in the background, blinds closed, and in the corner, a tiny bird's nest.

The apartment complex itself was a pimple on a main road that cut through a forested patch of land, conjoining two freeways. It was here in this liminal space that apartments and condos had been erected for those who couldn't afford Portland, encroaching on farmland and forest and reaping the monetary benefits of an ambiguously outdated tax code. Apartments hedged up against the odd hold-outs that had refused to sell – a rundown barn became an island, strangled with ivy in a two-acre meadow of nothing. There was sometimes a raspberry stand on the side of the road in summer. As it was between the dueling freeways, the apartment complex, besides being a place to live, was a popular turn-around spot for lost drivers often confused by the long yawns of highways linking suburb to city. This pattern tended to extend throughout all of Beaverton, leaving only a hiccup of space here or there for a strip mall or a grocery store, leaving one to wonder what Beaverton actually was at all.

Doreen walked out onto this connecting road and realized she hadn't put her shoes on. She was going to the grocery store – this would bring order to her day, she told herself. She struggled to unclench her shoes, phone, keys, and wallet from her arms, dropping everything at once. She slipped the shoes on and stuffed everything else in her pockets, embarrassed, but there was no reason to be; she was alone. The road was wide open. The rush hour current had come and gone and the artery was empty. The road was almost beautiful with its empty grey spine revealed, how it wound around through green. Entire colonies of birds were chirping and cawing overhead, merging together like white noise in the forest that flanked either side. Under the roof of leaves, the summer felt blue-green, not oppressive, not hot. Why can't my bird just live out here? Doreen wondered.

'My bird.' She said it out loud and laughed, which felt a strange thing to do, given the circumstances. The laugh shot through her with a quiver of both nausea and hunger, barging past more important feelings and thoughts that she was insistent on keeping bottled up.

She walked past other apartment complexes – the richer ones, the poorer ones – an empty lot, the barn covered in ivy. She passed a private school and a megachurch, then the sky opened up and the trees went away and she came to the strip mall right next to the freeway onramp, with the grocery store at the far end.

She cut through the parking lot and checked her reflection in the window of a physical therapy clinic to be sure of herself: She had the right shoe on the right foot, yes. She had her phone. She had her keys, her wallet. This was presentable. She pushed her long hair around, as you do. It felt weighed down and heavy like a dusty curtain on a stage.

The shopping center formed an irregular half-circle like one half of an opened clamshell. There were branches of burrito, hamburger and sandwich chains selling different variations on a theme and none of them was appetizing to Doreen, who had ordered food from every single one of these places over the past month. She half-expected to see Tyler, the delivery boy, stepping out of one.

She walked to the end of the half-circle, went inside the grocery store and wandered the frozen food aisles to cool off. The store was quiet and museum-like at this odd hour, not quite noon. The florescent lights overhead reflected in the white linoleum floor, looking like marble. Only mothers with babies in strollers trawled the aisles.

Doreen opened a freezer and let the cool mist swirl around her, washing her cold. She read a popsicle box. The radio over the loudspeakers played a four-count adult contemporary song, then it finished and played another one. There was an employee two fridges down, restocking frozen veggie burgers. Everyone seemed to be recalibrating after a late morning, just like her. Her devastation didn't feel quite as singular. She closed the door and the smell of frozen cardboard was all over her face.

She bought a sandwich and a soft drink from the grab-and-go café inside the store and sat down at a table tucked away in the corner. Everything was decorated with muted greens, browns, and gold – harvest colors, as if they were farmers in a field, as if this were important, psychologically speaking, for a grocery store.

She swallowed too fast. A fistful of sandwich landed hard in her stomach, shocking her system for a minute. She leaned back in her chair and tried to relax, but her leg bounced. When she was nearly finished, she made herself stay put. There was nowhere for her to go, she assured herself. Relax. She resisted the urge to take out her phone and drown in whatever news she could find about last night. She had trouble imagining anything not hysterical.

She noticed, sitting across from her, at the next table over, a woman staring right at her – not glancing for a quick moment, but staring right at her. They made eye contact. A jolt of shock, then sweat flamed over Doreen as she diverted her eyes and looked elsewhere, casually.

There was hardly anyone else at the cafe, why had she chosen the table right next to this woman? But then, when she thought on it, she couldn't remember seeing the woman sitting there when she had first sat down.

Across the room, at the window, there was a mother with a toddler, eating quietly. There was a group of construction workers on their lunch break in the corner and there was a student hunched over paperwork and books. But this woman...

Doreen still felt the woman's gaze locked on her. She looked up and out the window and in the corner of her field of vision, she could tell that yes, the woman was still completely fixated on her, staring at her.

The woman said something.

Doreen pretended not to hear, convincing herself she had to be talking to someone else. Or maybe not, maybe this is it, she thought to herself. My face is out there. On the news. Something about a witness hiding from the police. Surely her image was everywhere – a photo from an old high school yearbook or a crop of her face someone had pulled from the internet somewhere, pixelated and amateur.

She crunched up her sandwich box and stood up to go. Her knees popped.

The woman was still staring.

From the blurry edge of Doreen's vision, the woman's mouth opened, speaking again, Doreen saw squares of white teeth, smiling.

'Sorry, are you talking to me?' Doreen turned and asked – the first words she had said out loud to another person all day. She looked directly at the stranger. The action required a startling sense of bravery and she lost her breath for a moment.

'I was just saying I like your hair,' said the woman. She

smiled. She was sitting alone with only a cup of tea, no phone, no newspaper or anything else to occupy her attention. Her posture was alarmingly straight in context of the sleepy suburb around her, like a lonely cattail, curving above a pool. Her hair was a pale gold color, almost white – a brazen pale yellow sculpture that curved into a swooping shoulder-length bob. Her clothes and jewellery were equally pale and pastel if not completely white, and expensive-looking, luxurious. Her voice was solid and crawled right inside Doreen's ear as if its volume and tone had been calculated and hewn deliberately to fit there.

'Thanks?' said Doreen. She looked around, still reluctant to believe that this stranger was speaking to her, hoping maybe for a volunteer who wished to accept this compliment instead of her, but there was no one else. There were so many empty tables and here was this stranger that had appeared from thin air right across from her and complimented her hair.

The woman made a motion to say more, in fact, she was already talking, standing up and introducing herself, but Doreen was barely there, not listening. The woman extended her arm and handed Doreen a business card. A pale, key-lime rectangle embossed with a name and an address and a phone number. Doreen felt the card in her hand, the pointy corners, so she knew it was there, but her mind was a blur. She heard words but then she didn't because she realized that somehow she had fled. She was back outside under the sun.

She had run away. In the middle of a grocery store? I hope not, she thought to herself, amazed at herself. Amazed and trembling.

She turned her head back and forth in the parking lot like an exposed insect. She shocked herself with how fast she had flashed back outside. If she had said thank you to the woman, if she had pushed her hair around in that self-conscious but beaming manner, if she had even remembered to throw her trash away, she couldn't remember doing so. She didn't even bother reading the business card. She folded it up into a tiny little square and when she was back home, she deliberately threw it away.

CHAPTER 5

Back at the apartment, Doreen couldn't settle down. She opened the blinds, but then remembered the police were looking for her – the police were looking for her? She stopped herself, paused for a moment, but couldn't think straight. Pausing only piled on more madness. Yes, the police are looking for me, she thought. They knocked on my door twice. She shut the blinds and the place plunged into darkness again. The smell of the trash was still unbearable, the darkness and the heat. She couldn't take any more of this – this sinking feeling. In the dark, everything around her merged into a black tar. She needed it out.

With her feet, she kicked everything in the room into a giant pile on top of her mattress. Blankets, underwear, plastic bags, phone chargers, crumbs, wrappers – everything was gathered together. Her laptop crunched and broke right away and once the regret of doing that had passed, everything else was easier. Styrofoam snapped. Nasty leftovers leaked and spread. Pens and pencils and hair clips and notepads gathered. Somewhere under the heap, a glass of water spilled and the mess became wet. A sauce packet from a take-out box broke open and stained everything with rancid bitterness. She felt her shoes get wet, so she took those off and continued smashing everything with her bare feet. Organic squished against inorganic. Wet sheets sucked at her toes. Coldness became warmness from so much friction. Glass broke. Plastic shattered. Stale food crumbled, became wet and ripened with heavy smells. Doreen pushed everything into the center of the room. The entire apartment swelled and contracted into a soggy, black, expanding puddle.

After some considerable pulling and yanking, she extracted a bed sheet from the pile. It had once been white and was now a putrid dark yellow and soaked. She shook it out and spread it over the pile and used it as a makeshift garbage bag, folding and rolling the mess of things into one giant gunnysack. When everything except for the mattress had been gathered, she lifted the sack and threw it over her shoulder onto her back. Everything clattered inside and dug into her spine. A dark liquid leaked out from the bottom and trickled down her ankle. She steadied herself and wobbled to the door, then opened it and went outside, hauling the sack to the dumpster on the other side of the parking lot. The bird in the lamp watched this happen – this small, barefoot woman throwing everything away.

There existed the temptation to call for help. It had been there for a while and this was what Doreen saw it as – a temptation. Throughout her life, this was what she had been taught to see it as. Sure, help was available, but calling for it would be too easy, as if this feeling she had – this 'episode' it would be called – was something everyone went through, something corny, tacky, prescriptive, lowest common denominator – Doreen didn't want that. She shunned it as if there were some kind of value to be gleaned from suffering, like a club card that could be stamped enough times and free ice cream would appear. She ignored thinking about this any further because if she did, she would have realized that everything she was doing – sleeping all day, living alone in darkness, throwing away all her possessions – was in fact the purest, most alarming call for help and she was screaming it out into darkness.

And something out there was responding.

There were two police officers waiting for her when she got back from the dumpster. They hovered outside her apartment door, which she had left ajar, peering inside. She saw them from the parking lot and cursed out loud. She had no other option but to meet them. She walked back, barefoot, attempting to twist the panic out of her face. She pulled at her clothes to straighten them out but they were wet and covered with stains. She pushed her hair around into whatever position it had been in when that strange woman had complimented her.

The officers said hello and introduced themselves: Officer Palmer and Officer Solloway. She looked them up and down. They weren't some kind of Laurel and Hardy pair – they both looked exactly alike and exactly like cops. They were both in shape, tired, tanned, hardened, but not grizzled, not glamorous; more like manual laborers: muscle-bound by necessity. One of them, Officer Palmer, looked more evil than the other, but only because of the bags under his eyes, which made his eyes look swallowed, like two empty holes in his head. The other, Officer Solloway, looked just as off, but in the opposite direction. He seemed too eager for this kind of thing. His smile was painted on, as if he got off on this sort of thing. Doreen already felt her eyes rolling to the back of her head at the sight of him.

'Hi?' she said.

In the hours since they had first come by in the morning, the officers had grown more impatient with the task at hand. Officer Solloway, who couldn't stand these kinds of negligent homicides and showed it with a venomous, orderly rage, had refused to let the property manager off the hook – as if the old man had purposely designed the parking lot as a death trap just waiting to clamp its teeth. So they went back to the management office with all sorts of demands, with Solloway's voice rising in tone to match the level of severity of the killing. He strong-armed the poor property manager and for the rest of the morning and into the afternoon they watched as he compiled and photocopied lease agreements, rent receipts, vehicle registrations, parking lot assignments, building code checklists, contractor invoices – the entire history of the thirty-year-old complex was upended as if there was something there, some decision made long ago that would bring clarity and turn the white blur of the SUV into something sharper. The property manager had meant to ask to see a slip of paper – a warrant, or whatever – before allowing this intrusion, but the officers, the hyenas, were ravenous.

Solloway scoured through all of it. He read through the entire histories that were alive in these documents. Lives laid bare. An old woman living alone died two years ago in her apartment, 24-B. Her neighbor in 25-B had been the one to call and report her missing after a week of not seeing her out watering her plants as she did every night. Another woman in apartment 20-A had been arrested for drunk driving right outside the complex in 2004. In 1999 there was a series of noise complaints against a man in 14-C, and then they ceased. Another man moved from apartment 19-A over to apartment 20-B just this year, in January. 10-C needed the caulking fixed in the bathroom. A woman in 29-C owned two dogs. A woman in 14-A owned one car but had been assigned two parking spaces.

'Why does Whitney Green have two parking spaces?'

Solloway asked, pointing at the bit of folded paper like a bloodhound.

The property manager scratched his head and squinted at the parking and vehicle registry. He took the folder from Solloway and straightened out the papers, looking for an answer.

'Clerical error, I'm sure,' said the manager. 'No one gets two parking spaces, especially if they don't have two cars. I don't know of anyone here who owns two cars. Now, we've got someone with one car and one motorcycle, but that's an exception to the rule. There's not many parking spaces as it stands. We wouldn't let someone have two especially if they only have one car—'

'I don't need to hear you talk this much,' said Solloway. 'We visited Whitney Green's apartment this morning.'

'Twice,' added Palmer.

'Didn't seem like anyone was living there,' Solloway continued. 'There was a bird's nest in the porch light.'

The manager shifted around with a nervous twitch in his eyebrow, bullied into a corner. Whatever was becoming clearer to these officers – alarmingly clearer to Solloway – was surely their own germ of a revelation, inexpressible in easy answers.

'A bird's nest? I don't follow.'

They went back to the apartment for a third time. Palmer stood too close to the bird's nest.

'I like it,' he said – sinister Officer Palmer. He tapped his finger on the glass. The bird inside stayed put, only shuddering slightly, its tiny feathers flashing open and closed. When Doreen approached them from behind, she felt an unwarranted protectiveness for the bird and brushed it off, trying to summon confidence.

'Hi?' she said in the form of a question.

The men turned around and looked her up and down, no doubt surveying her untidiness. They looked at her bare feet, the stains on her jeans. Her hair was unkempt but she knew that to men like this it looked glamorous – voluminous and jujjed up. Even the woman at the grocery store had fallen for it. The stains could be overlooked.

The officers introduced themselves. Doreen didn't give them her name, but no, she was not Whitney Green. Whitney was gone, she said.

The men explained how they had come around earlier in the morning but no one had answered, how they had knocked and rang the doorbell and waited. The tone in their voice – in the voice of the one who was talking, Officer Solloway – was steeped in condescension. He listed off the things they had done and let them linger and fall in the air as if she should feel guilty or impressed or something else entirely. He said they were investigating a hit-and-run that had happened right outside her front door yesterday. She would have had the clearest view of the crime from her window, he said. 'If you bothered to open your blinds,' added Officer Palmer, still standing uncomfortably close to the bird.

The children. Doreen saw flashes of them right over her eyes. No sound. Faces.

She blinked.

She gathered all her strength – gathered all her mania – and funneled it into the act of monotonous dismissal. No emotion. She inhaled whatever was swirling around her and exhaled indifference. With only her chin, she brushed them off.

'I heard about the accident. It's terrible. I was at work during it. Didn't see anything.'

'Where were you this morning?'

'At work.'

'Is that your car over there?' asked Solloway.

Doreen stayed one step ahead of the connection he was trying to make. 'Yes, it is, but I take the bus to work, so it was here this morning. Sometimes I ride my bike,' she added. She had no bike and hoped they wouldn't ask to see one. She also hoped they wouldn't try to contact her work. She felt herself slipping.

'There's only a Whitney Green listed on the lease agreement for this apartment. But you're saying she's not here?'

'She's not. She's been out of of town. Visiting family. It's just me.'

'Where is she?'

'California.'

Whatever she was using to fuel her sense of ambivalence, it was running out too fast. She shuffled around the officers and went inside the apartment, closing the door enough so they couldn't get a clearer view of the vacant living room and the horrible residue leftover on the carpet and the bare mattress. Half of her face disappeared in shadow as she closed the door into a thin line. Officer Palmer made no effort to disguise the obvious craning of his neck to see behind her.

Officer Solloway leaned in closer as well, but closer to Doreen's face, exactly eye to eye. 'Did you know the two children? Harry and Leo? Or their mother, April?' he asked.

'No,' said Doreen. She couldn't help the sound her voice made, the crack in it. She should have said nope or nu-uh – that would have been flippant enough to be believable. She closed the door even more, further narrowing the space for her face.

'It's really too bad. Harry was only three and Leo was only seven.' Solloway leaned another inch closer to Doreen's hovering eye in the doorway. His voice dropped all condescension, going into a low murmur. His breath was uncomfortably warmer than the rest of the summer air. His eyes dipped into shadow. 'You know, when toddlers get hurt, sometimes they don't even break a single bone in their bodies. Babies are even more surprising, they're like jello – bounce right back up if you drop them, no problem; dribble a baby on the floor like a basketball, no problem. But once a kid hits three, or hits seven, and they get in that growth-spurt mode and they're not drinking breast milk every second – man, their bones will just shatter to bits. They'll spill right out of the skin like icicles. You ever get icicles over your porch here in the winter? Ever seen an icicle shatter on the ground when it falls?'

Doreen's eye betrayed her coolness and let out a series of impulsive blinks. Solloway was too close. Ethically too close. He was one muscle twitch from forcing his way inside her apartment, splintering the wooden door into pieces.

'Have you ever met your neighbors? Ever met the mother, April?'

She shook her head. Her eye was replaced with her ear for a second, flashing back and forth. No, she said wordlessly, she had never met the mother.

'Didn't think so. I know your type – everything's temporary to you. You watch the world go by; keeping an arm's distance, worshiping the Wi-Fi, not ruffling any feathers, sure as fuck not making any friends, at least not friends you keep track of, not real friends. You wouldn't have *involved* yourself with the mother. Not your crowd, even though she's probably around your same age. She's a nice girl. Dental hygienist. Single mom.'

'Now she's just single,' said Palmer from the side.

Everyone went quiet.

Maybe Doreen said, 'Sorry I can't be of much help,' or maybe even, 'Good luck, I hope you find whoever did it,' but she didn't hear it. She felt something leave her throat, some kind of definitive sounding mumble and the door closing on her vision – narrower and narrower until finally clicking shut.

When the officers were back down in the parking lot, getting in their car, Solloway heard the faint scraping sound of a lock being turned and a chain pulled across the door. He looked up at the apartment. The blinds were still shut.

'You wouldn't guess by looking at her that she'd be that weird,' said Palmer.

They both got into the car.

'We should have got her name,' said Solloway.

They drove to a fast food restaurant and ate lunch, then they returned to the station where there was other work to be done – the everyday business. There was a drunk driver still in custody from last night – not related to the hit-and-run. There was a paranoid man who had come in with a tip about drug-dealing neighbors. There was a teenager who had been arrested for shoplifting. A house had been toilet-papered. It was drug safety week at an elementary school and a volunteer was needed to teach a workshop. And at the end of the day, they were due to meet with April, the mother of the two dead kids, at the hospital – well, technically the morgue, but Palmer was the only one who would call it that out loud.

There was something about this hit-and-run that seemed off. Solloway felt it and he knew even Palmer felt some part of it, despite his moroseness, but neither one of them spoke of it. Solloway couldn't think of the words to describe it and he went about the rest of the day's chores with it lingering in his mind.

There was a greater level of severity to the tragedy of course – anything involving children was heightened to its own unique intensity. But there was something else. Possibly it had to do with the driver still not coming forward. They always did. Just last year, a woman was barely hit by the side mirror of a car and the driver had sped away. The woman hadn't even broken a bone, she was fine, no complaint, but the driver drove right to the police station an hour later and confessed to a crime that hadn't even been reported. The conscience of a normal, living human being was extraordinary in its ability to compel individuals to confession, often at the clerical expense of an already paperwork-laden police force.

Another time, a child had thrown a rock at a raccoon and killed it, and picked it up and carried it, crying, all the way to Solloway and Palmer in their squad car. The car's upholstery was ruined with raccoon guts, the kid required a trip to the hospital for rabies shots, the parents had to be brought in, the administrators at the police station spent hours filing the incident, a citywide investigation into a possible raccoon population problem was launched – which there wasn't – but that didn't stop a couple of bored, broken-home teenagers from shooting a few for fun, which provoked a whole new barrage of illegal firearms possessions, expired hunting license fees, curfew laws for minors, etc. All because of a kid with a conscience. Well, a weak conscience, and a rock, and a good throw, but a conscience by nature was designed to strengthen over time and that kid would never kill another raccoon again, never even think of throwing rocks again, become an animal lover maybe. It was the role of the police to encourage this growth in humanity.

It was this precarious song and dance of police and police-*work* that provoked Solloway into two different extremes depending on his mood, often ricocheting between them within minutes. On one extreme, he was a pure anarchist – he believed a police officer only needed an arm and a firearm, nothing else; no notepad, no radio, no dashboard camera, no municipal boundaries, no reports to file every time someone sneezed or forgot to trim their toenails. Just round them up. Lasso the bad guys and kick them out of town. Vigilantism.

His other extreme was the polar opposite: a totalitarian, gritted-teeth embracer of the laws of the land and the scuzzy lobbyists, faceless corporations, and zombie old men who had instituted them. A pious observer of rule and regulation in spite of logic and goodwill. The more boxes he could tick on a form the better, dragging his underlings and secretaries and partners through the muck with him.

He flipped on a dime between these two extremes – reprimanding a junior officer for missing something so petty and stiff in one moment, then lecturing that same officer about the need to shoot first, ask questions later, in the next. Only in rare moments of true ideological harmony – when he was able to float between these two attitudes – could he get anything productive done. And today was not one of those days.

So he kept the drunk driver locked up, along with the shoplifting teenager, who could not make bail and would be harassed and humiliated until he did. He made a secretary stay late and write down the tip from the paranoid man, word-for-word. He assigned a team of forensics to visit the home that had been TP'd. There was an eye-watering strain of spitefulness in the air and everyone avoided him, which only made him yell and call people over, point and shout.

Palmer, on the other hand, was an ideal partner for Solloway in that he was impervious to all of this – to rules or the lack thereof. He was a zero, almost permanently hollow, a waif of a soul, bending around whatever was in front of him. Solloway knew to give him tasks that appealed to his sick fascination with intimate human behavior, keeping him high throughout the day, knowing that keeping him happy would score him favors down the line. They shared a sort of code of silence between them, a disgusting brotherhood where one lifted up the rug while the other swept. Palmer had noticed Doreen's messy hair and the stains on her clothes. He told Solloway he knew exactly the kind of nut she was and he liked it. She was aloof, he said. I like that, he said again.

Solloway scoffed and shook his head, trying to act higher and mightier, trying to cover up the fact that he had been thinking the exact same thing.

They drove to the hospital and almost missed April, the mother, who was finishing the clinical process of death, surrounded by equal parts family and friends and flowers and hospital staff and paperwork. They found her in a back office, signing things, being touched on the shoulder too many times. She was green with grief and blue with hospital cold – how could someone be so sad in a place that was so sterile, Solloway wondered. She looked dehydrated, as if she had cried everything out of her. He told someone – using that flippant authority of his – to get her a glass of water, and that somebody, whomever, complied and went away, returning quickly with one. He took it and handed it to April, introducing himself and his partner, Palmer, who had already wandered off somewhere. April's voice was barely there, sounding more like a ticking clock, counting down to when she could finally get home and officially break apart, go into her boys' room and shatter.

'Did you ever see anyone living at the apartment complex, or maybe just a visitor, who made you or your children feel unsafe?'

'No,' she said. She turned away from him, obviously not wanting to do this – whatever this was – right here and now. 'I mean, no one specifically but I always told the boys not to talk to strangers – sorry, what is this about?' Her voice clawed at the air. 'What's the point of talking to you? My kids were run over, there's nothing to investigate, just go get whoever did it.'

'That's exactly what our intention is,' said Solloway. 'Unfortunately we don't have as many leads to follow as we would like. The security camera footage was lacking in clarity and no one at your apartment complex drives a white SUV like the one we saw in the available footage. We're looking for any information about anything: strange visitors, cars that pass through the complex often – I know people use it as a turn-around spot. Usually these kinds of things tend to sort themselves out, but unfortunately it's gotten a bit away from us at the moment and become a full investigation into vehicular homicide. We're treating this as if the driver was being intentionally reckless.'

April's face was glazed over. It had taken on a stony appearance. She was shutting down. Solloway was saying too many words that only added to the hospital's general sense of unfeeling.

'We'd like to get a formal statement from you,' he said. 'We can do that now and get it over with if you'd like. You can just tell us what you remember and then you can leave everything else to us.'

There was a stretch of silence.

'April?'

She blinked herself back from whatever abyss she had disappeared into. She breathed deep, too deep, triggering a warmth under her tear ducts that began vibrating.

'Can you tell me where you were yesterday?' Solloway asked.

The nurses fluttering around them shared uncomfortable glances and sunk away into the background.

April finally spoke.

'I was making lunch for them,' she said. 'It's on the counter still. I need to go home. Put it in the fridge or something.'

'What did you make?'

'Two sandwiches.'

'What did you do when you finished making them?'

'I went to call them inside. They had that scooter – they're only supposed to ride it when I'm out there with them. I saw them on the ground, both of them lying there, which I was going to yell at them for, but then I saw others standing over them, so I didn't yell, I didn't want to make a scene. So I walked over. I said hello and said sorry that my boys were playing in the street and blocking their car. I thought it was so weird. It was like they were pretending to be asleep there in the street. Kids do that, you know. They actually play dead in the street.'

The boys had been tucked away like fresh fruit. Palmer was down in the morgue, standing next to their containers, tapping a finger on the cold metal as if one of them would tap back.

The inorganic parts of the boys – their clothes, their shoes, their twisted scooter – had been bundled and sealed in clear plastic bags. The older boy had had a cell phone in his pocket. Its screen was shattered, but it still turned on when Palmer touched it through the plastic bag. The screen lit up. He took it out of the bag and moved his finger around the display, careful not to cut himself on the broken screen. He tapped through different menus. It had been childproofed – there was hardly any extra software added onto it and there were only a handful of contacts: Mom, Dad, Tommy, Tommy's mom, Samantha, Mrs. Taylor, Mrs. Stevenson, Mrs. Williams, Grandma. The phone was surely only meant to be taken to school, why had he had it in his pocket? There were no games on it, even the camera had been disabled by the parental controls.

Palmer opened the call logs. Almost all the calls were either to or from Mom, sometimes Dad. But there was another phone number. It was an unlisted number, one that hadn't been saved under a name in the address book, and the number had been dialed as recently as yesterday afternoon – nearly right at the time of the accident. Palmer scrolled down and the number kept showing up, peppered in the list of calls. Sometimes it had been dialed multiple times in a row, within minutes.

He took the broken phone out to the squad car in the parking lot and ran a search on the number. There was no police record connected with it. Next, he ran a general search and found a vehicle registry associated with it. A blue Honda, several years old. The name registered to it didn't look familiar.

Then he had a thought.

He noted the license plate number and reached into the back seat. He heaved the pile of documents they had taken from the apartment manager onto his lap. The cardboard box containing them all pinched into his legs. He weeded through lease agreements and tenancy forms until he found the tattered old folder with the parking assignments Solloway had found earlier. He opened it and flipped to the two cars that had been registered to Whitney Green. The second car – the extra parking spot the property manager had said was a clerical error – was for a blue Honda. The license plate listed matched the one Palmer had found in the state records, tied to the unlisted phone number. The car and the phone number belonged to a Doreen Durand. A Doreen Durand who had apparently been receiving phone calls from April's son, right up to the day he died.

CHAPTER 6

April's rage was astounding – misdirected, but not uncalled for, given the past twenty-four hours – so much so that Palmer and Solloway had to touch her – not restrain her, but just gently place hands on her shoulders to calm her down. It didn't help that Palmer had been sensational about it. 'Why would your son, Leo, be calling Doreen Durand's cell phone, even as recently as yesterday?' he asked, as if Doreen Durand was a name she should have recognized immediately.

'Who? What?'

April's entire head turned maroon and everyone was swept up in the drama, as if Doreen's phone number showing up multiple times on Leo's phone was somehow irrefutable proof that she was to blame for his death. Solloway struggled to calm things down while at the same time being tempted to fan the flames. He had to admit it was a strange finding and was only pushed further into the realm of consideration thanks to Doreen's strange behavior when they had confronted her earlier in the day. But there was zero realm of consideration for the chemicals of grief and rage pumping through April's system as she flew into conspiracy. She broke down further, right there in the hospital. Doreen was a pedophile who had been grooming her son and she ran him over to keep him from talking. Doreen was her ex-husband's new girlfriend, coaxing Leo to come and live with them; a kidnapping attempt gone horribly wrong. Who the hell was Doreen? She pushed Solloway and demanded he give her the phone, which Palmer held high above his head, almost tauntingly.

'I've never heard of her, but I'm going to kill her. What kind of sick person calls up a child on the phone?'

Solloway pleaded for some leveling. 'Let's all calm down. April, I'm begging you, don't let your mind turn this into something it isn't. All of the phone calls were placed from your son's phone. He was the one doing the calling and from the looks of it, Doreen only answered a handful of times.'

'She spoke on the phone with my son. Without me knowing. He's seven years old.'

Solloway glared at Palmer.

'I apologize for my partner's uncouth way of relaying unsettling news to other people, but I can assure you, April, that we will look into this as part of our investigation.' He had his arms outstretched like a militarized messiah. 'But I urge you, please, don't let this become any more than what it is – which, at this point, is unconnected to the tragedy at hand. What I mean is, don't get wrapped up in it. When we grieve, our minds have an unfortunate instinct to look for something to blame, really just a vessel to pour our anger into. Don't let Doreen rob you of your grief.'

April stonewalled logic and thrashed about for a while longer, then, after an hour or so, they ended up outside the hospital, next to the police car, in plain view of patients and staff entering and exiting the building. April's sister, who had been waiting in the lobby for the conversation with the police to be over, came running out to comfort her, along with an appointed grief counselor and a few nurses. The sister called their mother, who came speeding into the hospital parking lot, and the three of them wept in a mass of arms and hunched shoulders and Officer Palmer – who never had anywhere to be and never minded working long, overtime shifts – took out his phone and caught up on emails. By the time a sense of reason had finally reestablished itself among the gathering, the sun was setting and Officer Solloway stepped forward to brand a sort of ending to the day. He exchanged contact information with everyone involved and promised next steps, follow-up visits, counseling, the works. April and her family finally loaded up into her mother's car and drove home. The nurses went back inside the hospital.

Once everyone had gone their separate ways, Palmer and Solloway got in their squad car and sat in silence. Their day was not over. They stared at each other and noted the change in the air. Something was revealing itself to them like the bleeding yolk of a cold, raw egg.

They had to get to Doreen.

The connection wasn't logical, but the connection was still there, and now that twenty-four hours had passed, there was a sense of urgency. There was this empty line that demanded to be connected between the two children, the white SUV, and that strange, standoffish young woman. Doreen Durand. Solloway winced at his own ineptness. He recognized the absurdity of it. He was sure there was a reasonable explanation that connected each element, or, more likely, proved their disconnection. But there was still something else, something working underneath it all. It was the way Doreen had shuffled around the officers. The way she had slithered back inside her apartment. The giant bag of trash she had hauled to the dumpster. Palmer and Solloway sped through town back to the apartment complex, going through the facts, circling the edge of reason.

'Her phone number is all over Leo's phone, but she didn't think to tell us 'Oh, that kid that got ran over? Oh yeah, he called me just the other day'?'

'He called her on that actual day.'

'Right. He called her and then he died.'

'Why wouldn't she tell us that?'

'Now she's just made herself look more suspicious.'

'What was up with her clothes too? Why was she throwing all that shit away in the dumpster?'

'What the hell kind of a name is Doreen anyway? What is she, eighty years old?'

'And there was a bird's nest on the wall.'

They stopped speeding when they exited the freeway and noticed April and her family only a few cars ahead of them; they had caught up with them. They pulled off to the side and gave the women time to drive down the wooded road back to the apartment complex on their own, then they followed. They parked in the far corner of the parking lot, away from both April and Doreen's apartments, facing the trees. The setting sun striped everything in orange and purple. They had made plenty of visits to the different complexes out here over the years – noise complaints, assaults, squatters, plenty of drunk drivers thinking they had just about made it home. The apartments rotated their tenants, but the variety and frequency of crime were eternal. No matter how hard you tried, there would always be petty theft, loud parties, skinny dippers, wife beaters. The cycle was the same, year after year. It was as assured as breathing. Lately, Officer Solloway found himself sighing instead.

The two officers didn't prepare a plan of action. What were they going to do, break down the door and handcuff her? They just wanted to talk with her again and get clearer answers. Still, they said nothing to each other as they got out of the car.

They walked up the stairs to the apartment. From the balcony, they looked out over the parking lot and saw April's apartment opposite. Solloway imagined her inside, ripping herself into slivers – her life would never be the same. It was odd, he thought, how even after such a life-altering tragedy, you still had to eventually go home at the end of the day, squeeze your new self into your old home and smell the same old smells. It was likely she would leave someday, after the summer, after these endless twilights, and go somewhere far away and never come back.

Solloway knocked on the door of Doreen's apartment. The blinds were still shut and there were no lights on inside. He had forgotten about the bird until Palmer tapped on the glass of the wall lamp and this time the bird was startled. It flew out into the night, barely dodging them. The air swirled around them. Palmer laughed. He looked closer inside the glass at the bird's nest and grabbed the lamp cover with his hand. He shimmied it back and forth as if to screw it right-side up and dump everything out. The nest of twigs and dirt inside shifted.

'Stop,' said Solloway.

'Stop what?'

'Just stop. Leave it alone.'

Palmer let go and stepped back, bemused.

Solloway knocked again and rang the doorbell. They waited for five minutes, then ten minutes, but there was no sign of her. Finally, Solloway looked at his partner and sighed. He read Palmer's empty face – his black, hollow eyes still glancing at the bird's nest. Solloway pressed his weight into the door, assessing how hard he would need to kick to break it down, but there was no need.

It was unlocked.

It was even slightly, just barely ajar.

Solloway turned the doorknob and pushed it open. The tail of the sunset spilled inside. Their shadows blurred across the carpet.

There was nothing. The apartment was empty. There was only a dirty mattress on the floor and a few pieces of trash. The bedrooms were empty.

Doreen was gone.

CHAPTER 7

Doreen was a creature of habit. Or, of habitat, more accurately, and when an environment wasn't serving the rhythm that she had established as her life's current, she worked tirelessly to reverse course and correct it. She was experienced in expunging things from her life. Once when she was a little girl, she had two pet hermit crabs. She became preoccupied with the fact that one of them had a blue spotted shell while the other had a green spotted shell and she only wanted blue. Blue was her favorite color. Blue was this stage of her childhood. Everything blue, blue, blue.

After a thoughtful unraveling of the conflict in her four-year-old mind, the green-shelled hermit crab was made to disappear in a single, violent act. The crab soared from her upstairs bedroom window into the back garden where it was never seen again.

It was a cruel and violent example of her resolve – she was only four, come on, and her parents punished her for it – but that trait remained a part of her nature. It was almost matter-of-fact how she could do it, deserting boyfriends with hardly any warning, letting friendships dry out and blow away, changing courses of study in school as if she were examining these things with a fine-toothed comb, expelling any threat to what she knew she was or what she knew she would become. And what she *was* was not a perfectionist. She didn't grate on anybody's nerves or hurt anyone's feelings when she did this (at least, not majorly), she just knew who she was and pulled or pushed whatever or whomever needed to be in or out of her orbit. She was in tune with the shape of her life, almost like a medium, and if what she encountered throughout her life turned out to be a block that wouldn't fit, well then it wouldn't fit. That was it.

But these strategies were not working for her now. For as much as they had served her in the past, they were dismantling her current reality. Something had inverted. Something had gone terribly wrong.

The only thing Doreen could be sure of was that she was hungry again. Yes, hungry. That's the problem at hand, she thought to herself, pacing the floor, pacing for hours. The sandwich she had eaten earlier had been less filling than air and that strange, fancy woman at the cafe had ruined everything by talking to her. After the police officers left her alone – or, after she had closed the door on them, she couldn't remember – she waited a few hours in her apartment (pacing, pacing, pacing), then left and walked back to the same grocery store down the road.

HONK.

Cars honked at her. She was sure she was walking safely on the side of the road, not risking her life. Cars whooshed by. Whoosh, whoosh, whoosh, the occasional honk. There was more traffic now. Rush hour. These were all the people she would normally be snuggled up against in her own car. An endless chain of cars.

She crossed the street OK, no problemo. She waited for the green man. Clearly, it was green when she crossed. 'What?' she yelled at a car. Its brakes squealed right in front of her, little piggy, then HONK HONK like a goose – she raised her middle finger. They waited for her to move – she moved as fast as she could, she was sure of it, walking orderly across the cross-walk, not barefoot, no not barefoot. She crossed and the cars drove on. All of them drove on, filling every space in the parking lot like playing cards, dodging Doreen.

Inside the grocery store, the crowd was not as homogenous as before. Men and women in business attire and business-casual attire stormed the aisles. The grab-and-go station had been ravaged. Doreen rolled her eyes at the concept of dinner at six o'clock. For every gang of suits, there was an outlier swept up in the chaos – an old woman doing her weekly shopping at exactly the wrong time, a parent juggling children, a strange loner like Doreen – a barefoot vagrant with stains all over her clothes.

She lingered in the frozen food aisle as she had before, cooling off. Some part of her self that hadn't been discarded in the dumpster felt self-conscious surrounded by so many working professionals. She assured herself she looked fine. She still had her phone and her wallet in her pocket. Her keys were missing, but she was sure she could find them again.

Normal.

She tried to stabilize herself, standing here in her own business-casual clothes, tattered and torn like an intern from hell, and if anyone spoke to her, she worried her voice wouldn't sound right – not chirpy enough, not nonchalant enough. She tried hard – really hard – to think of a quirky answer in case anyone dared ask her why she was barefoot.

She stuck her head in a freezer and read the label on a carton of ice cream just like before. She closed her eyes and breathed in the cardboard and plastic and ice. The freezer next to her opened. She felt the air suction and pulse around her head. She opened her eyes and saw a beautiful, polished hand with almond shaped nails reach into the neighboring freezer. Doreen yanked her head out and tried to pretend she had been looking for something, embarrassed. She stopped when she noticed who the almond-shaped nails belonged to.

It was the same woman, the one who had said she liked her hair, the stranger. There was no way you could confuse her with anyone else. Her hair was still immaculate and the color of white gold. Her clothes were free from wrinkles, but folded in exactly the right places to hug her slender body. Her skirt and blouse shimmered in a way that suggested these were items no one else could afford, let alone have the audacity to wear to a grocery store. Despite luxury in abundance, there was a simplicity to her. She wore a silver watch, a minimalist necklace and no earrings. Her designer heels were powerful and heightening, but nude and not extravagant. The mist from the freezer swirled all around her.

Doreen meant to look away, to close the freezer and turn and leave so as not to be seen, but she couldn't do anything but stare. What else could she do?

'Hello again, what a nice coincidence,' said the stranger. Her voice was just as warm and even-toned as before. 'Are you as unprepared in the kitchen as me and came back for dinner?'

Doreen couldn't speak. She kind of laughed, but swallowed it, so it turned into a cough.

'Do you live around here?' asked the woman.

Doreen gathered what noises her vocal cords could make and stuttered. 'Sorry, but. Who. Are you? Sorry. Ha.' She touched her hair out of nervousness. The woman's eyes watched Doreen's hand for a split second, then went straight back to her eyes. Her eyes were blue, green, and brown all at the same time and stared right into her.

'My name is Violet Cascade,' she said. 'It's a pleasure to meet you – again, technically.' She extended a hand. Doreen shook it and said her name in return. The hand was like porcelain, but not cold and clammy like Doreen's or anyone else's that had just been inside a freezer.

'What are you looking for?' asked the woman, whose name was somehow Violet. Violet Cascade. Doreen heard it again in her head and was certain she hadn't heard it correctly. The strangeness of the name was enough to jolt her mind back into a state of feasibility – not stability, but words – English, A to Z, normal, whatever normal was – for five seconds.

'Dinner. I'm looking for dinner, I think. My day has been kind of a mess, actually. I don't usually come here twice in one day,' said Doreen.

'Don't worry,' said Violet. 'I'm just as bad.' She reached out and touched her on the arm. 'Why has your day been a mess? You seem to have managed it so far – you made it all the way to dinner.'

'There was a problem. There was this thing that happened—' Doreen stopped herself. What was going on? Who was this stranger? But the horror inside her was already spilling out, ravaging her thought process. 'Sorry, no,' she said, eating her words. 'There's just lots of stuff going on. A lot has happened.'

Violet's eerily perfect face loosened itself into a look of sympathy, somehow accomplishing the dual feat of looking both untouchable and completely empathetic. And the expression didn't create a single wrinkle. But her beauty wasn't flippant with youth – she could have been twenty and she could have been eighty. All of these features distracted Doreen from maintaining decorum. She stood there, unguarded, unable to hide her emotions, and Violet – whoever this was – had them ensnared.

'Is there anything I can help you with?' she asked.

'No, there's nothing. Sorry, for bothering you again.'

'You're not bothering anyone. If anything, I'm the one bumping into you everywhere. I don't mean to pry, but I don't like to see anyone hurting or in trouble. Would you like to eat with me tonight? Let me take you out. Let me help you.'

'No, that would be ridiculous,' said Doreen, laughing, but also, almost crying. She stepped back and began to turn away.

Violet's face transformed again – this time into a commanding, almost reprimanding look. A look of laser specificity. She took two steps closer to Doreen and grabbed her hand, not forcefully, but enough to make Doreen jump. Her voice was deeper when she spoke again. She was deadly serious.

'The word 'No' has detrimental effects when you use it the way you're using it. Please, it sounds silly for me to say, but don't ever say 'No' again today. You won't withstand it.' She spoke as if she was afraid it was the last thing she would ever say to someone. Then she let go of Doreen's hand and her face flashed back into a smile. 'Please, come to dinner with me. We'll eat at a nice restaurant – to hell with grocery stores.'

Doreen felt sick and flushed and under any other circumstances she would have had a stronger will to get away sooner. She backed up again. 'I'm sorry, I don't – I can't right now. Something's not right. I don't know what's going on. I don't know what I'm doing.' Embarrassed at herself and overwhelmed by this perplexing woman, she turned and ran away, knocking over a food display in the process. Her bare feet slapped across the white linoleum. Shoppers turned their heads.

She got outside and kept running, dodging cars that were still stuffing the parking lot. More working professionals were caught off guard, raising their eyebrows at this not-normal event cutting into their day. This weirdo-girl running past them as if there weren't appearances to keep up.

Cars flew down the road to the apartment and Doreen ran alongside them on the uncomfortable border between asphalt and nature, cutting up her feet. The black trees over-head arched into a tunnel and the sky was cloudless. She felt a shortness of breath in her lungs and in her current state, she knew it was permanent. She would never breathe normally again. She would never slow down. Her lungs slapped dry against her ribs. Chills ran through her body.

Reaching the apartment complex brought no relief. She stopped right in the middle of the parking lot.

She froze.

The police were back. She saw their car, parked off in the darkness, in the furthest corner of the lot. She looked up at her apartment. The door was open. The lights were on. The police were in her home. Their shadows moved across her closed blinds. Ultimate darkness swirled around in her mind, blacking out her vision. Then there was a screeching sound – a bird – no, it was a squeal. Loud and sudden. Red brake lights lit up her silhouette. A car jerked to a stop, inches away from her, trying to back out.

'Hey!' Doreen yelled. She slapped the back of the car that had nearly backed into her. Its red brake lights poured over the front of her body, creating angled, inverted shadows on her face.

Two women were in the car. An older woman and a younger woman. Their faces were muted in their surprise, as if they had been in some kind of solemn reverie, as if worse things had happened to them today than almost backing into someone. Doreen saw their puzzled faces in shadow through the back window. She looked up and saw the apartment they were leaving.

The mother.

April. There, standing outside her front door. She had been waving goodbye to her mother and sister. She was an empty vessel. Spent.

Doreen couldn't move. Her mind turned itself inside out, looking and not finding anything. Her only thought was a sudden desire for the car to keep backing up, run her over, and kill her. She wanted to lie down, right under the tires, let one pop right over her head. Her knees struggled to hold her up. The ground felt too close.

'Excuse me, can you move, please?' said the older woman out the car window. She waved at Doreen in the mirror, but Doreen couldn't snap out of it – she hadn't been able to snap out of it for a very long time, for not just hours, not just days, but months now, perhaps years.

She looked one more time at April – a long enough second for them to both memorize each other's faces – then turned and walked away. She walked out of the parking lot. She walked out onto the busy road. Without a care, without a rush. She walked deliberately. Cars and darkness and lights whirled and honked around her, barely missing her. The honking stirred up the birds in the trees above her. They sang and took flight.

SWISH.

She struggled to breathe anything but car exhaust and summer heat.

SWISH.

Another car dodged her and she stumbled dizzily from lane to lane. A traffic jam was forming. Brakes screeched, barely avoiding collision. A side-mirror flew by. Doreen fell onto her knees.

SWISH.

The asphalt broke the skin on her knees and stimulated tears behind her eyes. Her hair covered the ground. Her back arched downwards, folding in on itself – a jagged rock in the middle of a dangerous road. But she was bathed in light, a single light that poured over her. A car pulled up on her, not speeding into her, but perfectly centered, coming to a stop. White, crystal-clear headlights erased everything else.

A door opened and a woman stepped out – the most beautiful woman in the world. She walked, not ran, to Doreen's side and placed her arms around her small, arching back. She held her there for a moment, saying nothing, then lifted her up, not straining at all, as if Doreen's legs were compelled to stand, and the two of them walked to the woman's car.

The road was backed up almost to the freeway now, but no cars honked. It was as if they all knew who this woman was and that her presence overrode every sequence of a more practical reality. Their headlights formed a chain of light that fanned out into the surrounding woods and in a matter of minutes, once the two women were inside the car, everything began to move again. The unending chain broke apart, each light spacing further and further away from the other, fading away into the woods. The birds, finally quieting down. Everyone, going away.

CHAPTER 8

The Jaguar's engine barely made a hum. It took some time for Doreen's senses to return, but when they did, she was afraid she had lost some of them it was so quiet. It was like waking up in an empty, silent, dark room.

The first thing she saw were her ruined knees. They were bloodied and torn with dirt and pebbles. She didn't dare wipe them clean. Her first coherent thought was that she didn't want to make a mess in this smooth moonscape of a car.

They sailed through the trees and merged effortlessly onto a freeway. Doreen was in the passenger seat, but far back, almost curled up, as street lights passed overhead at increasing speed in a perfect single-file line. Violet, in the driver's seat, said nothing and piloted the vehicle with elegant, perfect posture. The was no music playing. Not even a tiny concerto at half volume as would seem only fitting. The air inside the car was filtered and pure, tinted with only the sanitary smells of leather and new plastic.

The freeway opened wide. They passed on-ramps and off-ramps and more lanes were added. The gray area between suburb and city slowly became more city. The streetlights became more densely packed, with varying degrees of orange and yellow. Traffic increased, but Violet maneuvered her way around slower cars with gentle, non-aggressive pirouettes. Doreen felt supremely dirty sitting in the car.

'I'm so sorry, you didn't need to do this,' she said.

'Nonsense,' said Violet. 'You were lying in the middle of the street. You could have been seriously hurt.'

Doreen rubbed her eyes. She felt unable to say anything reasonable or piece together a thought. She had wandered out into the middle of the street – what was she thinking?

'I'm sorry. I didn't mean to be out there – that road – that's a busy road. Just a mess – ' She tried to sound as if it had all been an accident. As if she had just misplaced herself like she had misplaced her keys.

Violet replied just as calmly. 'Don't worry. Don't say anything about it. Let your mind take a rest. You can take all the time in the world. No one is expecting any answers, least of all me.'

Doreen pulled at her eyelashes, which had become webbed and sticky from old tears and sweat. 'Thanks. Thank you . . . I'm sorry – you said your name was . . . Violet?'

'Yes. Violet Cascade.'

Doreen nodded. She was in awe. This bizarre, luxurious woman had swooped down and taken her away. Where they were going, Doreen had no idea, and any logical questions she could possibly think to ask were quickly forgotten, hidden away by this eclipse of a woman. She had saved her. She was a slice of the moon, peeled and placed carefully in this moment.

The Jaguar flung itself through downtown Portland without stopping, as if traffic were galloping away from them. Within minutes they came out on the northern end of the city and kept driving. Doreen wondered if they had gone as far as the Columbia River and had crossed over into Washington, but her mind was a blur and the night obscured everything. Eventually, after a long yawn of silent travel, they pulled off the freeway into a quiet stretch of city with wide streets and parked at a nameless diner.

'I hope this is all right,' said Violet. 'To be honest, I've been ordering delivery from my hotel every night this week and I'm not familiar with the area. I feel like a quiet diner is a good refuge for both of us right now, don't you think?'

Doreen nodded. It was perfect, actually. She had been ordering nothing but delivery lately too, she said. 'I'm happy to eat anywhere with a table and chair.' Already, she felt her mood lighten. It was as if Violet had an antenna perfectly tuned to the feelings of those around her – or just to Doreen – and was doing exactly what needed to be done. It was mathematical. Violet threw her a smile and they got out of the car.

The restaurant was intentionally moody in decor. There were rows of cushioned booths, yellow and green glass lamps, and a sculpted ceiling, all meant to look aged with old-world charm, when in reality it was a chain restaurant that had just recently opened – recent, at least, compared to the era it was trying to emulate. Intentions aside, it surpassed its goal and Doreen felt a warmth and comfort she hadn't felt in months.

Violet commanded the scene with ease. Of course she was the one in charge, she was in charge no matter where she went. She expected the best and she received it, even from a faceless franchised restaurant in the middle of the night. They sat down and she immediately requested a glass of water for herself, no ice, with two lemon slices, and a water, no ice, no lemon, for Doreen, with an extra glass of just ice and a small plate of freshly sliced lemon in case minds were changed. Somehow, the waiter complied with this request as if it were the most sensible thing. Doreen raised her eyebrows.

The menu was riddled with two-for-one deals and various amalgamations of 'endless,' 'bottomless,' and 'Friday Feast,' – terminology that didn't lend itself to a discerning palate – but Violet had the audacity to ask the waiter what he would recommend. Doreen waited for a wink or a smile, but there was no irony, and the waiter didn't seem to think so either.

'I'm personally obsessed with the curly chili fries, but the Santa Fe Chicken Burger is back for the summer and lots of people like that. It's got like this spicy mayo sauce that's really good.' The waiter was connected with this woman on a level no other customer had achieved all day. Doreen watched, amazed.

'Then we'll do the curly fries, no chili; two of the Santa Fe Chickens, but in a wrap, no bun. We'll also do the Goose and Grains salad, two potato skin sliders but if you can use sweet potatoes instead, please; a side of oatmeal; the Thai peanut salad; and one Ultimate Breakfast Skillet.'

'How would you like the eggs for that?'

'Hard-boiled, please.'

'Hard-boiled?'

The waiter looked around – the first time he exhibited any hesitancy – but Violet still had that look on her face that suggested that there was nothing wrong, absolutely nothing wrong in the entire world. Her eyes alone said she knew she would receive everything she had requested, no question, because she was someone who could ask and receive anything. She could command the sun. She was a prophetess.

'Yes, hard-boiled. With a teaspoon of sea salt on the side, if you have any.'

The waiter actually bowed, almost curtseyed, even, and said he would get right to it, and he meant it. He went back to the kitchen and sent her order to the front of the queue.

'So your last name is Cascade. Is that Cascade like the Cascades, the mountains?'

'No.'

Violet was strangely guarded about herself. As Doreen was

coming more to her senses, she felt an urgency to examine her surroundings – a careful assessment of this strange woman she was dining with and honestly what the hell was going on. But Violet was artful in dodging specifics. She couldn't exactly say where her last name came from, nor her first name. And Doreen couldn't think of other ways of asking without sounding too intrusive.

'Violet, like the flower?'

'Yes,' she said. And that was all.

Doreen drank her water and retraced her steps in her head. Maybe she had unwittingly entangled herself in the affairs of a high-priced escort, or an FBI agent – one whose operations were so classified, even her handlers didn't know where she was or what she was doing and she hadn't been seen for decades. Her age was a mystery and she outright refused to answer where she was from when Doreen asked.

'Honestly, from everywhere. I grew up all over the place. I bounce around.'

The curly fries came, then the chicken wraps, the salads and sliders and sides, and the sizzling breakfast platter that included two hard-boiled eggs on a small plate with a pile of salt.

'Thank you so much,' Violet said to the waiter and even touched him on the arm. She had complete control. It was as if she had inhabited the restaurant, merging herself into the upholstery. She took a sip of her ice-less water and looked at Doreen.

'Now, who are *you*?' she asked.

'I don't know,' said Doreen. She looked around the restaurant, as if she would find an answer in one of the movie posters or retro advertisements that were framed along the walls. 'I'm Doreen. My last name is Durand. I went to school here, graduated about a year ago, but stayed around.

I studied Political Science and thought about getting a law degree, or a teaching degree, but didn't, or at least, I haven't yet. I work for a software company called Mario's, which makes the little computer chips for exercise trackers and things like that.'

'But none of that feels relevant to you at this moment, does it? None of that is who you are.'

Doreen pushed around her silverware the way you were supposed to do at a moment like this – to stall and act preoccupied with the abyss. But she wasn't. She had thought about these things every single day, and Violet had worded it perfectly.

'No, it doesn't. Not at all,' Doreen said. 'And that's exactly how I would say it. Nothing feels relevant or worthwhile any more, and that doesn't mean I'm saying it used to feel that way – I never felt like I had a dream job or a perfect life planned out, but I used to have an *idea* of who I was, what I was going to do with myself. Mario's wasn't – isn't – the ideal job, but it's a way of getting me from point A to point B. But I've lost point A and point B. I've always had a good sense of what I need and what I want, but it's like that sense has gone numb. Or I've sharpened it too much and it's disappeared. Or gone dull. I have a habit of cutting out the parts of myself that don't serve a purpose, that don't get me to where I want to be, and maybe I've cut off too much.'

'And where is that?'

'Where is what?'

'Where you want to be.'

'It's not really a destination or anything concrete. Right now, I can't think of a thing I'd want to do or a place I'd rather be than just here, floating in the present, but I know I'm not really *here* either. It's more like a state of being that I need. It's who I'm supposed to be. But I've lost sight of that.

It's like I'm a battery that can only be charged a certain way. I've accumulated and accumulated until all of a sudden I've become depleted.'

It was the most Doreen had said to anyone in months. She looked down at her hands to make sure they were still there. She looked at the food on the table. She saw her tiny reflection in a puddle of maple syrup.

'I think I'm stuck,' she said after a while. 'I don't really know where I am at the moment. I've chopped off some limb I didn't think I needed and now I can't move forward. On top of that, there was this horrible accident yesterday – something truly horrific and I saw it all happen. Really, it was a real-life, physical *tragedy* that happened, and I saw it. But I—' She paused, cautious, but also because her voice cracked, then continued. 'I did nothing. I didn't do anything to help. I haven't even told anyone what I saw.'

Violet didn't ask what it was, she only nodded. Her hair barely moved when she did but she pushed it back into place with one acrylic talon. Even in the middle of her confession, Doreen couldn't help but admire Violet's beauty.

'I feel like a tree that's been pruned too much on one side and now I've grown around a house, into the shade, and there are all these people telling me I'm in the wrong place.'

'What people?' asked Violet. 'Who?'

'Everyone. Everyone I see. Everywhere I go I feel like I'm being watched by someone who's a witness to this terrible thing that I've sunk into, which doesn't make any sense.'

'It makes sense to me.'

Doreen scoffed and caught herself off guard. She stopped before she rolled her eyes. How could this make sense to a person so flawless?

'I can't imagine it does, but thanks,' said Doreen. 'You're this perfect woman. You're named after a flower.'

Doreen thought she saw Violet's face transform for a second, but then it was back to normal. What was that? A look of detachment? Dismissal? Anger?

Silently, they ate bits and pieces of the insane collection of food before them. Doreen found herself eating according to her taste buds, hopping from savory to sweet, avoiding citrus, wiping everything away with something starchy and plain.

Violet held up her hand and signaled to the waiter when they were finished. There was still plenty of food left, but Doreen was full. Violet hadn't eaten much, not even the two hard-boiled eggs, which sat alone and untouched on their plate. Doreen was wary of this. Here was this special request the waiter had had to fulfill and she hadn't even touched it. Still, he seemed pleasant enough when he appeared at the table and took Violet's credit card for the bill.

After they paid, Doreen made the uniquely restaurant movements – the deep breaths, the raising of the eyebrows, the looking around and stretching – that were meant to signal she was about to get up, but Violet wasn't reciprocating or noticing. She stayed exactly in her seat, not ready to move. Doreen took note of this and leaned back while the waiter cleared the table. The women sat in silence and watched him stack the dishes. The two eggs rolled around their little plate. He wiped away a blot of spicy mayo. When he was gone and the table was clean, Violet placed both her hands on top of the table and leaned forward.

'I'm going to extend you an invitation,' she said. She paused. She looked, for a moment, as if she were getting ready to spot a reaction in Doreen, then changed her mind, disregarded the utility of finding one and continued.

'I'm flying to Atlanta tomorrow,' she said. 'I have a few business meetings to attend. My plane leaves at seven o'clock in the morning. I want you to come with me.'

Now Doreen gave a reaction that was worth considering. She was totally surprised. 'What?'

Violet continued. 'Now, if this were for decorum's sake, I would say something like, 'You're more than *welcome* to come along,' or even 'I would *like* it if you could come,' but I believe in clear statements: I want you to come to Atlanta with me tomorrow.'

'I can't go to Atlanta—'

'How come?' Violet's tone changed. Possibly even soured. 'You can take a nice break. Your work won't mind if you're gone a few days. I'll be at my meetings, but you can go see the museums, see the aquarium, explore the city, take a day trip, it will be easy. Come with me.'

This was making Doreen upset. She suddenly realized where she was. She shook her head and got up from the table on her own. She came to her senses and her senses came violently back to her, colliding all at once in her head. What was she doing? Why had she come here? What about all of her things she had thrown away in the dumpster? What about all of her money she had wasted on fancy delivery meals? What about the kids? Those two kids, those children, those two dead children. The swarm of it all was enormous.

'Sorry, no. This is weird,' said Doreen. 'I don't mean to be rude, but this is weird. I don't know who you are but suddenly I'm here having dinner with you, out in wherever the hell we are – I don't even know where we are! I'm sorry, but this is over. I have to get out of here.'

She wove around the empty tables in the restaurant and made her way toward the exit, but when she reached the door, a hand grabbed her. A set of sharpened nails dug into her wrist. She cried and said, 'Let go of me!' but Violet yanked her close.

'Listen to me, Doreen,' she said. 'You think I know nothing

about you, but I know *exactly* about you. I know what position your life is in right now, down to the very degree and orientation and rate of decay. I promise you – I swear to you – if you leave this restaurant alone, you'll be closing the door on something that will never come back into your life ever again – *ever* again. Is that clear to you?'

The air hung in silence. The waiter eyed them from the other side of a glass partition. Violet relaxed her grip, but kept hold of Doreen's arm. They were illuminated only by the light of a claw crane arcade game. A hundred purple dogs and princess keychains stared up at them with cartoon eyes.

'This is your only chance, Doreen. You said so yourself: you don't know who you are. You've cut off too many parts of yourself, you've experienced real trauma. Come with me and let yourself heal. There are things in this world you won't believe exist and I can help you find them. If you walk away from that, you'll never have another chance. For your life's sake.'

She finally let go of her.

Doreen felt a propulsion inside herself, a kind of bubble that she hadn't burped yet, a cranky rudder on a boat trying to churn itself to life. A vibration ran up through her arm from where Violet had grabbed her. She wanted to run away, but she also wanted to crumble apart, break into a thousand pieces and fall through Violet's fingers. She sensed that there was something else here, something more than just flinging herself into simple, careless abandon with a stranger. Violet had reached and somehow pulled at something lithe and slippery from inside her. A discovery.

Doreen had once taken an impromptu trip to Las Vegas with Whitney. It had been Whitney's idea – back in the early days when their rooming together had been a novelty, and both girls were making a conscientious effort to become better friends.

They stayed two nights on the Strip and spent their days wandering casinos, pool-hopping, day-drinking into oblivion, and when the trip was over, Doreen felt like something was broken – and not newly broken, but broken and only just discovered. She and Whitney were different from each other, she had always known that, but there was a new dimension to it after the trip. They had gotten along, they had stayed up late chatting in their hotel room, they had memorized each other's drink orders, and even phone numbers, but somehow, against their best efforts, they had come home sunburned, reeking of cigarette smoke, and with a distance between them that neither of them had ever properly recognized before. There was a gulf of fear between them.

Was Violet just an extreme Whitney? Another A+ woman reaching out to her like some kind of pet-project or attachment issue? No. This was different. Violet had walked out into the road and had placed her arms around her broken self. And what was more – Violet was strange, stranger than her outward bravado suggested. There was something about her that Doreen could sense, a kind of insecurity or instability, a need to project perfection in order to protect something innermost, inconceivable.

The smell of after-dinner coffee hung in the air and mixed unpleasantly with Violet's perfume. She smelled otherworldly, fragrant like a flower – like a violet – but from a different world, not one with big corporations camouflaged as old-timey diners, not one with blind corners in busy parking lots, not one with cops intent on prodding the living until they die and the dead until they flinch.

Doreen goes.

She closes her eyes and nods her head.

All she says is 'Yes,' and the two of them disappear.

CHAPTER 9

Tyler the delivery boy just wanted to check on Doreen. He was in the area and stuck in traffic and the thought crossed his mind to stop by her apartment. He just wanted to check on her. See if she was OK.

For over a month, the two of them had established a routine that had amounted to several thousand dollars' worth of delivery orders – money that mostly disappeared inside the app, vaporizing magically to some billionaire in San Francisco, but her tips had been reliably generous and enough for Tyler to prioritize her orders above all others.

Money aside, there was something else that interested him in her that trained him to hover around his phone between six and seven every night when her orders usually came through. He would stay within radius of her apartment, rejecting any other orders that came in so he could grab hers right when it appeared.

She was an anomaly. A glitch in the system. Who ordered roasted lamb and polenta cakes one night and yellowfin tuna the next? How could she afford that? And she lived out here, in a municipally gray area better suited for warehouses and animal shelters and sprawling cinema parking lots than anything else. She seemed to exist outside the confines of money and class – and even space and time, what with her odd habit of keeping the lights off and the trash – so much trash – piled up inside her apartment. Really, what was up with that? And she was attractive but in a careless way, which was what Tyler liked the most. She wasn't grungy or intentionally disheveled, but beautiful without effort, and not too dolled up, but had good style and not in a try-hard way. Those were the depths of his ability to describe her. And aside from all of that, her expensive orders and lucrative tips had all of a sudden stopped coming.

There was no answer at her door when he knocked. The blinds were shut and the door was locked. The parking lot was empty save for a blue Honda. Summer noises from the main road swirled around the space like a stale echo, muffled by the surrounding trees. A pop song played from an open window and blew away. Tyler felt a surge of uncoolness and he wished he hadn't come. What was he doing here? He couldn't think of an excuse that made this seem at all appropriate, so he shook his head at himself and turned away.

A crunching sound came from the far end of the parking lot. Glass shattered and there was a loud thud that echoed around the complex. It made Tyler jump. He leaned out over the balcony and looked around for the source of the noise. In the corner of the lot a man was climbing out of a dumpster. He noticed Tyler watching and pointed up at him.

'Hey!'

The man got out and hurled a black garbage bag over his shoulder. The lid of the dumpster slammed shut.

Tyler looked around uncomfortably, unprepared for confrontation, especially with someone like this. He walked away from Doreen's apartment quickly, starting into a run when he was out of view of the man.

'Hey get back here!' the man yelled.

Tyler ran down the length of the building, into the stair-well, skipping steps. He made it out but the man had been faster, cutting him off at the bottom of the stairs. He grabbed him by the shoulders and pushed him up against the wall.

'What the hell, dude.'

'I'm a police officer,' the man said. 'Stop resisting.'

Tyler continued to struggle – the man wore no uniform or badge – but there was no use, he was overpowering, fit and burly, sweating through a gray t-shirt. He said his name was Officer Solloway – off duty at the moment, but investigating something in the area. There had been a hit-and-run at the apartment two days ago. Tyler's face continued to scrape against the cement wall. An elbow dug hard into his back.

'OK, OK, fine, please, stop,' he said.

Finally, Officer Solloway relented. They broke away from each other and tentatively relaxed. Tyler caught his breath, steadying himself against the wall. He noticed the black garbage bag on the ground that the man had been carrying. Its contents bulged and threatened to split the bag open.

'Maybe you heard about the accident,' said Solloway. 'Leo and Harry? Two little kids? Got run over two days ago?'

'I think so, yeah,' said Tyler. He hadn't seen anything about it.

'Do you know the girl that lives here?'

'Kind of,' said Tyler. 'Not really.'

'You were knocking on her door.'

'Yeah, I mean, I don't know why though. I didn't mean to come here, really. I was just checking on her. I'm a friend. I really don't want to get involved in anything.'

'You ran away from me.'

Tyler was nervous but tried to steel himself. Cops are pigs, he told himself. Come on. He had protested them once. He tried to remember what he had read in some of the pamphlets handed out.

'If you're a police officer, where's your badge?'

'It's in my wallet, in my car,' said Solloway. He instinctively felt around his body for these signifiers of authority: his badge, his gun, his radio.

'And what are you doing here, just digging through someone's trash?'

'Listen, two days ago, an SUV came blaring through this parking lot and ran over two little boys, killing them instantly.' Solloway stepped close to Tyler again, pointing a finger at him. 'We're gathering all the information we can and someone who we think might be a key witness – someone who might have seen it happen, who might help us identify the driver – is Doreen Durand, who lives here, and we can't seem to get hold of her anymore. So if you've had recent contact with her, or know anything that might help us, I need to know. Her apartment is empty, cleared out.'

Tyler shifted uncomfortably. 'Look, it's weird, but I'm her delivery boy.' He told Solloway about the extravagant meals, how Doreen had been ordering them every night for months until just the other day, when she had abruptly stopped. As he said this, he felt his allegiance to her slipping away – she was just another customer in a matter of seconds. 'She's gone?'

'Gone,' said Solloway. 'We entered the property last night. Cleared out.'

The two of them stood there in silence in the shadow of the building, with Doreen's apartment up above as if it were a portal into a different world and neither one of them knew how to proceed. If there was any logic behind why the two of them were here, some cosmic sequence of math that drew both Tyler and the officer here together, it had been an apparition. There was no logic. What was between them now was emptiness. What had once been so close to them – this strange Doreen – was now far-flung. They might as well have held a séance.

The two of them went their separate ways. Solloway went

back to his car and threw the garbage bag in the trunk. Tyler went back to his motorcycle, opened the delivery app on his phone and made himself available. Almost immediately an order came in for spring rolls, fried rice, orange chicken, and fried calamari rings. Twenty-dollars total. He knew it wasn't Doreen immediately – she would never have ordered from the restaurant, she would never have spent less than fifty dollars. Still, he looked back up at her apartment, as if she would suddenly appear in the doorway. Across the parking lot, Solloway – the man who claimed to be a police officer – was doing the same thing. Waiting and watching, not moving.

After some hesitation, Tyler shook off his unease and accepted the new delivery order, started his motorcycle, and drove off. A few more days went by where he thought about Doreen, especially around dinnertime when the delivery requests would flood his phone. A few times he would scan the list for her address, but then, eventually, he stopped. Sometimes if he was ever in the area, he would suddenly think of her, but then, as more time went by, he didn't.

CHAPTER 10

There had been no other leads. No tips. News of the accident had been picked up nationally – albeit as a footnote during a morning show – but a barrel of public rage was directed at the case and the police department was unprepared for the onslaught. April had released the cutest photo of the two boys to the media. She had accepted donations for the funeral. A memorial fund was being talked about. The mailbox on the blind corner had already been torn out. And on a Saturday evening, free from work, Solloway could not pull himself away.

He went home and emptied the garbage bag out onto the floor like a man possessed. There was something wet – a half-empty pop can or something – that immediately soaked the carpet in his living room, so he kicked everything over onto the hardwood in the kitchen. He cursed at himself for making a mess because there was no one else there who would. He lived alone.

He should be doing this at the police station. He should be logging this activity as part of the official investigation. He should have a reasonable excuse for hounding this periphery witness. He shook off his conscience and plowed through his shame.

The trash was Doreen's. There was unopened mail with her name on it that confirmed it. Most of the trash had been bundled together in a bed sheet, which Solloway unraveled and sorted through. There were wrappers, plastic bags, receipts, half-eaten meals, books, utensils, plugs and cords, a laptop, Kleenex, pens, coupons, a hairbrush, clothes, lotions, blankets, crumbs. All of it spread out onto the floor, layer after layer, a life revealing itself. Solloway was revolted by the smells but also felt a strange attraction to the mess, as if the messier it got – the longer he let it sit there and percolate – the more it would burn a hole through the floor, revealing a whole new place to explore, a hidden chamber underneath his house.

He was embarrassed. He never felt the temptation to do this sort of thing in his job. He had *almost* never done something like this – to intrude in this kind of way – and doing so reminded him of the one other time he had become obsessed like this.

He dug through Doreen's things and opened her mail and examined her receipts and inspected the different residues of food and fought waves of shame. He paused and solidly declared out loud that what he was doing was an intrusion, practically perverted, and vowed to get it all out of his system right then and there, and yet . . .

It was clear that Doreen had really thrown *everything* away.

Under a jacket, there were sets of keys – she had thrown away her keys. There was a diploma with her name on it, crinkled and wet. There were financial documents. There was no phone and no wallet, but there were two purses and a backpack. There was fifty dollars in cash. There was a roll of half-used toothpaste and a spatula coated in grease and a bit of egg. The audacity of these things seemed to justify Solloway's act of intrusion, as if it were somehow permissible given the circumstances.

He pulled out the laptop. The screen was cracked but it had a full battery. He wiped a smear of cream cheese off the keyboard and turned it on. He opened Doreen's saved documents and web browser, her music library, her photos, but there was nothing of interest. Her social media passwords were saved, so he weeded through those, but there was nothing out of the ordinary, barely any recent activity and nothing from the past few weeks. Her email had gone unchecked for weeks and only consisted of order confirmations from the delivery app.

An odd fantasy entered his mind: maybe she had been the one who got killed. Maybe Doreen had been hit by the same car that day and died and they had somehow missed it. How else could she have just vanished like this? How else could she have seemed so off, so ghost-like when they spoke with her out on her balcony? Because she was dead of course. Solloway thought about movies where this kind of story played out and lost himself in the fantasy.

Doreen reminded him of a former colleague, a woman named Sophia, who had once worked in admin at the station. Over a number of strictly professional years, Solloway had cultivated a sort of relationship with her – not sexual and not really even romantic, but intimate and close. A work wife.

He considered her special and it seemed healthy and reciprocal to everyone involved. It got to the point where it was expected they would eat lunch together whenever they were both at the station and their schedules allowed for it. Neither of them had much of a life outside of work, certainly not Solloway, who was working long hours as a rookie cop, so their conversations were freewheeling, there were no repercussions or topics that were out-of-bounds. They vented to each other. They bantered back and forth about the news of the day, politics, movies, each other's families, girls Solloway was dating or thinking about dating. They asked each other weird questions – far-out, off-color questions that relieved some of the high pressure at work. 'Would you rather accidentally kill someone who was innocent, or mistakenly let someone go free who was guilty?'

Sophia was settled in a long-term relationship and was finishing a second degree at school on her spare time. Solloway was in over his head with work, struggling with discipline and career ladder politics. In their separate lives they were two solid rocks, completely apart from each other, but somehow, under these circumstances, they each found a small, carved-out space inside themselves where the other person could sit and visit, like a treasure. They recognized the singular sense of specialness their relationship took on. And if there was ever an intruder – the peppery taste of office gossip or the threat of a job transfer or a change of schedule – Sophia had a way of taking that foreign thing and throwing it far away, out into a nether-space where they could watch it and be unaffected.

'You're a cop,' Sophia said once after a comfortable stretch of silence.

'I'm a cop. Weird, huh?'

It was the only time Solloway had ever expressed real, reflective surprise at his life.

Their lunch breaks sometimes lasted too long. Solloway was reprimanded sometimes, but never seriously. They gave each other Christmas presents. They remembered each other's birthdays. They each confided in one another what they *actually* wanted to be doing with their lives – because no one, even if they have their dream career, is ever doing what they want.

And then, without warning, Sophia disappeared.

Solloway had trouble remembering. Had she mentioned something about leaving? Had she got a new job? Did she get married and fly away? Did something terrible happen? There was no one to ask. In fact, it was him that other people asked.

'Whatever happened to Sophia?' they would come up and say.

Even Officer Palmer had asked him. 'Where's your little girlfriend?' And Solloway had no answers.

He went to human resources and asked what happened to her.

'She put in her two weeks' notice two weeks ago. And that was two weeks ago, so she's gone now,' they said. There was no reasoning. Or, actually, there was reasoning – the most reasonable reasoning of all: she was gone.

'But she never told anyone,' said Solloway.

'She put in her two weeks' notice. I'm not sure what you mean? Was she working on some kind of project with you? Her replacement started the other day, his name's Monty, have you met him? She trained him up pretty well if you need anything.'

It was a shock. Solloway once held a forty-year-old woman in his arms as she died of a gunshot wound. He was the very last thing she saw in her life – not the ceiling fan above them, not the radio buzzing on his shoulder – she only saw him, this complete stranger, cradling her. That was the most disturbed and raw Solloway had ever felt during his time in the force and the only time he ever felt like that again was when Sophia left. Desertion. This woman with whom he had shared a pure connection, had poured fragments of his mind into, had laughed harder with than ever before, was gone.

He went home and expected an answer to appear the next day and there was none. He waited a week, then a month for something to make sense, for someone to hand him a card from her that they had forgotten to give him, for a missing paycheck she would have to come back in and collect and *voilà!* here's why I'm leaving, hugs, kisses, have a great summer, goodbye – just a goodbye, that's all. But there was none.

One day, he indulged – the first of many indulgences – and found what he could of her online. There wasn't much, just one privacy-protected social media page. On it were only a handful of photos that had been left unprotected and they each contained a Sophia he had never known: there she was with her boyfriend in Hawaii – she had never told him about that trip. She was rock climbing in another – a hobby she had never mentioned. There was a group photo of her with people he had never seen before or heard about. Even her boyfriend didn't look like the boyfriend she had brought along one year to the office Christmas party. Who was this person and why had Solloway spent every day with her? Had it all amounted to nothing? He was stupefied.

He was paired up with Officer Palmer that year. Dreaded Officer Palmer who had received two citations for misconduct and seemed perpetually on the edge of a human rights investigation. What had been given to Sophia had been given and what was left inside Solloway was turned inward and wrapped up, burrowed away to fester. He developed a sadistic rapport with Palmer that hinged on mistrust, sarcasm, and laziness; a distaste for authority when it worked to their advantage and a stringent devotion to authority when it also worked to their advantage. If what they encountered during their shifts together wasn't dark comedy, it was pure darkness, it was bleak, it was two kids killed in a hit-and-run, holy shit. He never would have said some of the things he said with Palmer around Sophia, and then he realized, maybe she had done the same.

Solloway didn't want to become that guy – the office troll, in love with and then spurned by the receptionist – but he knew that that was the appearance it was taking on. He hadn't been in love with her, at least, not in the way he had loved other women. He was teased for it. He unjustly laughed along with the jokes with the hope that they would stop, but he was still teased. He got angry, more prone to lashing out. If he had ever been on the cusp of figuring out what exactly he had had with Sophia, any actualization was ruined by Palmer, by the boys' club, by the drudgery of the everyday and by not having anyone to talk to about it any more.

He saw Sophia in Doreen's things, piled there on his kitchen floor, sticky and smelly. He saw a woman who had seemingly up and left without explanation, escaping definition, and leaving chaos in her wake. He pored over every item, every article of clothing, every receipt, every uneaten crust for some kind of sign, for an explanation; an easy answer that would slip out and tell him exactly what went through a mind like that.

The longer he sat and stared at the pile on the floor, the less sense it made and the more humiliated he felt for having let it suck him in. Humiliated – yes, it was *her* fault, this loser Doreen. Another woman who had left him high and dry, probably due to her own insecurities – she had to have millions – her misbegotten career choices, whatever they were; her singledom; perpetual adolescence.

Solloway curled his hand into a fist and smashed it through the laptop screen, completely shattering what had already been cracked. The screen went green and purple then permanently black when he punched it again. He flipped it over and tossed it aside.

Then something caught his eye: a small green square that had been underneath it. The square was paper, but folded up so many times that it was bulging and almost spherical. It was thick, almost like artist's paper, almost cloth-like; the kind of paper that has to soak in water before being run through a printing press. Solloway unfolded it carefully. The green expanded like a tiny bug and revealed nothing at first. There was no ink on the card, so he almost didn't see the delicate embossing that had been distorted by the folds. It was only by the luck of the angle of the light that he noticed the words. He brought the card close to his eyes and tilted the card so the letters outlined themselves in thin shadows. The first thing he saw was in the corner of the card: an address – an address in Portugal – and a phone number. And in the center of the card was a name, or at least, two words that had been placed next to each other. Maybe it was the name of a business – some uppity marketing company or a cyber-security firm. Or a florist. Something involving flowers.

Violet Cascade.

ATLANTA

CHAPTER 11

The dolphin show was enough to remind Doreen of what her crippling depression had done to her. A trio of the world's most intelligent animals were jumping up out of the water in tune with cinematic music and seemed to watch her sitting up in the highest, furthest-away seat she had found. They locked eyes with her every time they flew out of the water. They did flips and shot through hoops and caught fish in their mouths and still they watched her, noticing how inelegant she was. 'Did you see that one up there?' they said to each other between tricks. 'Up in the far corner? Don't you think she seems out of place? She's not smiling.'

A dark purple dome covered the arena, giving the impression of a night sky or a deep, dark sea. Ocean-inspired patterns were projected onto it and moved around. Jellyfish and seahorses – abstract and stylized, pink and teal – and also, inexplicably, stars and planets. They were at the bottom of the ocean but also shot out into space. Was there a difference?

Depression. That was the word for it. Doreen thanked the dolphins for showing off their blunt precision, as if they had helped her name it. They were so exacting in their movements. Everything they did, they did with intent, as if to say 'If you're going to be depressed, be depressed, go through the motions like we go through these hoops, there's a fish at the end.'

She named it now. She said to herself, 'I am depressed. I am a depressed person, so that's why I didn't do anything when

I saw two kids get run over by a car and that's why I threw away all my possessions and that's why I'm here now, in Atlanta, with a stranger with a weird name, who flew me in her private jet and dropped me off at an aquarium, watching a dolphin show by myself.' Her emotions took a sudden dip – turned off, actually – and she wondered if Violet would have a phone charger she could borrow as the map she had been using to navigate the city had sucked up almost all her battery. This thought popped up in her mind and she realized she was stable enough to get a move on. If you can worry about a phone charger, you can get up and get on with things, she told herself.

She left the aquarium and rode a bus through midtown. She got off a block away from the art museum where it had been arranged for her to meet Violet at the end of the day, but paused for a moment in front of a giant church that had caught her eye. Long cement steps led up through a tan portico under imposing Corinthian columns. There were three enormous wooden doors at the entrance and all of them were closed. A breeze that was trying its hardest to be refreshing passed by and blessed her with a warm shiver. It was evening almost suddenly – the time on Doreen's dying phone surprised her. The sky was dark orange, fading purple, and both the sun and the moon were somewhere up there, dancing around each other the way they did in the summer. She looked across at the museum down the road and wondered if it would still be open, how she would get in. She contemplated not going so as not to let Violet be the one to have to abandon her – *Doreen* would abandon *her* instead; just hang out here on the steps of faux-Rome forever.

'Are you lost?' said a voice.

Doreen turned around. A handsome man in a suit was leaning against one of the columns.

'Doreen Durand, right?' he said. 'I'm Tom. I'm Miss Cascade's assistant.'

He came forward and shook Doreen's hand. He was too handsome, too angular, too hard to look at because you couldn't just look, you had to stare. Each of his features was the perfect shape, the perfect size, the perfect color, the perfect consistency, like the painted portrait of a man, not an actual human. His wet pebble eyes widened. His plush lips parted into a smile.

'The art museum is down that way. This is a church.'

'I know,' said Doreen. 'I just wanted to take a look at it. The bus dropped me off on the corner.'

'The bus?' He said this as if it were the plague. 'You should have called. I could have come and picked you up with the car. Did Violet give you my number?'

'Maybe. She gave me a lot of things, I must have lost track.' Doreen laughed and tugged at her shirt – Violet had given her a brand new set of clothes before they left Portland. The clothes were simple, just a light top and dark jeans, but they had come in boxes wrapped in ribbon, folded and pressed with a stunning degree of care. She had also given her a plain gold necklace – a thin strand of gold with no pendant or charm – that hung nearly invisible around her neck, resting along her clavicle. 'I guess I'm just a little overwhelmed by everything. I wanted to take the bus.'

Tom shrugged. He didn't seem to understand or care. Doreen could sense his singular loyalty to his employer and no one else. 'We should get a move on,' he said. 'Violet is just finishing up at the museum.'

They crossed the street and walked down the block. They reached the museum but the doors were locked. Tom pulled and pushed on all six of the front doors but the thick glass wouldn't budge. A janitor inside running a vacuum didn't pay attention to them. Tom took out his phone and called Violet to let her know they were there.

'She'll come get us in a sec,' he said when he hung up. He put the phone away and leaned against the door. Doreen shuffled around and watched him in glances, trying to read his expression. Was this business as usual? Was it normal for his boss to fly around the country, trapping strange, lost women and taking them away? Was he always tasked with shepherding them around? He was stoic and unreadable.

Doreen broke the silence between them. 'So how long have you been working for Violet?'

'A few years.'

'Do you enjoy it?'

'Yes.'

Silence again. The ambiguity of the entire situation festered. She tried to push through it. Tom seemed young – surely there was a default kinship there, a baseline under-standing where she would be able to ask the questions she wanted answered.

'Look, I don't mean to sound weird or anything, but who is she? What does she do? I don't know if she's told you about me, but we kind of just met.'

Tom laughed and shook his head. 'That's something you should ask her then, if you really want to know. She does a lot of things.'

'Like what?'

'She owns a lot of businesses. Museums, galleries, univer-sities, shopping malls, wineries, pharmaceutical plants, a few historic palaces in Europe and Asia, oil refineries. She's an activist, a movie producer, a lobbyist, a saleswoman, a banker. She's an heiress. A lawmaker. A free agent.'

'I've never heard of her before.' Doreen's eyebrows were

raised. She was beginning to sense a sort of charade running behind the scenes, the long con.

'That's how she likes it,' said Tom.

'Who did she inherit her money from?'

'She didn't inherit anything from anyone.'

'You just said she was an heiress—'

'An heiress to her own wealth.' Tom stood slightly more upright, annoyed. Less annoyed at Doreen than annoyed at something else. He was searching for the right words. 'You have to understand that she's been around a long time. A very long time. Her network reaches everywhere in the world.'

'What companies does she own?'

'You would be surprised.'

'Then name one. What galleries does she own? Does she own this museum?'

'No, not this one.'

'Then which ones?'

Tom laughed and sighed. 'Look. Violet doesn't operate the way you would typically expect someone like her to operate. She moves through the world at a different frequency than you and me. Her businesses are a smorgasbord, her bank accounts are infinite, she negotiates stocks, bonds, mortgages, acquisitions the way a gardener rakes up leaves – but she's nowhere. You can't find out a thing about her and there's a reason for that.'

Doreen's incredulity was left hanging, still displayed across her face in a smirk. She took a few steps back and crossed her arms. Tom was a zealot and maybe that was his purpose – puff up Violet's resume with nonspecific nonsense, herald the angel before she arrived.

'You don't believe me,' he said.

'Sure, I believe you,' said Doreen. She resigned herself.

A light fragrance pulsed through the air, changing

everything. It pushed invisibly against the back of Doreen's head and wrapped around to her nose – the smell of berries in winter, a pinch of salt water and cloves.

'Sorry, I meant to tell them to keep the doors unlocked for you.' Violet had materialized behind her from nowhere. 'You must be exhausted.' She extended a perfect wing and touched Doreen on the arm. She wore the same pastel outfit from earlier but also a thick, white cape. Worn by someone less alluring it would be called a poncho.

'You're probably famished. We'll go to the hotel now, but I want to show you what I've been up to all day.'

The door opened for Violet, somehow, without needing a key. Doreen walked with her through the lobby, passing the janitor who smiled at them and possibly even bowed his head. They walked through a darkened exhibit hall and down a set of stairs. Violet's heels tapped out a pleasant rhythm. Tom trailed silently behind them. At the end of another long corridor, they went through a large fire door into an underground loading bay where everything was bathed in yellow industrial lighting. Parked in the middle of the large, nearly empty space were two semi trucks and one black Jaguar, which Tom went to and readied. Near the trucks was a group of men who were gathered around two large objects on the ground wrapped in tarps. The objects were each the size of a whale and had been tied with rope and bungee cords to a series of wood pallets.

Violet had bought a statue.

'Procured,' was the word she used, but it was more complicated than she had anticipated. The statue had to be split in half in order to fit inside the two semis and that's what she had been doing all afternoon – supervising the cut, along with the museum curator and the artist, who had already left and flown back to Montreal. 'So as of today, it's officially mine, and now I've just got to find a place to put it. I'm thinking desolate. Abandoned. A void. Somewhere it can be alone. Near an ocean, maybe.'

She explained this all so matter-of-factly, as if it were perfectly normal to purchase a massive statue and have it shipped wherever you wanted. Doreen found herself nodding along as if this truly singular administrative headache was somehow not completely unrelatable.

A final series of negotiations was made with the group of men over the care and storage of the halved statue, and Doreen and Violet both got in the back seat of the Jaguar with Tom driving. They sped through the city for yet another traffic-less moment and arrived at a luxury hotel. Doreen had never felt so whisked away and seamless. The museum door had opened for Violet right away. They had stopped at no red lights. Violet hadn't signed a form, or showed a card, or reached for cash, or raised a finger for anything or anyone. The world was hers.

'You look tired. You're probably hungry.'

Violet instructed Doreen to lie down on the bed. She touched her hand to her forehead. Doreen didn't worry about the grease and grime her forehead had accumulated over the course of the day only because she knew Violet's hands had to be impervious to that sort of thing. She was sure Violet saw her body as merely a jellyfish or some other mushy sea-thing, similar to the ones she had poked and prodded earlier that day at the aquarium.

'I'm OK,' Doreen said. 'I had a fish sandwich for lunch.'

'They serve fish at the aquarium?'

'I know. Barbaric, right?'

Violet laughed, flashing a million-dollar smile. Her face was almost iridescent. Unfathomably smooth, but also unique, incomparable. She paused and looked closely at Doreen.

'Are you sure you're OK?' she asked. She seemed to be peering into Doreen, trying to see something inside her eyes. The expression on her face was almost one of nervousness and Doreen had to look away, embarrassed.

'I'm as OK as I can be. I think I'm finally coming out on the other side of this ... this *thing* – whatever this is. I'm finally realizing that I actually dropped everything and ran away with a crazy rich woman in her private jet.'

Violet broke into another agreeable smile. Both of them laughed. 'What you need now is food and sleep,' Violet said. 'And tomorrow, that's all we'll do. Food and sleep. I've got no other appointments and have no intentions of leaving this hotel. There's a great gym and spa downstairs we can grab a massage at. We can relax.'

Doreen looked around and noticed the second bed next to hers. They would be sharing the same room. It wasn't an uncomfortable thought, just not one that lined up with the kind of person she thought Violet was. She had assumed she would have booked herself another room – an executive suite in a completely different hotel, like she had done in Portland the night before. Or maybe not book another room at all, but fly off into the night to roost somewhere. Instead, she was still here, in fact, she was sitting on the bed with her legs folded up, grinning. She seemed almost girlish, eager to chat the night away.

There was a knock at the door and it opened. Tom entered, bringing with him a push-cart filled with food. Again, a strange assortment of tastes. There were biscuits and a stew, a small bouquet of seafood samplers, pastries, two strawberry shakes, hamburger sliders, a spinach salad, and a slab of red licorice crusted with sour sugar crystals.

Nothing matched. It was the kind of meal a space alien would order.

Violet thanked Tom and told him that was all they would be needing for the rest of the night. She let him take her white cape, her matching white wallet, and her phone for safekeeping.

'Doreen, your phone probably needs to be charged, I'm sure,' she said. 'Do you want to give it to Tom?'

'Yeah, that would be great, actually. It's totally dead.' Doreen took out her phone and handed it to him as if this were perfectly normal, as if it would be audacious for her to charge her own phone. They shared a look. She wasn't sure what kind of look it was, but it was a look. Something shared. Doreen had no idea how old Violet was but she knew Tom had to be around her own age, twenty-something. To a certain degree, in terms of life experience, they were equals, and when he took her phone and their hands made momentary contact, she felt this awareness. Tom's face wore a kind of anti-smile. Not a frown, but an opposite, inverted expression from a foreign land. Doreen tried to ward it off. She faked a smile of her own and said thank you.

Where she was, what she was doing, whether she should eat a hamburger and then a shrimp cocktail or the other way around was all irrelevant to Doreen and that was exactly how Violet seemed to want her. She wanted her to be comfortable and that was what she became. Their conversation devolved. They became sarcastic and jolly. They talked about the statue Violet had bought. She couldn't describe the design of it very well – she said more about the kind of place she wanted to put it. They talked about the food. They talked about the ethics of aquariums – if a performing dolphin and a caged starfish could recognize their predicaments on equal levels. Doreen told Violet about how starfish can be cut in half and regenerate themselves into two new starfish and Violet wondered if that could happen infinitely, if something like that could split itself into bits again and again, regenerating into new people. They talked about Atlanta. The weather. What they had seen that day.

'I walked by this beautiful church near the museum.'

'The tan one? With the columns? It's gorgeous, isn't it?'

'It looks like a mini-version of the Parthenon in Rome.'

Violet laughed and held a hand up to her mouth while she finished chewing. She apologized and pushed her hair away from her face. 'Listen Doreen, I'm going to warn you – we're going to have a lot of moments together where I seem like a know-it-all. That's not exactly the truth, but I'll admit to being one on just a few occasions, like now.'

Doreen laughed at this elaborate addendum. 'What do you mean?'

'There's no way to say this without sounding like a know-it-all, but I think you mean the *Pantheon* in Rome. The *Parthenon* is in Greece.'

'What did I say?'

'You said Parthenon.'

Doreen pondered, then burst into a smile. She slapped Violet playfully on the knee – the first time she initiated physical contact with her. 'Oh my gosh, no – I knew that! I *know* that, really, I do. I meant to say that, I took art history. Parthenon, Pantheon.'

'Potato, potato!'

Their laughter was a release. The air around them warmed. Their voices flew out into the night through open windows. Atlanta glistened beyond them.

'We should go there,' said Violet.

'To where? Rome or Greece?' Doreen was still smiling.

'Either one. Both. We can go the day after tomorrow if you

want. That would be a nice trip.' Violet pursed her lips and looked up at the ceiling, thinking through a calendar in her head. 'I'll have to deal with the statue again in two weeks. I was going to stay here in Atlanta until then, but there would be no point since my other appointments fell through.' She mumbled this to herself, sorting out her engagements, then her voice grew louder. 'I think that could work, actually, if you wanted to. Do you want to? Would that be fun? We could just go to Rome if you think it's too much. Have you got a passport? I can send Tom back for it. Actually, it might be faster to just order a new one direct from the State Department. I'll make a call tomorrow.'

Doreen tilted her head. Her smile was still there but had gone askew. 'You're crazy. Just go to Rome?'

'What's crazy about Rome? It's one of the oldest cities in the world.'

'I didn't say Rome is crazy, I said *you* are crazy.'

Violet had a nervous look on her face again as if she had forgotten for a moment where she was, looking suddenly insecure. Then she tossed out one last hearty laugh and leaned back onto the bed. Resting on one elbow, her body curved with a mathematically pleasing slope. Her chest, hips, and legs were like three separate units, but all working in perfect harmony, commandeered as one sole enterprise by her head. Doreen pushed away her food and joined her, lying side by side, ignoring the absurdity. A single light from the ceiling wrapped them in a perfect circle.

'I'm glad you're here,' said Violet, whose age, identity, and agenda were written plainly on her face, but in an ancient language.

'I'm glad too.'

CHAPTER 12

Tom woke them up in the morning. He entered the room with a suitcase, which was filled with new clothes all for Doreen. He drew back the blackout curtains and let the morning pour into the room. A routine was enacted. It was something that Tom had honed and perfected to the point of appearing casual while he went about it. He sliced open a fresh lemon, put a wedge of it in a glass of water, set it on Violet's nightstand, then placed a pair of slippers next to her bed, right where he knew her feet would land. He went into the bathroom and turned on the shower and the fan. He laid out a tray of lotions, serums, perfumes, vitamins, and makeup. When he came back into the room, Doreen was just being woken up by the smell of coffee beginning to brew.

'The suitcase over there has new clothes for you. And some shoes. Bath stuff, cosmetics, that kind of thing.'

'Thank you, Tom,' Violet said before Doreen could. Tom nodded and was at her side with reading glasses and a news-paper right as she sat up. She took them and he adjusted her pillows to cradle her back. She put on the glasses. She opened her free hand and the glass of water was placed in it, she didn't even need to reach or ask for it. She drank, then Tom took it away.

Doreen watched this dance from her bed, lying on her side with only her messy head poking out of the covers. She stayed burrowed there all morning, watching Tom straighten up the room, then Violet rising from bed, showering, dressing, already telling Tom about their plans to fly to Rome, telling him to prepare the private jet, to make a call for Doreen's passport and have it ready for them. It was overwhelming, the morning, how it shone a light of realism onto what Doreen had done, how she had ended up here, and she thought that if she remained still enough, she would melt into the bed, turn into a sheet and be tossed into the laundry where there would be someone else who could make sense of all of this for her.

Eventually, she fell asleep again.

She slept through most of the day and woke up in the afternoon with her stomach growling. There was a glass of water and a sandwich on her nightstand. She sat up and took a drink and looked around. She was alone, but she heard movement coming from the other side of the door in the adjoining living room.

Doreen had hoped her mind would have figured things out on its own while she slept, but it didn't seem like it had. Everything was still as it was. She was a bundle of loose threads. Part of her felt reinvigorated, as if her head had been whipped around with such a force by the past twenty-four hours that it was finally screwed on tight. The insurmountable task of figuring out her life no longer seemed like a vague cloud, but a logic puzzle – a highly difficult one to complete, but at least something tangible, something that could be compartmentalized and digested.

She took two bites of the sandwich and went into the bathroom. Her new suitcase was there and from it, she took out new underwear, a shirt, jeans and socks. There was also a plastic bag filled with toiletries and cosmetics, which she laid out on the counter in an orderly row, marveling at the brands. She disrobed, carefully removing the hair-thin gold necklace she had been wearing, and showered. When she was done, there were the toiletries and cosmetics waiting for her – a routine begging to be commenced, an old rhythm her body seemed to beg her to play, and she obliged. She put on deodorant and lotion and a negligible amount of makeup but the sensation of it – of bringing order to herself – was like drinking sweet spring water after days of nothing but salt and sand.

She decided she would turn herself in.

'Well, not turn myself in,' she said to herself in the mirror. 'Turning yourself in is something you do when you're guilty of something. Turning yourself in is what the driver who killed those two kids will have to do. What I'm going to do is volunteer my support. I'm going to take ownership. I'm going to move forward with intent. I'll fly back to Portland, go straight to the police.'

She paused and thought about the amount of time that had passed. It was hard to tell. Steam filled the mirror. It had been three days since the accident, she counted. That long? It felt as if it had happened only hours ago and she was just waking up from that nap-of-the-damned she had taken right after it happened. She reached for her phone to search for the legal consequences of leaving the scene of a crime as a witness, but she couldn't find it, then she remembered. She had given it to Tom last night. A sudden chill ran through her. Tom shouldn't have her phone. No one should have her phone.

Her thoughts came undone in a complete reversal. A shudder of nerves threatened the two bites of sandwich in her stomach. The bathroom was awash with gold but there was a darkness in the corner. There were giant steamed-up mirrors, but no windows, and the darkness doubled in on itself over and over. There was a child's voice coming from somewhere – the vents, the non-windows, the tile, the beads of moisture. She caught flashes of children in her mind. Just generic children. Faceless. Nameless. Leo and Harry are our names, the faceless children said, reminding her. She gasped and shook her head, backed up against the cold marble wall. She clutched the side of the sink to steady herself against a tide of dizziness. She watched the veins in her arms pulse and tried to focus.

Her toothbrush would coax her back to stability, she was sure of it. She stood upright in front of the mirror like a soldier and brushed her teeth for longer than was necessary, slowly reeling herself back to reality, feeling the mint sting her gums and tongue. Foam mixed with blood. She rinsed, put everything away neatly inside the suitcase, and assessed herself in the mirror. It was one of the better versions of herself, she thought, though she was sure there were at least twenty others somewhere behind her eyes, running amok, trashing the place. She breathed in and out until she was convinced that her smile was genuine. She felt sure of herself – more sure than she had felt in ages. She knew what she needed to do.

But when she left the bathroom and went into the living room, where Violet was speaking on the phone, already arranging a hotel for them in Rome, she realized that no matter how much inner zest she could scrape together, she was no match for this all-consuming woman who had collected her.

'I'm not going with you to Rome,' said Doreen. 'I appreciate all you've done for me – this has truly been something I'll remember for the rest of my life – but I have to go home.'

She said 'home' with too much of a hollow sound in her voice and Violet noticed. There was an echo. Doreen continued, but Violet held onto this failure in tone like a cat finding an insect with a broken wing. She turned curiously to face her.

'Seeing this incredible life you have has been empowering for me, as a woman,' Doreen said. 'It's inspiring. Your graciousness has been more than I could have ever imagined possible for someone and you've made me strong enough to face the things I need to face. I'm grateful we were able to meet, honestly, it's been a truly life-changing few days. So thank you. I'm going to be able to go back to Beaverton with a real game plan and take charge of my life. I'll go to therapy, talk to friends, maybe move back in with my parents for a bit. I think I'll start doing more volunteer work, eating healthier.'

Violet was perched on the couch, looking up at Doreen in awe. Her attention was rapt. She nodded, her mouth covered by her hand, but she couldn't hold back any longer. She giggled and broke into an enormous fever of laughter. Her face broke apart with smiles.

'I'm not trying to be funny,' Doreen said more forcefully, miffed. 'I'm leaving. I'm not going to Rome, OK? I need my phone back so I can get a taxi to the airport.'

Violet kept laughing, swallowing up whatever Doreen said. Her face shook and swelled. She struggled to stop herself, wiping tears from her eyes. Doreen was annoyed.

'Oh my, I am sorry,' said Violet, finally. 'I'm sorry to hear that, really. Oh dear.' She laughed for a minute longer, red in the face, then cleared her throat. She stood up and went to the kitchenette and poured herself a glass of water. She took a new lemon and cut it in half with a knife, put a slice in her water and threw the rest in the trash.

'I know you're only saying what you think I want to hear,' she said from the sink. 'I guess I'm laughing at the idea of ever being someone who would want to hear something like that.' She turned back around, looking Doreen up and down.

'What kind of an impression have I left on you, I wonder. No – ' she paused, suddenly, truly concerned. 'No, I really do wonder. It's a strange thing for me to do but I'm wondering. I'm wondering...' Her voice faded away. She tapped a finger to her head and frowned, then shrugged it off.

She sat on the couch and drank slowly. She dialed a contact on her phone. 'You can come back up,' she said and hung up. Then she said to Doreen, 'Please, sit down. Let's talk.'

Stripped of her confidence, Doreen lowered herself onto the chair across from Violet, who still chuckled to herself and shook her head, but also made these strange, upset faces; transfixed with both giggles and concern, thinking deeply.

'So that's what you think this was?' she said finally. 'That this was some kind of self-help, empowering pow-wow, girls' retreat? A women's conference? What are you doing, thanking me, as if I've actually done a single thing. No, Doreen, our adventure hasn't even started yet.'

The front door clicked open and Tom entered, expressionless. He closed the door and remained standing there while Violet kept talking, paying no attention to him.

'What were you expecting?' she asked Doreen. 'That this would be some kind of rah-rah orgy out at a winery someplace? "Thank you for empowering me" – I don't believe that for a second. What does that mean? Empower you? I would never give anyone my power – I would literally fall to pieces if I ever did that, I would die.'

Doreen opened her mouth to speak but Violet spoke over her, louder, aggressive, agitated.

'You think this is closure?' she said. 'I'm supposed to buy that pathetic excuse of a testimony you just gave? You want to get out of here because you're getting scared. To be polite, you're telling me what you think I want to hear, which is just groveling, isn't that right? I recognize groveling – I smell it. I get it every day; people groveling at my feet. I'm afraid you've sorely misunderstood my intentions, Doreen. As if I would want to mold you into some hotshot honey – yes, by all means, get empowered, right in the ass, right on top of the capitalist pile just like me and become the oppressor in ten easy steps. The cycle continues. How trite.' She drank the last bit of water in her glass and looked up at Tom then back at Doreen. 'I have to admit, Doreen, I think I would have fallen for it.' She tapped her head again with her finger. 'I'm not as clued into things as I usually am, I'll admit. I think I would have even accepted this little *resignation* of yours if there hadn't been a very interesting development in the past few hours that betrays your facade of normalness. You're not the kind of animal you try to be, Doreen. In fact, you're exactly the kind of animal I knew I found when I first saw you.'

The darkness from the bathroom had caught up with Doreen by now. It was so obviously there, clinging to her, pulling at her from the edge of the bedroom doorway with its tendrils. She looked all around. Violet stared at her, trying to read everything in her face. But still, Doreen warded it off. 'Sorry, I don't know what you're talking about. Really, I just need to get back home. I have to be at work tomorrow.' Her voice was so small.

'Home,' said Violet, repeating her. She tapped a finger on her chin and crossed one leg over the other. 'I still don't buy it, Doreen. I really don't. And I wish I didn't have to be confrontational like this, but if it's the only thing that will keep you here . . .'

She opened her hand and Tom appeared at her side instantly. He placed Doreen's phone in her hand.

'You received a voicemail last night. Someone from Mario's called. They didn't say their name. They were wondering if you'd be returning to the office soon. You can call them back later when you find the time but more importantly, I'd like to ask you about a rather disturbing string of voicemails that we found.'

Doreen felt her pupils expand. The brown of her irises peeled away to reveal only black. There was a ringing in her ears. She made a movement to brush her hair away from her face but her finger got caught in the thin gold necklace around her neck. She couldn't remember putting it back on after her shower.

Violet saw her fear and smiled – but in her perfect manner of communicating, her smile wasn't sinister or malicious, it was incomprehensible. 'Don't worry,' she said. 'You're not in trouble for this. But I'd like to know about these messages, really. I think there's key information in them that might explain why you're here right now, why you and I were brought together.' She paused, then added, 'It's a little boy, isn't it?'

Doreen shifted uncomfortably. Her voice was scratched and worthless but she said she thought she had deleted them.

'Nothing's ever deleted,' said Tom.

Doreen breathed rage through her nose and looked at him and then at Violet, steeling herself. She went inside her mind for a moment. She admitted to herself – or, maybe she even said it out loud to everyone in the room – that she knew this wasn't a normal story. This wasn't a normal story about a normal girl learning about life the hard way. This wasn't about a woman scorned – a Hitchcockian broad fleeing the scene of a crime, plagued with consequence. She knew there was more. There was darkness, yes, but there was also gray – an ambiguity. A level of profundity she couldn't yet reach, no matter how far she dived. It was this deepness that had caused her to flee. She couldn't reach the things that were there.

But something had reached her. Something had found her in that darkness – in that deepness. Violet Cascade.

Violet sat far back in the couch. She didn't smile or laugh any more. Her face was motionless. She didn't speak. Her head was locked into place and her eyes were wide as could be as she listened carefully to every word of Doreen's story.

CHAPTER 13

'Boobie boobie fat ass fat girl boob girl stupid fat fart pussy bitch!'

That was the first voicemail Doreen received.

It was only a few days after Whitney left, in the middle of the night. She had left her phone on silent, so she slept through it, and the voicemail was there in the morning when she woke up – this bizarre mishmash of words.

'Boobie.'

It had to be a child, was her first thought. The voice was a boy's, but high-pitched and nervous. He said the words with a hysteria, as if he were being dared to say them. He was barely comprehensible. She had to listen to the voicemail three times before she could understand all the words he was saying.

Where did a kid learn those kind of words?

She would have shared it with someone. She would have laughed it off and played it out loud on speaker, but she had no one. Her roommate was gone. Instead, she let the words linger in the air. They embarrassed her. The call had come from a blocked number, so it couldn't be traced. She thought through all the people she knew, old friends, people from work, and if any of them had kids. Most of them didn't and the ones who did had babies, not bratty kids that, unfortunately, could talk, could work a cell phone.

There were four missed calls and one new voicemail the next night, which again, Doreen found in the morning when she woke up.

'Bitch bitch bitch penis dumb fatty fat ass boobie bitch!'
She was annoyed this time. What kind of environment was
this kid being raised in that had taught him it was OK to do
this kind of thing? It was kind of sickening.

This was occurring at the same time as the beginning of the
end for Doreen. The strangers had just finished their parade
of showing up at her doorstep unannounced and taking all of
Whitney's furniture away. The plumbing was starting to act
up. She was catching a whiff of something in the air every now
and then. An irony, fishy kind of smell. A serial prank caller
didn't do anything to ease her general disdain for the world
around her. If it took a village to raise a child, she thought, it
took a world to raise an asshole, and the world seemed ready
and willing at the moment. Screw everyone.

The next night was more of the same. Then there was nothing
over the weekend. And on Monday night, she caught him.

Her phone lit up neon blue at two in the morning and she
was awake – she was beginning always to be awake at this
hour now, sitting on her mattress, which she had moved into
the living room. She leapt at the unknown number when it
appeared on the screen and answered.

There was silence on the other end.

Static, then a rustling sound, and muffled giggling. There
were two voices. Two different boys on the other end, giggling.

'Do you have boobs?'

'I do,' said Doreen.

The boys erupted with laughter and hung up. They didn't
call back.

There was a week of radio silence between Doreen and
her tormentors and she assumed they had moved on – had
been caught by a parent finally or had found a new phone
number to dial incessantly. Then one night, promptly at two
in the morning, there was one final barrage. She missed the

first two calls – the phone was buried under a tangled mass of blankets, clothes, and clutter. She answered on the third call and again there was silence on the other end. She said, 'Hello?' and stayed on the line, listening. This time, there were no giggles in the background, no whispers. She looked at the phone, checking to see there was still a connection. She put it back to her ear and listened.

There was a tiny voice on the other end.

'I'm sorry.'

It was a feather of a voice. It was the same boy from before, but zapped of its bravado. It wasn't frantic and it didn't seem to have an audience this time. It was only him.

'It's OK,' said Doreen. She paused, she had never scolded a child but assumed she should in this instance. A lesson not-learned right now would be a lesson not-learned for the rest of his life. Or something. 'You shouldn't do that to people. It's very rude to say those words. Even though you're on the phone with a stranger, it's still not nice and can hurt people's feelings. You can hurt people's feelings even over the phone, even a stranger's.'

'You're not a stranger,' said the little voice.

'I'm not? Then what am I?'

There was silence. She heard the boy on the other end contemplating hanging up.

'What's your name?' she asked. 'Don't worry, I won't get you in trouble.' Then she suddenly dropped the parental tone in her voice, surprising herself. 'Actually, no, I really don't care, to be honest.'

'You don't?'

'No, not really.'

'Why don't you care?'

'Well, it's like . . .' Doreen stretched out on her nest and yawned. She kicked away an old garlic dipping sauce that was empty. 'I think your prank calls are gross, but I'm not going to go out of my way to find out who you are. I'd rather you just stop calling me. As long as you don't do it again, I don't think I should go out of my way to get you in trouble. You're just a kid anyway. How old are you?'

'I'm seven.'

'There, see? You're just a kid. Seven is too young for that sort of thing. And what about the other boy who was with you the other night? I heard him giggling in the background.'

'That was my brother.'

'Well now you have to make sure he doesn't do prank calls either. It's a vicious cycle, you see. You do one thing, your brother does the same thing again, and on, and on. You probably learned those bad words from your parents and you don't even know it.'

'You're weird.'

'You're weird. You're the one calling me in the first place.'

There was more silence, but it was a closer, more comforting type of silence. The boy on the other end didn't know how to carry on a conversation but he wasn't hanging up. And Doreen was fine – this didn't seem strange to her, at least, at the moment. There were weirder things happening to her.

'So, what's life like for a seven-year-old in the world today?' she asked.

'It's nice.'

'I can tell. You've got your own phone. You're up at two in the morning. You've got a cool brother who you can do prank calls with – but remember, you're not supposed to do those any more. Maybe when you're older you can do some, but when you do, you should do them to people you know. Just prank call your friends, not strangers like me.'

There was a pause and a muffling. Then the little voice spoke one last time.

'My name is Leo,' it said.

The call ended and the line went silent.

Doreen checked the call records to see if the boy's phone number had been recorded at any time, but it hadn't. All the calls had come in as blocked. She put down the phone and watched it as if it were a departing party guest who might change its mind, but there were no other calls.

'But I don't see what any of this has to do with me going to Rome with you,' Doreen said to Violet now. She said this with zero confidence. This forced revelation had shaken her up and weakened her. It was as if all the feelings she had been trying to ward off were now outside her, a shadow standing next to her, a phantom.

'It has nothing to do with Rome, you're right,' said Violet after a moment of contemplation. She spoke with her hands. 'It's all very unrelated. Disjointed. A lot like the way you described yourself to me when we first met. Tell me, did you know who Leo was when he told you his name?'

'Yes. He was a boy in the neighborhood – well, in the apartment complex. I didn't know him personally, but I had seen him outside. His mother was always calling for him, yelling his name when it was dinnertime, that kind of thing. He was ...' Doreen paused. Her voice didn't quiver because of the tragedy, it quivered because Violet seemed to know all of this already. The woman's expression was calm and focused on every word she said, nodding along as if she were a music instructor making sure Doreen hit all the right notes. 'He was killed just the other day. He was run over by a car. He and his brother. They both died.'

'Were you shocked when this happened? When you found out it was him?'

'No, I didn't really register that part of it at the time. I didn't register any of it, and I think that's what's causing all of my problems right now. I'm not registering the things around me.'

'When you saw him on his scooter and then when you saw the car hit him, did you know immediately it was the same boy that had been leaving you voicemails? The same boy you had had the conversation with on the phone in the middle of the night?'

'Yes, I knew it was, him, Leo. I recognized him. He played outside my apartment a lot – sorry, how did you – how did you know I saw it happen? And how did you know he was on a scooter? I never said that.'

Violet looked impatiently at Doreen and then at Tom, as if this were somehow his fault, as if he was supposed to have briefed her on something. She seemed frustrated at the flow of things.

'Doreen, there's something happening that you're not allowing to exist in the forefront of your mind. It's the fact that I might possibly have known all of this before I even met you that day at the grocery store. Why you're avoiding that fact, I frankly cannot figure out.'

Doreen wheeled this over in her head. She tried to see a timeline of the past week, but things blurred, things hid themselves from her.

'You're wondering who I am, where I come from, what I'm doing with you. Now you want to know how I know that you saw Leo and his brother die – something you've never disclosed to anyone, not even the two police officers who knocked on your door shortly after the accident. Yes, I know these things.'

Doreen breathed in deep and felt herself sinking further. Violet leaned forward and held up three fingers.

'There's only three possible solutions to how I know so

much – all three of them are reasonably valid. The first possibility is: I did it. I was the driver in the white SUV and that's how I know it was a white SUV that killed Leo and Harry and that's how I know you saw it happen because I saw you peeking through your blinds when I did it. I smashed right into those boys and kept driving and didn't look back and then I tracked you down and brought you here because that's what I do, I'm insane and sick in the head.

'The second possibility is: I'm with the police. I'm a detective and I've been spying on you. Tom here is my deputy and we're about to put you under arrest for deserting the scene of a crime and we might just accuse you of the crime itself because you're the easiest answer. *You* have no alibi, *you* have a disturbing connection to the victim, and we can probably make it out that *you* fled the scene of the crime in your white SUV and so good on us, we got you. We've entrapped you.'

She flipped her hand when she doled out this mock decree. She leaned further forward in her seat and grew suddenly bigger and closer, encompassing everything in Doreen's field of vision like a full moon.

'But the third possibility is something less concrete. The third possibility is that I've found out who you are, tracked you down, and learned your story all on my own – not because I'm a police detective, and not because I'm the bad guy in the SUV, in fact, I have nothing to do with any of it. You could say I learned these things about you, but a better descriptor in this case would be I *inferred* them. I felt you out. I received some sort of indication that you were over there, in Oregon, going through this strange ordeal, which means that there are things beyond our control that somehow work in harmony with what we see in the light – a kind of shadow that runs alongside us, as we traverse these tricky intersections. And if that third possibility is true, then you have all the reason in the world to stay with me.

'I sense your fear, Doreen, I really do. But I think your fear is different from the kind of fear you would have if you believed one of the first two possibilities. If I were a police officer or the driver, you'd be fearful, yes, but you would have acted by now. You would have accepted who I was by now and done something, but you haven't. Instead you're lingering in this mysteriousness because you know it can't be that easy. You can't place me. And if you can't place me, then what am I? Where are we?'

A silence passed between them. The opposite of a draft of air. There was the faintest of muffled sounds coming from outside their hotel room, housekeepers making their rounds down the hall, tired plastic wheels rolling over carpet.

Violet stood up and walked across the living room to the window. She looked out at the buildings surrounding them. Tom left the room and went into the bedroom to make the beds and straighten things up. After a stretch of time had passed, Violet also went back into the bedroom. Then, when she came back out, she was dressed in black workout clothes and her hair was pulled back with a thin black headband. She put on a pair of running shoes and tied the laces. Her singular smell of lilies and ginger and ice was just barely detectable, like a crushed petal blowing away.

She finished tying her shoes and faced Doreen.

'If you walk away from the third possibility, you'll never discover it again, Doreen. I promise you,' she said. She spoke in a hushed, holy voice. 'But if you stay, if you can at least continue to linger in this realm a little while longer – think about what can happen.'

Without another word, Violet stood up and left the hotel room with Tom in tow. They might as well have dissolved into the air or flown out the window. They would be back, Doreen knew. But when they returned, she would be gone.

Leo didn't call Doreen again until the morning of the day he was killed. He had been wanting to call her again, but he didn't know what to say. He didn't *love* her, that would have been weird, but he wanted to talk to her again. He had never talked to an older person like her before, and the way she had been mad at him about the prank calls – she had been mad at him in a different kind of way than how his mother would usually get mad at him. He had been searching for a reason to call her again and he finally found one: there was that bird outside her door. He was riding his scooter around with his brother, Harry, when he noticed the progress it had made. Doreen's house light was filled with sticks and dirt and the bird was inside it, making a nest. Leo watched it fly in and out of the lamp, building a little home, and he thought that this would be the perfect thing to call Doreen about. He called, but there was no answer. He thought to leave a voicemail, but decided not to – he didn't know what he would say.

CHAPTER 14

Doreen waited in silence in the empty hotel room to be sure they were really gone. She didn't know what Violet was expecting her to do – stay put? As if this was the final test of her loyalty to her? Maybe she was just giving her time alone to sort through her thoughts and really they were right outside the door, waiting. Surely they wouldn't stop her from leaving, that would be kidnapping, but still, she was fearful and rolled these possibilities over in her mind.

She went to the door and looked through the peephole. There was no one in the hallway. She let a few minutes of silence pass, then sprang into action, running around the hotel room, gathering her few possessions. She grabbed her wallet from the nightstand. Her phone – where was her phone? Tom had handed it to Violet. Violet had walked into the bedroom with it. Where had she put it? Had she left the room with it? The hotel was spotless, there was nowhere to misplace (or deliberately hide) a phone. Doreen traced Violet's movements. She checked the couches, she walked to the window and went into the bedroom. In the bathroom, she tried opening Violet's suitcase but it was locked. A tiny padlock was on the zipper. She pulled as hard as she could but it wouldn't budge. The phone had to be in there. She ran back to the living room and dialed her own phone number on the hotel phone. Sure enough, she heard a gentle vibrate coming from the suitcase.

Her arms shook as she tried to yank open the zipper again.

She tried prying it open at the corners. There was a loose thread in one of the seams, and she pulled it hard, pinching deep red marks into her hands.

'Come on!'

She cursed and heaved the luggage upright on its wheels and made for the door – she would take the luggage with her. It wasn't stealing – her phone was in there, and Violet had put it there. And Violet had put her here. She had brought her all the way to Atlanta.

'What the hell am I doing?' she said out loud, remembering two nights ago, how she had stumbled out into the busy road outside her apartment. Of course Violet had found her there, she thought. There was no mystery. Crazy attracted crazier.

She burst out of the hotel room into the hallway and ran, disoriented, to the elevator, but the thought crossed her mind that they might be there, waiting in the elevator for her, or waiting right in the lobby on the other side of the doors. Maybe they had the place surrounded at all exits. Maybe there were more of them than just Violet and Tom, a whole network of billionaire drifters.

She took the stairs. She threw the suitcase down every set of the ten flights of stairs, hoping it would burst open if it landed hard enough and she'd be able to get her phone out. A housekeeper on the fourth floor poked her head into the stairwell to see what all the commotion was, but Doreen blazed past her, not bothering to explain.

At the lobby level, she stopped to catch her breath. She composed herself and put the suitcase up against the wall. She left it there and ventured stealthily back inside the main hotel, peering around every corner as she walked into the lobby. There were two people at the front desk helping a family check in. There was a man at the breakfast bar watching a football game on TV. There were two kids looking for the pool. No sign of Violet and Tom.

She hurried back to the stairwell and walked down the opposite end of the hall, following the signs for the gym, and found her. There she was. The back of her perfect head was bouncing up and down. Doreen watched her through a glass door. Violet was running on a treadmill with her back to her. There was a TV on in the top corner of the room playing a daytime courtroom show.

'Doreen.'

She jumped. A hand gripped her elbow. A strong, perfectly constructed hand.

'You found us. Are you all right?' said Tom.

'I'm fine, yeah. I was coming down to talk with Violet some more, but we just did. We just spoke now, actually, so now I'm going to go back up to the room. I just had a question about Rome, that was all.'

'You did? Just now?' His grip loosened slightly, but he kept hold of her elbow. 'Did you want me to escort you back up? Do you have a room key?'

'Nope. But yes. I mean yeah, I have one. A key. I'll just go back now, don't worry.' She moved as forcefully away from Tom as she could without looking like someone fleeing. 'I was thinking I might go lie down again. It's all still a little overwhelming. I'll see you back up there.'

Doreen was backing away and turning the corner just as fast as Tom was opening the door to the gym and going inside. When she was out of sight, she sprinted back to the stairwell, grabbed the suitcase, and ran through the hotel, through the lobby, out into the parking lot. The heat outside blasted away the veneer of air conditioning that had been chilling her body and she started to sweat instantly, but she didn't stop running. She ran out of the parking lot, out onto a busy downtown street – busy with cars on wide streets, not busy with people on sidewalks. She looked out of place. The hotel was on a little island, with a freeway entrance down every direction she turned, and nameless glass and brick buildings fencing her in. She settled on a direction and ran. The air was pumped with heat and pollen. She felt her nose begin to sting. She ran alongside the six-lane stretch of road for two city blocks and reached a shopping mall that had been built as an afterthought in the footprint of a skyscraper.

Doreen searched the mall directory and found an office supplies store. Dragging the suitcase behind her, she went inside and bought a pair of scissors and rushed back outside in minutes. She knew she couldn't stay at a busy mall so close to the hotel, but she couldn't stay on a main road like this one. Surely Violet and Tom were just discovering the empty hotel room now.

She ran through another stretch of city for five more blocks until she reached the entrance to Piedmont Park. Breathless, she squeezed out what energy she had left and ran as far inside the park as she could, away from any of the bordering roads. She pushed through crowds of people, running past playgrounds and wading pools filled with children and their parents, through stretches of field and multiple games of soccer and frisbee and flag football, dragging the heavy suitcase. She crossed a small footbridge over a pond into an area of the park that was less manicured, under plenty of sheltering trees. She wove her way around piles of sunbathers and found a space under a tree where she could be alone and out of sight.

Without waiting, Doreen took the scissors, and with no pretense for public sociability, she sliced into the suitcase. The woven nylon and leather and plastic were tough, but not uncuttable. After a few minutes, her hands were sore, but she had made an opening, which she could fit her hands in and peel the suitcase open like a stubborn clam. A sunbathing couple near her watched with eyebrows raised behind their sunglasses, but she didn't care.

After great difficulty, the two halves of the suitcase fell open and there was her phone, resting right on top of a sweater. Doreen grabbed it and held it above her head, beaming with success, and finally, collapsed. She lay right on the grass next to the suitcase in relief and exhaustion. She breathed deeply and wiped sweat from her face. She could call a taxi to the airport and be on the next flight to Portland by evening.

Her conversation with Violet had clouded her mind but now she was free – free to go back to her initial decision. She would go back home, go to the police, explain her story, her depression and mania: how she couldn't bring herself to come forward earlier because of her chance encounter with Leo. Yes, she knew the voicemails from him were weird, and yes the fact that she had had a private conversation with him was even weirder, but none of that meant that she had been deliberately avoiding the tragedy. If anything, her connection to the boy meant she wanted to do all she could to help find the driver who caused the tragedy and bring justice.

'That sounds trite,' Doreen said to herself out loud. She was on her back, looking straight up at the sun, imagining the scenario in her mind. She blinked with every flicker of light through the canopy of leaves above. As casually as they could, the couple that had been watching her got up and left.

There was four-thousand dollars in cash inside Violet's suitcase. It was hardly shocking, given everything else that had happened, plus the amount was probably pocket change to her. Doreen counted out the rolls of fifty dollar bills and lined them up in a row. The cash was the only outlier among the mundane contents of the suitcase, which Doreen riffled through. The clothes were all designer brands and impeccably folded, made from silk and organic cotton and high-fiber woven things. There was also a book on learning advanced Portuguese. A French novel. A tin box of breath mints. Vitamins. Serums and lotions that were probably worth more than the cash.

The cash was drawing stares from other sunbathers. Doreen tucked the rolls away and closed the suitcase, though she couldn't seal it because of the inconvenient way she had cut it open. She used her phone and bought a plane ticket to Portland with an early-evening departure time, then called for a cab to come pick her up on the corner outside the eastern entrance to the park. Easy enough.

The taxi arrived too quickly, when she wasn't even halfway through the park. When the driver rang she had to plead with him to wait.

'There's not really a place to stop around here, miss. I got cars honking at me.'

She started running, cutting across a playground like a wild woman fleeing for her life, dragging the open suitcase, leaving a trail of socks and underwear in the grass behind her. A dress got caught in one of the wheels.

'Excuse me? Hey? Hello?' strangers yelled after her but she kept hobbling along.

The driver eyed Doreen's luggage situation with caution. He picked it up as politely as he could and threw it in the trunk.

'The airport, right?'

'Right-o,' said Doreen. She sunk into the back seat, relieved. She tried not to act as if she had been abducted by aliens, but it felt that way, like she had just woken up from some horrible operation. 'I. Am. Outta here,' she sang. It had been months since she had ever said something like that, used a tone of voice like that. 'Outta.' That was something she would have said to Whitney, back when she had more pretenses. She felt like she was creeping back into a discarded layer of skin. Maybe, she thought for a second, her things would still be in the dumpster when she got back home.

The driver's name was Lloyd; it was printed on a piece of paper inside a plastic slip on the back of his chair. He drove with less grace than Violet and Tom, but he was fast, speeding through what Doreen assumed (and hoped) were back roads.

'They're not gonna let you on the plane with a bag like that,' he said.

'I'll buy a new one there. Sorry, I need to make a phone call.' Doreen was slick, speaking and thinking a mile a minute. She held her phone in a hurried-executive kind of way with pure, unnecessary flourish. Tap, tap, tap. She was high on the thrill of escape. A pendulum that was on too strong of an upswing.

She called Mario's and the co-worker she was friendly with picked up. But the co-worker didn't sound as friendly as she usually was. She sounded aloof and offish. There was static. Their manager was out for lunch, but she would tell him to call her back as soon as he could.

'That'd be great,' said Doreen. 'I'm literally on my way to the airport now and my flight's right at five o'clock, so have him call me when he gets in. Or, wait, actually, no I don't think he even needs to call me. Can you just let him know that I'll be back in the office tomorrow? And don't tell him I'm in Atlanta, I'm still *sick*.' She let out a conniving fake cough and giggled, which somehow seemed more sickening than a real one. The co-worker didn't laugh.

'I'll tell him, but I think he needs to talk to you, so don't be surprised if he calls.'

'Sure, no prob. Is everything all right? Busy day?'

'Pretty steady. A big order came in out of nowhere from a wireless blender company, so we've been tackling that. I'll have him call you, OK?'

'Right. Great. See you.'

(If it had been a few years ago, Lloyd the taxi driver would have rolled his eyes at Doreen, but by now he was used to how her type tended to act. Yapping on the phone. He accepted that this was just the way they were. Uppity. Not self-aware. Bad tippers in the sense that they tipped either nothing or huge, gaudy, mawkish amounts of money. He bet she worked for one of the big advertising agencies in the city. The big five. How come everything needed to have a big five? Monopolies full of pure pomp and no circumstance. At least the traffic wasn't too bad. They arrived at the airport in a jiffy and there she went: She was one of the gaudy tippers, shoving a handful – an actual hand's full – of fifty dollar bills into his hand.)

'Shit, miss, this is too much. Are you kidding?'

'Not at all,' she said.

Lloyd changed his tone. He almost matched hers in peppiness. He suddenly remembered the duct tape he kept with his emergency supplies and offered to tape up her suitcase, 'Just to hold you over till you can get a new one,' he said. He cinched it closed with a corset of tape.

Doreen was grateful. She smiled and waved goodbye to him when he pulled away from the curb.

Things were going swimmingly but then there was a delay at the check-in desk. Doreen was made to wait in line for almost thirty minutes – crossing into the threshold of possibly missing her flight – and when it was finally her turn to present her documents and tag her bag, there was another delay. Normal issues, computer errors, she reassured herself. She had only just purchased the ticket online, there was sure to be a syncing error. She tried distracting herself while the desk agent tapped away on the computer, looking up her information, frowning for some reason.

Mario's should look into partnering with an airlines or an airport, Doreen thought. Maybe she would pass along the tip to the sales team. They could have some kind of wireless airport sensor thing that took care of all this check-in stuff for you automatically. She couldn't think any less vaguely but it calmed her down. The airline desk agents were consulting with one another now – looking over Doreen's ID. She felt a flea of panic awakening just below her neck. A wireless airport sensor thing, sure, that'll do. That's a good idea. A sensor thing that knows where you are at all times no matter what. Yep.

Something wasn't right. It was like her senses were heightened. Her brain zoomed out of her skull and she was able to see her surroundings from overhead, laid out like a mathematical grid. She saw the snaking line of people behind her. A pair of security guards a few yards away. Three desk agents – one of them making a hasty phone call, the other two coming back to her. 'I apologize, ma'am, but we're having a slight technical issue verifying your ticket. If you'll please wait just a few more minutes, we'll get this sorted for you.' Doreen smiled and nodded as you do, and held out her hand to take back her ID, but neither of the agents gave it to her. They were still consulting it. She knew she wouldn't get it back.

She backed away from the desk slowly.

'I'll just wait over here,' she said. 'I'll get out of the way so you can help another customer.' The two security guards were listening to a call on their radio, sauntering over to the desk. The desk agents were flagging them down. 'I'll just be over here.' Now she was very obviously beginning to walk away, abandoning Violet's suitcase. She was almost beyond the line of other passengers.

'No, ma'am. Please wait here. It'll just be a minute,' the desk agent was panicking as well and commanded her to stay. 'I'm fine, really. I'll be right back. No problem.' She ducked through the crowd of people, tripping over suitcases and dodging trolleys. She pushed out into the main thoroughfare of foot traffic, half skipping, half walking. At the doors, she looked back. The security guards were looking around for her. The desk agents were on their tiptoes, trying to point her out in the crowd.

Again the yin and yang of climates assaulted Doreen when she ran back outside. The sun was waiting for her, glittering off the black-hooded car services and taxis. Shuttle busses puffed clouds of exhaust. She ran down the drop-off point and hailed the cab that was closest to exiting the driveway and practically crashed inside, slamming the door behind her.

'Go now please. Fast. Go!' Her face reddened, embarrassed at herself. She sounded like an action hero, but she couldn't help herself. These were the sick things adrenaline made people do. She almost smacked the back of the driver's chair. Edward, said his framed plastic nameplate. She told him to go anywhere but back to the city.

'What's north of here?' she said.

'The city.'

'Well then go south.'

He grunted a confirmation, openly rolling his eyes at her, but Doreen didn't care. She turned around and watched the airport disappear. A security guard had just run out the main doors, looking around frantically. A line of sweat prickled across Doreen's forehead, contrasting too harshly with the car's air conditioning. She sank back into her seat and closed her eyes. There was a pain in her stomach. She hadn't eaten anything except for two bites of a sandwich. She almost wished she could be back there – not back there with them, but back in that bed, still asleep.

'Argh,' she said. 'Grrr.' She couldn't hold the noises back. She beat her head in frustration. There was nothing she could do. Her name must have shown up on the desk agent's computer with a red flag next to it – her name was tagged, she was wanted by the police for questioning, maybe there was even a warrant out for her arrest. That was what was happening, right? She wasn't being crazy? They had kept her ID. She felt both her pockets. She had nothing but her phone.

'Ahhh,' she groaned again. She had left her wallet back with them too. She visualized it now, sitting on the counter. She had nothing to pay the cab driver. She cursed out loud.

'You all right?' said the driver.

'I'm fine,' said Doreen.

'So, how far south are we talking here? Stockbridge? McDonough? Macon? I don't go all the way to Macon.'

'Sorry, I have to take this.' Her phone started buzzing. It was Mario's. Her manager.

Edward the driver sighed and shook his head. These people.

'Nice to hear you're feeling better, Doreen,' said the manager. There was hardly any background noise, which meant he wasn't at his desk with the rest of the team. He had to be in a private office. Hardly anyone used the private offices. 'I've been meaning to talk with you,' he said. He continued with niceties for a while longer, like a conductor tapping his baton then pausing, dramatically. 'You see, I value honesty, Doreen. And I don't mean to pry, or judge, but if you have an interview for another job, you can just tell me. You don't have to take all these sick days, honestly. No one is going to be mad if you're honest, but because you've been continually lying to me, I'm not left with very many options.'

'Sorry, what?'

'I know you've been thinking about quitting for a while now. Quinn actually mentioned something about a two weeks' notice she thought you had already given me and that was almost a month ago.'

'Who the hell is Quinn?'

'Uh—'

'And who the hell told her I had done that?'

'Quinn is the girl you're friendly with. At least, I thought you were friends with her. She told me you said you were quitting. That you had drafted your two weeks' notice. I was actually worried you had given it to me and I had lost it. I just want to make sure we're on the same page here.'

'No. No, there's no page in the first place. This isn't a thing. I don't know who told Quinn whatever she thinks she knows about me, but I'm not quitting. I'll be at the office tomorrow. Nothing's changing.'

A drama unfolded across Doreen's face. Quinn? That was her name? Surely her life had split in two and there was another Doreen that had done all this, that had made friends with a girl named Quinn and had drafted up a two weeks' notice and had formally quit her job and flown away to a better life. Why was she this Doreen and not that one? Where could she find that one?

'We'll talk then, OK, Doreen? I'm sure we can reach a conclusion here. You sound like you could use some rest.'

'I don't need rest. I don't need to talk to you. I just need to be back to normal. I need my life back!'

She began to cry. She hung up the phone without saying goodbye and screamed this time. A full-throated roar. Her oesophagus rippled and scratched against itself and her face turned a violent shade of red.

'Hey, lady, you need to take it easy. Come on. What's going on?'

'Fuck you!' she snarled.

'All right, you're done! You're out of here.' The driver jerked the car over three lanes of traffic and took the next exit. He peeled into a Waffle House parking lot and ordered her out of the car. Defiant and feral, Doreen shouted, 'Fine!' and slammed the door. The taxi squealed out of the lot and left her there.

She screamed again into the air. Blood welled up into her face. She dropped her phone and eventually dropped everything, all of her gone limp. She collapsed into a heap and sulked right there on the curb.

The parking lot was nearly empty. She felt as if her brain had hit the ceiling of her skull, broken through and blasted out into the sky. She waited for the sensation to pass and for her thoughts to grow stale. Every few minutes, she felt a current of blood and feeling drain from the top of her head to her toes. Her thoughts slowed their endless cycle. Job, wallet, suitcase, sanity – they flashed in her mind and she had to tell herself that none of it mattered. She went through them like a checklist every few seconds. Job, wallet, suitcase, sanity – nope, still don't matter, they're nothing. She stayed put for an hour and did this as the Earth and an early moon above it kept spinning.

The sky turned pink. It refused to turn dark blue or even purple. It was pink with clotted cream clouds, showing off. An enormous Waffle House sign lit up yellow and buzzed like a beehive. The seven o'clock crowd of regular civilians was leaving the restaurant, some of them satisfied, others filled with regret – families and people on their own, groups of teenagers – none of them batted an eye at Doreen slumped on her side in the corner of the parking lot. She was just part of the eight o'clock crowd now. A night patron. The kind of person whose life circumstances had misaligned them from appropriate business hours. She pulled a few blades of dead grass from her hair.

Her past felt fictitious. The hard asphalt beneath her, the damp sweat in the small of her back, the hot mouth of Atlanta's night sky. These were what felt most real to her now. Everything else was just a delusion or a mockumentary or a flash of light across a knife before it stabbed into something.

She was missing a shoe. When did that happen? At the airport? Some time before that? She kicked off her other shoe so she could at least commit to a look. What else did she need to lose? A limb? She picked up her phone but dared not check it. She extended her arm and held it out away from her. She dangled it, pinched between her thumb and forefinger above the ground and let it drop. It fell onto the asphalt again without a scrape. She put her chin on her knees and stared at it – how this stupid phone had caused her so much trouble, or at least enabled most of her trouble. Inside it was that empty space between her and Whitney. The violated space between her and that delivery boy, whatever his name was. The weird space between her and Leo. What had that space been?

She was sore when she stood up. She arched her back, breathing in and out. There was a black wall of trees behind the Waffle House. That would be a good oblivion, she thought. She picked up her phone and walked, then broke into a run. The crumbly asphalt poked the bottoms of her bare feet. She ran behind the Waffle House, to the very edge of the parking lot, right up to where the pavement turned into litter-strewn grass and a steep embankment. Her muscles contracted and she threw her arm forward, flinging the phone out into the oblivion. It cut through the air and spun like a windmill, a rectangle blurring into a circle. A whooshing sound. Then it was gone.

A big gulp of air filled Doreen's lungs. She breathed in and out. She forced herself to smile. Her lungs filled with air again and in just the right way, enough to jiggle a grain of dopamine in her dead brain and remind her of two things: that she was OK – really, it would all be all right – and that she was hungry. Absolutely starving.

She waltzed into the Waffle House barefoot, which everyone seemed fine with, as if there were worse things in the world. The tile floor was untrustworthy and darkened by grime, but it was luxuriously cold to the touch. A waitress sat her at a booth by the window and Doreen smiled a smile that had to be forced and phony, but she knew the importance of it. The act of smiling. She made it enormous and operatic.

She was free of everything. She had no phone, no wallet, no shoes, no cash. No way to pay for a meal. So why not order a huge one? Fill herself with senselessness? Her only plan was to eat until she died, and if they kicked her out before that, her plan would be to sit in the parking lot until she died. And if they made her leave the property, she would walk until she died. Her life was an open, unwritten prescription. It was romantic in the sense that her sails needed only the slightest of breezes and she would carry on forever and then not.

The table conjured up food. Pop, pop, pop! Pancakes, burgers, and fries. She ordered everything on the menu in rounds, bringing the waitress back multiple times for another ice tea, another hash brown, another BLT. There was no Violet-special here. No conflict of interests. Just different shades of gold and brown and different extremes of salty and sweet. She ate a T-bone steak, a double cheeseburger, hash browns covered in sausage gravy, hash browns covered in melted cheese, tomato and chicken on Texas toast, and ham and scrambled eggs – not hardboiled. She drank two liters of Diet Coke and a pint of orange juice. She ordered waffles with every main course and so eventually there was a stack of nineteen sticky plates that had each held one waffle. Her tastebuds shriveled from salt and grease, then expanded and swelled with swishes of pop and maple syrup.

Around midnight, her stomach was nearly non-functional. The food Doreen put in her mouth no longer joined an orderly queue of digestion, but was pushed into whatever open space it could find in her body. A jalapeño had lodged itself somewhere behind her kidney. A bit of egg yolk was seeping out of her ear.

Just as the gravity of eating food and the gravity of paying for it became very real issues, a woman dressed in white, gray, and cream levitated into the restaurant. The glass doors opened for her automatically. She hovered inches above the floor, somehow, but it made perfect sense: Why should she even dare touch a perfect heeled foot on a Waffle House floor? She gestured to the waitress as if to say, 'Oh, that one by the window? That one's mine,' and she sailed over to Doreen and sat in the seat opposite her. They sat and stared at each other for an hour, wordlessly, studying each other. Maple syrup pooled then dripped off the edges of stacked plates like a shishi-odoshi.

At promptly two in the morning, the two women stood up at the same time. Violet placed two rolls of fifty-dollar bills on the table and thanked the waitress for her service. A little bell by the door jingled when it opened and closed. She wrapped an arm around Doreen and whisked her away into the silent cascade.

PART TWO

PORTLAND

CHAPTER 15

They found the driver.

Not Solloway and Palmer, but Paulson and Cho – a pair of detectives who became involved in the case after a third day of no leads. They were senior officers who worked well together. So while Palmer was dicking around and Solloway was obsessing almost to an illegal extent over a missing witness and reading the tea leaves of her trash, Paulson and Cho did the more sensible thing and checked traffic cam footage from all the cameras on the surrounding freeways.

They spotted fourteen white SUVs from around the same timeframe as the accident. They cross-referenced their license plates with the DMV's registry and made house visits to the three drivers on the list who had either multiple or serious previous charges on their records. One was a college student with two speeding tickets, the other was an older man with a drunk driving offence from three years ago. The third was a former reality TV star, a woman named Molly, who, on the day of the accident, had been driving all over Portland, going to meetings to negotiate her contract as the new spokesperson for an outdoorsy health supplement startup – she volunteered this information right away when Paulson and Cho turned up at her house, including the fact that she had been lost between two parallel highways and used an apartment complex's parking lot as a turn-around spot. Her voice turned off after she said this – just completely went flat and empty – then she fainted. Officer Cho caught her before she hit her head on the floor. They called an ambulance just in case, and they let her recover. They got fluids in her and sat her down in a chair. It took only about ten minutes for her to unspool her confession in her living room, as if she was finally making sense of it for the first time.

'You know what, I thought I heard a strange sound that day. I thought I had scraped a curb or something, a speed bump. You know armadillos? They have them in Texas. I was once driving in Texas and hit an armadillo and it was as if I had run over over a log. I thought it was an armadillo, but we're in Oregon, so I knew it couldn't have been that. I thought it was a cat or a coyote or a speed bump, those things are everywhere.'

Her voice trembled. She was digging the truth out from the back corner of her mind and that was the hardest part – putting it into words. It was a conversation with herself.

'Yes, I remember seeing two kids. They were definitely there when I hit the bump. Maybe they threw something at my car? Kids throw things like that. Water balloons. Maybe I clipped one of them with my mirror? In fact, yes, you're right, I think I remember seeing one of them in the street in my rear view mirror. I thought he was too close to the car. Oh my God, if I did anything to hurt one of them, I'm so sorry. I was in such a rush. I was stressed out and lost, late for a meeting. They always say parking lots are the most dangerous places, more dangerous than the freeway. If I clipped him with my side mirror I'll never forgive myself.'

She knew they were dead. She had seen the news. She hadn't even needed to see the news. She knew the second it happened that she had run them over. It was only a matter of neurology now – Paulson and Cho just had to sit patiently for the emergency floodgates in her brain to dissolve and be there for the unpleasant deluge of anguish. She was carted off to the hospital in a stretcher, tended to, then taken to the police station.

The case was closed.

April, the mother, experienced a vitriolic, Biblical sense of justice and her mind, her worldview, her relationships, were never the same, and why should they be? She left her apartment and eventually left Portland, never to return.

Her feelings on 'the matter,' as she came to describe the deaths of her two sons, wavered daily, sometimes hourly between bouts of guttural, animal grief. She thought of those elephant mothers who sniff over every crevice of a corpse with their trunks and trumpet into the sky, and saw herself. She also felt plateaus of ambivalence. There was sometimes a numbness – a result of the crater blasted into her head by the initial grief – a permanent ringing sensation in her ears and an inability to gain weight, lose weight, get out of bed, do what was acceptable and 'right' in a 'matter' like this. She quit her job, she ended friendships, she started new ones.

During the height of the investigation and the search for the perpetrator, 'the matter' took on a life of its own, becoming a nightly news spectacle for a week. A ten-minute segment where viewers could live vicariously through April's grief and flirt with the trauma from a comfortable distance.

There was a funeral for the boys – a clumsy, surreal affair, with two tiny little coffins for two tiny little boys, like a pretend funeral, a funeral for two bugs. There wasn't enough wailing, April thought, there wasn't enough food, there weren't enough photos of the boys to use for the slideshow. A whole kindergarten class showed up and sang a song. Her ex-husband showed up with his new family. It was awkward and uncomfortable and she had to remind herself constantly what it was for.

She took a trip to England a few months later, to visit her

older brother and to escape the grief circus. A portion of the money she used to pay for the trip was money from a memorial fund the city of Beaverton had helped shepherd donations into following the accident. This was a no-no, apparently, or at least, from a PR perspective, as if April was supposed to know or care, as if the money was anything but money that had landed in her bank account in one lump sum. People who had obsessed over the tragedy saw this as an affront to normal, performative grief and it was reported on in a slew of viral news stories for large outlets, written by twenty-somethings in New York who prowled local news for content. They saw the cute kiddos and their dumb mom who let them play in the street and *voilà!* She faced a violent backlash online, with one enraged donor even petitioning to get his money back from the memorial fund. But sure enough, two days later, there was a backlash against the backlash, and April was rewritten as a kind of Joan of Arc. Her quick vacation to the Cotswolds with her brother became a Revolutionary Act of Self-Care, said the new articles. This Woman In Oregon Lost Everything And How She Grieved Was Incredible.

When everything finally faded away, she was left with little more than what she started with: two ghosts. Tasks were left incomplete. Relationships that had been reinvigorated by grief were re-ingrained into the woodwork. She got a new job and moved to a hidden corner of nowhere in Oregon, a place called Diamond Lake. Dark clouds became dull clouds. Sure, there was sunshine again, she supposed. Hikers in the summer, skiers in the winter. Whatever makes you happy.

Back at the police station, they had been testing out a new cloud-based software for filing casework. It was nothing groundbreaking like body cameras or lighter sentences for drug offenses or diversity outreach initiatives or bail pay reform or the defunding of private prisons. It was an online filing system that supposedly streamlined the more administrative side of policing and it was the fault of this internet-of-things, responsive-design, brand-integration, mumbo-jumbo that caused Doreen Durand's case file to slip away into an unnoticeable little corner where Solloway could have her all to himself. Why there was ever a case file created for Doreen in the first place was ethically up for debate – Solloway had ordered its creation during one of his when-the-mood-strikes bouts of authoritarianism.

He wasn't creepy about it, he insisted, when Palmer of all people confronted him about it after seeing her file still open on the shared network drive, under Solloway's recent history, months after Molly had been arrested and charged and everyone had moved on.

'She's technically still an open case, so technically the case should be worked on,' Solloway said. 'That's all.'

'Yeah sure. Let me know how that goes,' said Palmer. He winked and Solloway tried not to feel disgusted. Their partnership hinged on these exchanges and trade-offs.

Solloway tried to move on. He bundled Doreen's soggy trash together and stored it away – he didn't throw it away, but at least he cleaned it up off his kitchen floor. It had been left there for weeks and the wood was permanently warped with water damage and he busied himself with DIY methods to repair and replace the spot, ripping out planks of mold. He worked on it every night for two weeks but still, the memory of Doreen lingered there, weighing constantly on every one of his thoughts.

He kept her bundle of trash in a sealed plastic bin in the garage, renewing a pledge with himself each week, then each month, to finally throw it away, but he couldn't bring himself to do it. Sometimes, often in the middle of the night, he would think of something – some new idea, some reason for Doreen's disappearance – and he would creep out into the garage, tip-toeing away from his own shame, and unpeel the plastic lid on the box, just to inspect it one last time. The plastic would suck and flap around the air that would escape immediately, damp and unspeakably soured. He would dig into the trash, the socks and soggy cereal, the wires and sparkling black glass. Covered in the mess anew and finding nothing of interest, he would seal the box back up, push it away but only for so long. He was revolted at himself.

New leads cropped up – but only cropping up because he was still needlessly investigating. They were never anything substantial, but enough of an excuse for Solloway to keep talking about Doreen as an aside. Her car was still at the apartment, the landlord said she was still paying rent – he mentioned these things in passing, slowly noting them down in her case file like a growing shrine to an invisible goddess.

'Duh, probably because she still lives there, dude,' Palmer would say. Leave it alone. But if you can't, at least leave me alone.

Solloway never mentioned the more curious leads, the ones that didn't make sense to him, because how he discovered them was disturbing. Doreen was never home. She was paying rent and her car was there, but she was never home. She did not come back to the apartment for days, then weeks, then months. Solloway knew this because he often visited. He would park in the corner of the lot and watch. He never confessed this to anyone because even Palmer would take it into consideration and weigh it, along with every other behavior Solloway was exhibiting, against the edge of reason.

More time passed and the lease on Doreen's apartment was not renewed. The car was towed away. The last remaining things in her apartment – the mattress, some basic cleaning products – were thrown away. He watched as the landlord cleaned out the apartment one weekend. All day, maintenance workers stomped in and out with their carousel of supplies, a vacuum, a vat of cleaning solution, some touch-up paint. Exhausted by nighttime, they finished and packed everything up and left the apartment and closed the door – but didn't lock it – had they locked it? Solloway couldn't tell from his vantage point. The apartment was empty and they had kept the door propped open all day, so it would be easy to forget to lock it.

He had to be sure. No, he didn't have to be sure – there was no reason for him to check, nothing to be gained. There was nothing requiring his presence, but here he was and there he went. Solloway got out of his car for the first time in hours. He listened to the night and waited to be sure of the silence. There was nobody coming or going, no neighbors with bright opened windows, there was the cover of darkness.

He walked up the stairs to the apartment, stepping lightly, moving slowly, preparing the excuses in his head if anybody saw him. He reached the door and waited there for a moment, holding the doorknob as if it were the hand of an old friend. He breathed in and turned it slightly to the right, then tried turning it a bit more. It didn't budge. He turned it to the left then to the right, back and forth, harder this time, but it stayed put.

Locked.

A warm bulb of anger swelled up inside him. A wetness of humiliation and embarrassment trickled out from his eyes. He could have ripped the doorknob off the door and flung it down into the parking lot below but he held himself back. He breathed out hard, chastising himself for his stupidity. What was he doing here? He turned around to go but something whipped around his head in the dark. A shadow nipped at him behind the ear. He yelled and ducked.

Swish.

He flung his arms around in the direction of the sound, smacking the porch light off the wall. Glass shattered. He spun around and hit a soft, weightless thing in the air. It flew and broke against the wall and fell to the ground, feathers askew. It struggled to get back up, fluttering but broken now.

Horrified and spooked, Solloway ran. He sprinted down the stairs and tripped over himself getting back into his car. He slammed the door shut and let out a scream, ripping his throat apart with fury. He smacked the steering wheel repeatedly as he sped off into the night, trying to forget, trying not to be what he had become, trying to pull away but knowing that he had already gone too deep, absorbed too much, latched himself.

By the time he was back at his own place, he had convinced himself he was fine. He convinced himself it hadn't been as he remembered. The lamp had fallen, yes, but on its own. A faulty screw. There hadn't been a bird, it was the wind, or a spider web he had walked through. No bird, not at all. He had only been there to check on things, make sure the door was shut properly, the crime scene secured.

And as if it were a spell, the next morning things could not be proven otherwise.

Solloway went back to the apartment as soon as he could and wandered outside, observing. The broken light was gone, replaced with a new one, nice and clean on the wall. And there was no sign of this phantom bird, no sign of a struggle, no unseemly residue, not even a feather on the ground, not even a broken nest, a broken egg, not even a single blade of dried grass blowing away in the breeze.

CHAPTER 16

'Isn't that weird, though?' Solloway asked the landlord, strictly as a concerned friend of Doreen's, not a police officer. 'She just disappeared?'

'I wouldn't say it's common, but it's definitely not rare. We get dine-and-dashers all the time. Young people most of the time. They're in town for school or a job, then they're done and gone but mommy and daddy's rent checks keep coming until the lease is up. Leaving the car is a little strange, but I mean, it's not like it was worth much anyway. She was probably just a spoiled brat and couldn't be bothered with it.'

'She wasn't a student, though. She had steady employment.'

'Yeah but she was still a kid. Kids are older these days, aren't they? There's kids living in these apartments pushing forty. There's one kid who's been living here for almost ten years – a thousand-dollars in rent every month for ten years. That's over a hundred-thousand dollars in rent. You could get a pretty nice house with that kind of cash, but it comes to me instead. And what do I do with it? I hire some guys to come trim back the ivy every couple of years, maybe buy new laundry machines. I don't make the rules.'

Solloway nodded silently and thought for a moment. Every thought in his mind began and ended here at this place. Doreen had vanished and the afterburn of her image was all he had left, an invisible bird flapping around his head. 'Has the apartment been leased again?' he asked.

'No, sir. Not yet. I've got two viewings booked for tomorrow morning, but nothing concrete.'

Solloway said there was no need, he would take it. He put down a deposit and signed the lease agreement that same day.

'We've still got some deep cleaning to do. I've got some carpet guys coming tomorrow, but it'll be as good as yours this weekend.'

Again, there was no need, Solloway said, and he moved in that night.

Now with the key in his hand, the door unlocked and opened. The apartment seemed larger than he remembered. There were two bedrooms and one shared bathroom, but the rooms were spacious, wider than what was necessary – probably decided upon and built back when square footage wasn't translated into dollars and cents as stringently as it was now. The floor creaked and bounced with age. Whoever had designed the print for the linoleum kitchen floor hadn't even tried to mimic the look of real ceramic tile. The carpet was beige and bristly, especially in a swath in the center of the living room floor where there was a stain the color of rust.

Solloway paced around the empty rooms the way he imagined Doreen had paced them. He looked out the front window in the living room the way she must have looked out the day the children were killed. She would have seen it happen – but it's been solved, he had to correct himself. The case was closed. But telling himself that didn't make it feel any more true.

Is this weird? A cop finds a possible witness to an accident. The witness disappears, but the mystery of the accident is solved without her. Justice is served. A former reality TV star goes to jail on felony vehicular homicide charges. There's closure. But the witness is still gone. And the cop is stuck on finding her. He wakes up in the middle of the night thinking about her, every single night.

'Honestly, I don't think it's weird. It's probably wrong for me to say, but Molly was the *worst* on that show. What was the name of it again? Where they were stuck on an island with those hot guys? Did you ever watch it? She was such a bitch. That show probably turned her into an alcoholic. Was she drunk when she ran them over?'

Solloway was on a date with a woman he had met over the internet. He clicked and she appeared. He had been doing this for a while now. He would click and they would appear, then disappear. Some stayed for a while, taking up space in his mind but never enough to forget about Doreen.

'I think that's beside the point,' he said. 'I'm asking you if you think it's weird.'

'Weird she was on a reality show? Not really. Everyone goes on reality shows.'

'No, is it weird that I'm still trying to find the witness?'

'No,' she paused. 'I don't know. Aren't there usually lots of witnesses? You're the cop, not me.'

'There was only one witness. A girl named Doreen Durand. She was home during the accident, which happened right outside her window, but she lied and said she wasn't there and hadn't seen anything. Now she's gone and I can't stop thinking about her.'

Solloway's date shifted uncomfortably in her seat. She looked up and watched new people entering the restaurant.

'I don't know anything about being a police officer, but I would assume it's normal to think about that kind of stuff since it's your job. But then again, the way you just said "I can't stop thinking about her" kind of sounds like she was an old girlfriend or something. I mean, everyone needs a work-life balance, you know? But again, police work – I don't know the first thing about it – maybe it's different. Maybe you have to take it home with you.'

Silence passed and a calzone was stabbed a few times.

The date recovered, but slowly. Solloway was able to climb up to other topics of conversation that didn't include Doreen or the fact that he had moved into her old apartment – he would never confess to that. Things were pleasant enough to prolong the date and order dessert. But the temptation was still there. The urge to circle back to Doreen and her car and her phone calls with the boy and the bird nest on the wall – all of it was always there, in the back of his mind. It was truly all he ever thought about.

The date ended on good terms, but back at his apartment – Doreen's apartment – Solloway was alone. His date had agreed to another date, sure, any time, and that was that. Click, click. He had invited her inside and she had declined, but nicely, genuinely. Click, click.

The apartment was quiet. The forested area surrounding the complex did a good job of filtering any freeway noise. It felt almost nest-like.

Entire months passed by like this, until slowly, the apartment became his own. Solloway's sudden occupation of this space no longer felt like an intrusion. The façade of him belonging there actually started to look nice. He mounted a TV on the wall. He bought a new couch. He got plants. He decorated the place sparingly, under the guise of modern minimalism, as was the fashion these days, but in reality he kept it that way in case an unspoken guest showed up. Not a person – not even Doreen – but an idea. A thought. A development that suddenly unearthed an answer.

He often neglected the couch and sat instead in the center of the light stain on the carpet as if it were a prayer circle and hoped for something to happen – an old friend of Doreen's would turn up or a piece of mail addressed to her would provide all the answers he needed: a coupon for flying lessons, a newsletter for a neurological institute, a court filing, a letter from overseas.

The biggest clue he had was also the biggest mystery: the business card with the words Violet Cascade embossed on it. Solloway kept it on the windowsill in his bedroom and the sun had turned its key lime color to mint. The thick paper had softened and the embossing on the card had nearly rubbed away but the name could still be read, as well as the Portuguese address and the phone number.

He had dialed the number obsessively in those first few weeks and now he dialed it only once in a while. He had used the office phone at the police station to call it, and then, when he was asked why he was making so many international calls to Portugal, he bought his own calling card and made them from his own home.

No one ever answered. There was an answering machine, but it had no greeting message. The phone would ring and ring and ring with a foreign-sounding dial tone from another side of the world, then there would be a loud beep and then silence. After a few minutes there would be another beep signaling the end of the call. Solloway's messages were succinct and formal at first: 'Hello, this is Officer Solloway calling. I'm looking for a woman by the name of Doreen Durand. Please call me back as soon as you get this message.' But now his messages were unhinged, free-flowing, as if he were having a conversation with an old, frustrating friend.

'Please come back. I know you're out there. I hope you're all right. We would still very much like to have you help with our investigation.'

* * *

His girlfriend overheard him once. (His girlfriend now was the girl who, a few months ago, had been his date. She had miraculously but very casually become his girlfriend after a short while and things seemed to be fine. They got along well enough. Solloway liked her and he even felt what might be a grain of sand of love.) They had spent the night together at her house after a wine-soaked dinner party where Solloway had been looser with his words and had let flow his confessions about work, about what he could get away with, about his partner, Palmer, whom he referred to as a devil who was bound to get embroiled in 'Some kind of police brutality horror show.'

His new girlfriend – her name was Cara – had been mortified and she regretted taking him to meet her friends so soon in their relationship. She spent the remainder of the night trying to iron out his disastrous first impressions and they both passed out in her bed, exhausted, not speaking. In the morning she heard him downstairs talking to a woman on the phone.

'Please, I just need to know where you are. I need to know why you went away. Why did you have to go? Where are you?'

She trained her ear to the direction of his voice. No one seemed to be talking back to him. He was leaving a deranged voicemail, or, more accurately, he was talking to no one, flitting back and forth between formalities and vibrant, emotional pining. He sounded rawer than she had ever heard him before, more emotional.

'We have important business to discuss. Please, for God's sake just answer the phone.'

Cara flushed with embarrassment. She tucked her head under her covers, shocked at the kind of guy she had picked up – no, not just picked up, they had turned it into a formal thing, a relationship. She groaned. Luckily, she thought, she hadn't fallen for him completely. He was sweet, he was attractive, and he was not much else. There was nothing in him that would hook her too strongly. If anything, this drunken reveal of naked psychopathy endeared him to her in a way – a sick, unhealthy way that she was able to recognize and stop from becoming 'a project,' but an endearment nonetheless. She wanted to know more about him – specifically about this woman, this Doreen Durand. She obviously meant everything to him.

Cara kept the relationship casual.

The last bit of information Solloway pored over was the Portuguese address on the business card. Of course Solloway looked it up. He bookmarked satellite images of it online. He knew exactly how to get there from the airport. He knew what the weather there was like every day. He knew how to say simple phrases in Portuguese like hello, how are you, and have you seen a woman by the name of Doreen Durand?

ROME

CHAPTER 17

Rome was wheat, oil, tomato, onion, basil, salt, and water, and somehow these ingredients were the perfect distillation of a primordial joy, whether baked, fried, boiled, or simply left raw. Everything Doreen ate was this alchemy, perfectly brewed to make her forget about Leo and Harry, their mother, the police officers, her work, her direction in life or lack thereof. The trip played out like a shallow dream or a cliché-ridden movie. Everything that she had expected Rome to be it either was exactly that or exceeded.

'Well there it is,' she said. 'The *Pantheon*.' They stood in front of it and looked up. She nudged Violet on the shoulder. They both smiled at each other as if this were one big, thousand-year-old inside joke between them.

'Pan, not par,' said Violet. She nodded agreeably and winked.

'It's huge.'

They stared up at the temple. The columns were larger than brontosaurus legs and little birds flew around them, looking like tiny fruit flies. They went inside and watched the pure sunlight pouring through the oculus above, the air cold and rock-scented. There was a constant low echo that was older than the voices that fueled it.

Next they walked to the Trevi Fountain and watched the clot of people surrounding it, eagerly tossing coins in by the second like a flooded slot machine. Violet explained the tradition and the proper technique for tossing the coin over your shoulder and Doreen rolled her eyes. They hovered around the edge of the crowd, unless of course, as Violet explained, Doreen wanted to go throw one in, otherwise she wouldn't be able to come back to Rome.

'That's the *only* way to ever come back to Rome?' asked Doreen.

'Absolutely the only way.' Violet smiled.

'It can't be that hard to come back, I thought all roads lead to Rome.'

'They do, but this is the faster way.'

'How's it work, someone collects the coins at the end of the day and traces yours back to you and registers you with a travel agency?'

'That's exactly how it works.'

The women laughed and clutched each other. They continued their endless wander, dancing down side streets, ducking into hidden churches, laughing but full of awe at how wonderful life had suddenly become. It was as if the world had injected itself with a higher octane of romance and excess and drama and clear blue skies. Doreen knew this was owing to the fact that Violet's millions were lubricating the wheels of each day – they never encountered lines at attractions or waits at restaurants or poor service – but she wanted to believe in something more cosmic. She wanted to believe that a new hemisphere had somehow made stable everything in her life that wasn't.

After one full week in the city, Doreen finally became more of the self she knew she had always been: practical, assured, sarcastic and dry, but earnest and teachable. A wreck of a person was finally coming back to herself.

She noticed it one night during dinner. They were laughing about the fiasco their private tour of the Vatican had turned out to be. Their tour guide had been confused at first, as he had been expecting a full group of tourists.

'"*Sir, I booked the whole tour.*"' Doreen mimicked Violet's voice. 'The poor guy was so shocked.'

'It was the quickest way to do it,' said Violet, laughing. 'All the normal private tours were booked-out for the next month, so I had to buy up all the spots. I don't think that's completely unreasonable. I don't know why he didn't believe us.'

'The cash you pulled out sure made him believe. He fell right in line after that.'

'That's what cash is for.' Violet sipped her water. 'I'm sorry for that, really. I hope it didn't ruin the experience for you.'

'It didn't. If anything it made it more memorable.'

'Oh no, in that case we need to go back and rewrite the memory. Let me take you again in a few months. We'll do a proper one-on-one tour with a good agency.'

Doreen laughed and brushed her off. 'No, it's fine.' Violet had been doing this more and more often – over-correcting some innocuous hiccup.

'All right, but let me know if you change your mind.' She sat back and watched Doreen, still unsure. It was a strange, wayward expression, but she seemed to recognize it and tried to snap out of it. 'I guess I shouldn't expect any sort of Audrey Hepburn in your personality.'

'No,' said Doreen. 'None at all. I should have warned you from the get-go. I mean, I adore Rome, but I'm not going to fawn over it. Actually, that's the surest sign I'm back to normal. I'm impressed but not overwhelmed. I'm content but not stagnant. I'm not ...' she searched for the word in the air, 'Yippy.'

'That feels true,' said Violet. 'You're definitely not yippy. Happier, but not yippy. Maybe summery.'

Doreen agreed. The summeriness of her recovery was almost disconcerting to her, which was just how she approached things normally – not mistrusting of happiness, but prone to go at it with a scalpel to make sure there wasn't anything more to the story. And there wasn't, or at least, there was nothing more to their spontaneous trip to Rome, their happy whim. There was no mystique, in fact, after one whole week in the city, the two of them were finally getting bored.

Violet listed off on her fingers the attractions they had seen as they made their way back to their hotel. The Vatican, the Colosseum, the Roman Forum, the Spanish Steps, the food, the food, the food, the day trip to Pompeii, the day trip to the beach. All done and done.

'What else should we do?' she asked.

Doreen said she didn't know. She didn't mind the long stretches of time with nothing to do or the days that were becoming open-ended. It was as if they certified the authenticity of the trip and that of their friendship. It made Violet more human, and yet, she seemed to be having a problem with that.

'Maybe we can go back to the gallery where you saw that painting you liked. We can talk to the dealer about making a purchase. Or there was that pasta making class we saw the other day – I'll call them up and see if we can book one of the instructors for a day.'

Doreen was afraid to say no outright, so she only laughed and shook her head, being nothing but politely tentative, non-committal, but by the next morning, Violet had grown even more frantic. Her reaction to the boredom was like a body fighting off an infection. She trawled their hotel suite listing off things they could do, each one more extravagant and therefore easier for Doreen to suggest otherwise.

'How about Venice, is that close?' Doreen suggested half-heartedly, not bothering to consult a map.

'It can be,' said Violet. 'Should I call the plane? Or were you thinking by car? Tom can drive us.'

No, no, no, Doreen chanted and tried to calm her down. She stretched out on the bed and reached for Violet as she walked back and forth. She grabbed her by the hem of her shirt and tugged playfully on the thousand-dollar fabric – something she wouldn't have dreamed of doing just days ago.

'You gotta relax,' she said, practically singing it. Violet visibly flinched when she said this. 'Let's just do nothing today. Let's take a nap. We can go wander around later and grab dinner.' She reminded Violet of how she herself had suggested this very idea back in Atlanta, how she had said they would do nothing but sleep and eat all day. Now they would have a few more relaxing days in Rome, then they would be off to meet Violet's statue. 'Our statue,' Doreen said, so comfortable and nestled into this world she had been absorbed into.

Violet smiled and stopped and paused to think this over. She seemed hesitant and unsure – a rare feat for her face – as if it were one of the first times in her life she was expected to surrender herself to someone else's plans. She stood completely still and closed her eyes. After a moment, she nodded her head, compliant. She would do nothing. Instantly, she slumped, almost subordinately, onto the bed, and assumed a position that could only be described as text-book napping, as if she had never been lazy herself, but knew the gist of it and how to play along. This wasn't lounging pleasurably as she had done at the hotel in Atlanta, she was completely, not mildly, zonked.

A thought crossed Doreen's mind: What if, as she was recovering from the brink, Violet was sinking down into it, as if they were on a see-saw together. If one of them was up, the other was down. Opposites, eternally swirling around each other. One's high dependent on the other's low. The thought crossed and kept on moving.

Later that night, after a full day of nothing, they were at another cavernous restaurant in the hidden nook of an alleyway. Candlelight blurred orange across the stone walls and wood tables and there were no windows, as if whoever designed the place had intended to tuck patrons away like little bats, wrapped up and hand fed. They ate the usual combination of tomato, basil, garlic, and oil here, but this time it was divided and multiplied by scallops, asparagus, pears, and blackened mushrooms in frilly gestures of modernity. Violet drank water as she always did, but Doreen was comfortable enough – had been comfortable enough for the past week – to order wine for herself, an expensive kind, and pay for it all with the credit card Violet had given her.

'What are you thinking?' Violet asked during the meal.

Doreen smiled. Dozens of candlelights intersected across her face, simultaneously covering her in shadow but also in no shadow. It wasn't the first time Violet had asked the question.

'Nothing actually,' Doreen said. 'I don't think I'm thinking of anything for once. Why do you ask?'

Violet shook her head and Doreen saw a hint of nervousness, as if she had a stomach ache, a wince of nakedness – Doreen had noticed it a few times lately.

'I just want to know what's inside your head,' Violet said.

'I guess I *am* thinking of something,' said Doreen. She brushed aside the odd way Violet had said that: what's inside your head. She was used to her strange sentence structure. It was often odd, but there was never anything that required parsing, she was exact and specific at least in that sense. 'I'm thinking about how I'm more of myself now. I feel sturdier.'

'You do seem to have a firmer grasp on yourself.'

'I'm comfortable. I guess anyone would be comfortable if they were whisked away to Rome like this. But I'm beginning to think I'm strong enough to face what I have to face in my life. I know I left everything behind – I've left my job, left my car, I spent almost all of my money. Soon I won't even have my apartment any more – my lease is up for renewal at the end of next month. But that's all beside the point. What I wonder is if I'll be able to face the accident – the accident in and of itself, yes, but also what my reaction to the accident was. I want to know why I didn't do anything. Why I froze.'

'I think the explanation is simple enough,' said Violet. 'You saw a horrific thing and your body went into shock. On top of that, you had a strange, coincidental connection with one of the boys and you were worried about how that would look, even though your innocence was clear.'

'But I don't think my innocence is clear at all,' said Doreen. Violet blinked and opened her mouth as if to speak, but no words came out, as if she were shocked she hadn't gotten something perfectly right. Doreen pretended not to notice. 'I don't think the boy – the prank calls – had anything to do with my reaction. It was more like this kind of zapping. I've never felt anything like it before in my life. It was like the world had fallen through a funnel but I was still up at the top, unable to go through it. I felt this incredible sense of isolation, like I was alone, but under a magnifying glass, like I had been deserted, but by my own doing. It was as if all the loneliness I had been feeling in the months leading up to the accident – this kind of spiraling madness – had finally filled me up with as much dread as I could possibly take, right to the brim, but the perpetrator of all that dread was finally revealed to be just me, or an inversion of myself, no one else.

I want to figure out what that was and I want to make sure it never happens again.'

Violet was staring into her empty glass, slowly turning it, watching the single lemon slice inside. She looked like a mournful queen in an old oil painting, without a single blemish, unnaturally stoic and expressionless.

'Are you all right?' asked Doreen after a moment had passed. 'If anything, I want to know what's going on inside *your* head. You've done so much for me and I still hardly know you. I feel like I've reached this point where I'm almost OK enough to go back and face my life and all its consequences, but – this might sound silly – I feel as if, somehow, you're not done with me.' She laughed nervously, even more when Violet showed almost no reaction. 'Or I feel like there's some purpose for me you haven't told me about yet – if that makes any sense. I feel like there's a lot more going on inside your mind than in mine.'

Violet hesitated. She stopped turning her glass but was still looking down at it and not at Doreen. One of her diamond earrings flashed a pinprick of yellow light like a traffic signal. She touched the part in her hair as if to make sure it was still there. She moved a strand behind her ear, but her short bob didn't allow for it so the hair fell right back to where it was. This kind of war with the self seemed unnatural for her.

'To be honest, I've been recharging,' she said. 'The past week has taken a lot out of me.'

Doreen began to apologize. She didn't need to be there still, she said. Her tagging along had to be a nuisance; she knew she had overstayed her welcome and was just as stumped as to how to politely disinvite herself.

'No, no, don't be silly. Both you and I know that that's not reasonable. I brought you here – I still *want* you here. There's more to be done – you just said so yourself.' She swatted Doreen's persistence away, but her voice was shaky. 'I'm recharging my way of seeing things, my perspective. My mind feels like a pair of binoculars right now and I need to readjust the vision one degree at a time. It's a slow process.'

She shook her head, rattling around whatever was inside it, knowing what she needed to say, but struggling with the words.

'Tell me, Doreen, do you remember the circumstances surrounding our first encounter? Do you remember that evening, and then the following evenings? Do you remember that day in Atlanta when you tried to run away and then I found you? We still haven't really spoken about those days.'

Doreen was silent. Up until now, the two of them had looked like two successful young women having a lively dinner, dressed up like masterpieces in designer clothes, thick hair and clear skin. Now with a few simple exchanges, both of them seemed to have shrunk. Doreen nodded and said yes, of course she remembered. Why was she bringing this up?

'It's a difficult balance to strike,' said Violet. 'Between the intensity – dare I say the spirituality – of those moments, with where we're at now.' She looked all around the restaurant and then down at herself. She looked at her hands. 'I've spent a long time observing the process of how a human builds herself back up after a raw, fraught experience like you went through and the walls they put up as safeguards. They have no other choice but to do it – it is *building*, after all, there have to be walls – but it's probably the most taxing thing for me to see. The real work for me is maintaining my usefulness after the initial encounter, the initial connection.'

Doreen felt the wine pulse at her temple. She tried to make sense of what Violet had just said and tried to match the seriousness she was suddenly entrenched in. 'You mean you're like a crisis worker? Like how a 9-1-1 operator or an emergency room doctor has to help people through all these traumatic things, but they eventually need to get some help too?'

'No,' said Violet. 'No, that's not at all what I mean, actually.' She shifted in her seat, flickering in the candlelight. She looked around the restaurant again. 'I don't think this is the right place to tell you exactly what I'm trying to tell you. Would you mind if we left?'

Doreen said of course and the two of them gathered their things. Doreen paid the bill using the credit card Violet had given her – making a funny show of it, saying what a burden it was for her to pay for it (the wine should be held accountable for the tired joke) but Violet didn't laugh. Her mind was elsewhere. Doreen saw this change in her countenance and willed herself – even with half a bottle of wine in her – to join her on that plane, or at least make more of an effort.

Leaving the restaurant, the women walked south, crossing the Tiber river and back into the ancient winding streets, turning left, then sometimes right, shuffling through enormous crowds of tourists then passing through long stretches of empty alleyways. They walked in a silence that threatened to become uncomfortable with tension, until they reached an enormous piazza that opened up with a nighttime yawn of cobblestones, fountains, dim street lamps, and people – some scurrying off to hotels, some haggling for money, some wandering aimlessly, some inebriated and giggly. They found a bench at the far end. Violet seated herself in an unnaturally passive way. A group of revelers nearby were laughing and clinking glasses at an open-air restaurant, and Doreen was certain she saw Violet wince in pain at the sound.

'Tell me what you want to tell me,' said Doreen. 'Please.'

Violet was almost unresponsive. She was staring at the

fountain in the center of the piazza with complete focus, as if she were estimating the amount of water bubbling out of it.

'You mentioned walls,' said Doreen, trying to prompt her. 'How people eventually put them up – because we're people and people have to have walls. And I understand what you mean. I've watched that happen to some of my relationships where I thought we had connected on some level, or at least shared something together for a moment, but then things suddenly become blocked off and unreachable. I don't want you to think that now that I'm more stable means I've blocked myself off to that initial connection we first had. I mean, I don't ever want to *be* in that kind of mental state again, but I want to always keep that intimacy we had – we *have*. We definitely still have it. Even with all of this.' She gestured around at all of Rome and also, inexplicably, her hair, which earlier she had curled into heavy waves for their night out.

Violet turned to her. It wasn't clear she had heard anything Doreen had just said. Her voice was low.

'I'm going to speak in plain terms and I expect for you to follow me,' she said, looking Doreen in the eye. Doreen nodded in agreement, but there was no possible way she could be prepared for what Violet was about to say as she took a deep breath.

'When I first saw you at the grocery store,' she began, 'I knew what had happened to you. I knew about the two boys. I knew you were going to be at that grocery store. I picked you out – I felt it. You: Doreen Durand in Beaverton, Oregon, near Portland, working at Mario's, seeing what you had just seen. I was all the way in Atlanta and I felt what was happening to you and I flew to Portland the morning of the accident. It was one of the strongest sensations I've ever felt in my lifetime. When you asked me what I was doing in

Portland, it was a lie. I was there only for you. I came with the intention of meeting you, assisting you, retrieving you.'

Doreen was still. There was the temptation to smile, to be sheepish about what Violet was saying. 'So you're psychic, is what you're telling me,' she would have said, had the moment been light enough. But her heart pounded.

'From any normal perspective of the world and what we know about it, what I'm saying comes off as crass, I know,' said Violet. 'I've spent a long time crafting the best way to relay what it's like for me to have this type of ability, but I'm afraid the best descriptor I have for it is it's a type of intuition, but stronger. It's a blend of prediction and inference. My senses are heightened to a point where they can feel miniscule, undetectable shifts in the world. I'm as comfortable doing it as a fish is comfortable in an ocean. It's like breathing. When I first sensed you and the accident with the boys, it was like a typhoon. I had felt large presences like yours before – I've predicted plenty of disasters and tragedies around the world before they've happened, as well as good things, triumphs, wins, peace, good news – but yours was different. With you, the exact pinpoint of who you were and where I could find you made itself available to me with more clarity than ever before.'

Doreen nodded as if she could accept this all as fact. It felt ludicrous to do so. The wine inside her clouded her thinking and she had to be sure she was understanding Violet correctly. She cleared her throat. 'And when this happened – when you found me – that's what drained you? It took some kind of energy out of you?' she said. She struggled to find the appropriate terminology.

'Yes. But also, I think it has to do with the general change that there's been inside you. Really, my power is only the ability to see the authentic that resides beyond whatever has been built around it. With you, since you had already stripped away so much artifice before I came along, it made your signal all the stronger, and now that you're coming back into a normal presentation, I've lost the signal, and I'm afraid I lack the ability to help you any further.'

'I think that's understandable. You've done enough for me already. I don't expect you to still be my – I don't know – my guru or something.'

'No.' Violet waved her off again. 'There is more to our meeting, I know this. I have more of a purpose to serve you, but I just haven't been able to tap into it yet. I thought it would become clearer to me once we came to Rome. I still hope it comes to me, but I don't know. I've never been strung along like this before.'

'You've done this sort of thing before?'

'No, not like this. Never without seeing the end goal first. Take Tom for instance – I've got his severance package all ready to go for when his eventual end comes. All of life is contractual. Even if it doesn't serve me, I know what my role is and where it ends. Operationally, my interactions have usually been fairly rote. Oh, I know this can't make any sense to you; this is all new. But for me it's very old, ancient, even, and when something different like you comes into the mix – it's – it's thrown me off balance.'

Violet's voice trailed off. The two women went silent for a while. They stayed sitting on the bench and watched the crowds of the night slowly whittle away to only small groups of people or individuals who crossed the piazza alone. The emptiness became deep enough that the splashing water of the fountain could finally echo around the space in soaring loops. The sound was as if all the ancient buildings around them were applauding together.

'I believe you,' said Doreen. She touched her hand to

Violet's knee. 'You probably don't need people to say that to you since you've had this ... ability for so long, but for my own sake, I want you to know that I believe you. I don't know what it is exactly, but I understand the truth behind it. And I'm grateful you found me, really. I hope I can help you figure out what you're supposed to do next. You helped me, now I can help you.'

Violet thanked her and wiped what could have been a tear from her eye. They watched the world pass a while longer, then stood up to leave. Slowly and silently, they linked arms and disappeared among the dark figures crisscrossing the night.

Doreen felt the pull. She wanted to feel the warmth and the magic of the city – the light clouds of cigarette smoke and diesel fumes pushed away by summery Italian breezes, the yellow flickering streetlights, the late night foods slowly, comfortably, cooling off – but she felt the pull instead, the pull of something else. She felt Violet's warm body next to hers and recognized the makings of a sisterly bond, of friendship bracelets, braids, and all, but there was also the overpowering pull. A chain link, cold and metallic, that clanked and snapped as it pulled her, not maliciously, but with a sense that made Doreen instantly regret having told Violet she believed her. Because she didn't. She couldn't, for fear of all the things it would entail.

CHAPTER 18

The morning blasted away any sense of the sacred from the night before – or whatever that was, Doreen thought to herself when she awoke. She tried to remember. She tried to think. But there were distractions around her like cawing birds.

Violet was already up, chattering away about plans, preparations, things that needed to be done, things that had been on the calendar for months and had slipped her mind. There was a meeting. She had forgotten. Something big and fancy. There had been a knock at the door – an unforeseen knock – and Violet had leapt from the bed. Tom was there, handsomely suited, holding a leather-bound folder of documents. Both of them were trampling around the suite.

'Fong and Partners,' she said. 'How could I forget. The semiconductor plant.'

'—Kwon and Partners, actually,' Tom corrected her. 'The fracking investors.'

'The frackers, of course. This stuffy hotel's making me forget. The frackers. Fracking in Colorado.'

'—Wales.' Tom seemed just as surprised as she was at her lapse in memory and just as uncomfortable with having to correct her. It was apparent what an anomaly this was. The businessmen were downstairs in the lobby, Tom said. They had flown out from Seoul. A conference room had been booked. 'Shall I go ahead and start the meeting? I can go over contract amendments with their legal team for now—'

'It's fine,' Violet snapped. She was suddenly furious and maniacal. She spun around the hotel room, gathering pieces of herself together, changing her top, ditching a scarf, grabbing earrings, reasserting control. 'We're fine. You see what happens, Doreen? If you never reschedule a meeting then they'll come to you. Always make them come to you. All the way out to your stuffy hotel in Rome. When they want your money, you make them come get it. Only go to them when you're just about ready to die. But we're good. We're fine now. Everybody's fine. They can wait a little while longer. We'll all go down together.'

Doreen stuck her head into the fray. 'All of us? I'm fine to stay up here. I don't mind.'

'I said all of us.'

Doreen and Tom shared an apprehensive look that nearly put them on equal terms for the first time. They had both noticed it: the shock of forgetfulness rippling across Violet's face. It was as if entire years had sputtered apart like folded papers in her mind, names and faces blurring, mixing and matching. She was trying to recover but both Doreen and Tom had watched it happen. Neither of them knew exactly how to proceed other than to be carried along in the flow and fury.

Fracking? Doreen felt the familiar sting of corporate guilt she used to get philosophically caught up in at Mario's. Tom had mentioned oil refineries in his vague list of what Violet actually did for a living, but now that the vague was becoming specific, Doreen was suddenly wary. What other morally ambiguous businesses was Violet involved in? She wished she had never asked. But then again, after spending every day with her and seeing how she operated, did it even matter?

Was moral ambiguity the only option once you reached the apex of wealth? And then there was that added layer of mysticism that Doreen couldn't even start to wrap her head around. She had a pounding fogginess in her mind.

'Doreen,' said Violet when they were in the elevator. Her tone was firm and direct. 'This hotel is stuffy, don't you agree? Even the best hotels grow stuffy after a week.' She stated this as a fact. 'Let's have you go find us a new one while I sort out this meeting, is that all right? Fresh lodging for our last few days in Rome.'

Doreen said she agreed. She said so in the new tone of voice she had honed specifically for addressing Violet in these instances, as if it were perfectly normal for a luxury hotel with daily housekeeping and nightly turn-down services to grow 'stuffy'. Part of her wanted to see this purported meeting, see this physical evidence of Violet Cascade, but a larger part of her was too afraid. She avoided eye contact with her the whole way down to the lobby. She didn't want to see the eyes of the weakened woman of last night – who had been lost deep in thought, who had revealed her innermost fears – and the mask she wore now, the chicanery, the fuss.

On her own but still high from the chaotic morning, Doreen went out into the city in search of a new hotel and quickly found she wasn't good at this, at making the sort of high-minded decisions of taste Violet was used to making daily. Personally, Doreen would be fine at the nearest American chain she could find, but she knew that wasn't Violet's style. Surely she wouldn't flat-out refuse to stay at a Hilton or a Marriott, but Doreen imagined it – Violet would have a severe, anaphylactic reaction if she had to sleep between generic, starchy sheets; rinse her mouth with sweetly iron-tinged faucet water; eat stale blueberry muffins and drink coffee made in a microwave from a sachet of powder.

That was the reaction Doreen imagined her having, but maybe she wouldn't. Maybe she didn't really know Violet at all. She had seen two drastically different sides to her in a span of only a few hours. She wasn't sure what to make of her any more. Apparently she was some kind of psychic prophetess who had come to Portland with the express purpose of saving Doreen from herself, but, strangely enough, not saving the two little boys who had been in actual physical danger. Had she been sitting by herself in the grocery store, just waiting for the moment they were run over and killed? 'What the hell,' Doreen said out loud, stopping in the middle of the street, realizing for the first time the implications of everything Violet had told her last night. She felt dizzy. She hoped these psychic abilities were sporadic, not selective, but then again, it would fit the profile for someone involved in the business of fracking. But then again, there were no psychics.

There were no psychics, right? There's simply no such thing, Doreen thought to herself. For a businesswoman at the height of corporate prowess, sure maybe it felt like a superpower to be so charming, to be so infinite, to snap your fingers and be in a different country, but it wasn't mystical. It wasn't foreordination, it was mostly just good genetics. It wasn't spiritual intuition, it was simple logic and maybe an inflated sense of the self. It was maybe psychosis and a good hairdo.

And fracking? Surely a psychic could see the ills in that. Doreen was full of these fragmented questions and none of them sat comfortably within her, but she also knew that searching too deeply for answers now would be an affront to the stability she had so carefully regained over the week. She

tried to breathe, disregard, and move on. Stability was only a
series of latches that needed tightening, locking, and leaving.

The sky was clearer and brighter over Rome than in most
other places in the world. It was as if the sun saw the city
approaching on the horizon and leaned in closer to get a
better look at the domed roofs, the terraces, the spaghetti
layout of the streets. Doreen felt the curious prickle of warm
sunlight through the chilly morning breeze.

Tourists were just beginning to clot the streets and she
walked in the direction of fanciness and capitalism. She
followed the parade of Guccis and Pradas and Herméses
and McDonalds' like a migratory bird seeking out familiar
patterns in the wind. Her idea was to find something blunt
and American – a Tiffany & Co. or a Hard Rock Café or a
Nike store – then find an Italian hotel next to it. She knew
there was no logic, but it felt right to her; something about
how if an Italian hotel could break through the wall of inva-
sive American chains, it would be good enough for Violet.

Falling right in line with her strategy, Doreen performed
a pirouette in front of a Burger King, and right away she
found her hotel. The face of the building was stucco and
white rock. There were shutters and hanging flowers on all
of the windows, suggesting authenticity, but the signage was
sleek and modern, one-of-a-kind, as if a giant had written
the hotel logo in red cursive right onto the wall.

Inside, she asked the woman at the concierge for the nicest
executive suite available. There was a quartet of flags around
the woman's nametag, indicating the languages she spoke,
but all she said was 'OK,' and took Doreen's Violet's credit
card. A suite on the top floor with the best view of the city
was booked and Doreen took the room key and went up to
inspect.

All the normal trappings of luxury were there: the claw-foot tub, the giant paper-thin TV, the separate living room and kitchen and closet, the master bedroom with a bed the size of a small hotel room and a glass-cubed shower fit for an exhibitionist. Everything was silver and gold and decently tacky – a faux gold gilding around everything, mirrored cabinetry, doilies under the kitchenware.

But like something dead and rotting in the walls, Doreen detected a garish American influence, and grew suspicious. She inspected the logo printed on the guestbook and the stationary. She dug her toes into the carpet. She fluffed the pillows. She sensed that there was only a veneer of Italian, masking something else; she could taste it in the air.

The remote control – she recognized the remote control for the TV. She had seen this model before. It was the size of an ironed dead mouse, with buttons arranged esoterically. She picked it up and immediately banged it against the glass coffee table, cracking it open like an egg. The face of the remote popped off and she examined the innards. She gutted the battery and tossed it aside.

Yep. Mario's.

She could recognize a Mario's sensor in anything, no matter what form it took. She remembered these remotes – Mario's had put out a press release about the partnership, how, thanks to Mario's sensors, consumers would never lose their TV remote again. The hotel suddenly became immeasurably cluttered. Inside the remote were the deals between company, parent company, holding company, Chinese factory, financial trust, marketing agency, freelance photographer – everyone present during every conference call squeezed down to this dead rat black plastic.

Doreen wondered if Violet saw all those things behind a simple remote control. Maybe the world was so noisy for a psychic, she had to just let some things happen. Let frackers frack. Let dead children die. Doreen looked out of the tall bedroom windows and imagined Violet on the other side of the city, having her meeting somewhere behind the host of domes and spires that reached up into the sky like moss. She pictured her in her mind.

'Can you hear me?' she vocalized in her head. She thought long and hard.

It doesn't work like that, she imagined Violet saying in reply. Nothing ever worked the way it should, even for psychics. How convenient.

She couldn't possibly have been serious.

Last night, in the fog of wine, what Violet said had made sense. Being in touch with something unknowable certainly fit with her general brand of mysteriousness, but now, like all morning-afters, any sense of the sacred was blasted away by the light of day. It wasn't only skepticism Doreen felt, but a profound sense of So What. Even if there were psychics, so what?

'Yes, but what's the point?' she would ask her old room-mate sometimes, when she would go on about a boyfriend, or a career plan, or a trip to Vegas. So what? Even though Doreen shouldn't have been one to scoff and question the utility of such things as she had none of those things herself.

If there was any one thing Doreen feared, it was a cult of personality – both not having one, of course, but also getting sucked into one. She recognized she was someone particularly susceptible to them, and the orbit surrounding Violet had proven to be the perfect climate for that to happen. Maybe this was what she had intended to have happen, she thought. Maybe Violet prowled the world for the depressed and disillusioned and made them her next assistant or driver or flight attendant on her private jet. Maybe she was a psychic but of the carnival fair, keeping you holed up in her magic tent, doling out platitudes while some rapscallion assistant stole your identity and tanked your bank account and sold you a fortune cookie on your way out. Luckily I've already tanked my bank account, Doreen thought. Self-fraud.

During her trip to Las Vegas with Whitney – that chipping rock of a vacation – Doreen had eaten by herself at a McDonald's two blocks away from the Strip. She was lost, hungry, and inebriated, and while she ate her Big Mac, she watched two fat trolls playing cards at a neighboring table. They were fluffy and pink and sweating, had red eyes, and used coarse, French fry freckled language. They were fastidious. Doreen looked closer at their card game and saw not casino playing cards but social security cards and driver's licenses. They shuffled the cards with their greasy fingers and laid them out in different arrangements on the table, pointing at different ones, commenting on others, making note of certain things. They were two roly-poly con artists with an entire deck of humans at their fingertips. Gods.

She caught up with Whitney that night at a drag show and told her all about them. 'I saw these two crooks and they had all these stolen social security cards just out in plain sight,' she said. But Whitney couldn't hear her over the singing of a Whitney Houston, whom Whitney was yelling at, eager to tell her that her name was Whitney too.

When the Whitney Houston finished, a loose interpretation of a Tina Turner came out and the girls left for drinks with a herd of other men and women they had semi-befriended during the show – or Whitney had befriended, while Doreen had watched in awe at this version of her roommate she had never witnessed back home, one that was calculating and actually successfully conversing with strangers, finding common-denominators, 'clicking,' as they say. It caught her off guard. One of the first things Doreen had admired about Whitney was how, once, when their neighbors had left them a plate of Christmas cookies on their doorstep as a gift, Whitney had done nothing. After they finished off the cookies, Whitney threw away the paper plate along with the unopened greeting card, never thanking or even nodding in recognition at their neighbors – she had seemed so defiantly against social performance. But now she was here in Vegas, asking Doreen which of the men in the group she preferred – drunkenly, yes, but not in the drunken manner Doreen expected. There wasn't a hint of satire. This was exactly what Whitney was wanting to do.

The rest of the trip proceeded like this, the recitation of familiar Las Vegas beats, with Doreen on the bleary-eyed sidelines, wondering, often out loud to no one, if everyone around her was actually being serious.

Whitney had never even thought to ask how Doreen had ended up by herself at a McDonald's outside the Strip, as if this were normal.

Doreen had told her, though, right there at the drag show, competing against the soaring Whitney Houston. 'I walked there by myself because I'm tired and out of my mind! Did you even notice I was gone? I'm sick of all of this! What the hell are we doing here? Why did we come here? Is this what my life is going to be now? I'm going to live in Beaverton but tell boys I meet in Las Vegas that I live in Portland? Is this what *you* want to do?'

Whitney had heard just a selection of those words. 'Vegas *is* hot as hell!' she yelled back, nodding. The Whitney Houston on stage jumped another octave and turned a rhinestone encrusted arm up to heaven, smiling like she knew it was the brightest thing Doreen would ever see.

Doreen threw the broken remote into a corner and stormed

out of the room. She went back downstairs and handed back
the key to the concierge.

'Changed my mind. TV remote didn't work or something.
Keep the deposit. Bye.'

She ran away. Back into Violet's arms.

CHAPTER 19

Can you really read a person's mind? Is it something that lays itself out like a book and doesn't change? And if you can get in there – screw off their scalp, unclench their skull, look inside the folds of their brain – is it so easy you can call it reading?

Violet is a child. She's a baby. She's sitting up in bed, sitting the cartoonish way babies sit, but she's screaming, surrounded by people who watch helplessly. Pain courses through her tiny body. Her skin is blotchy and red. It's as if an old man, an evil being, made entirely of needles, has wriggled through every one of her nerves.

The same pain returns again and again for years. She accustoms to it. When it's there, her senses are at their most physical and primal as she scans her body with her mind, searching for areas that aren't bursting into flames where she can take refuge. There is the sensation of infinite awareness when she does this – first, taking stock of every fiber of her body, then spreading outward, outside of herself, becoming hypersensitive to the immediate environment. It's as if her mind spills. Somehow, she overhears a group of elderly women whispering about spontaneous combustion, about people in their homes, doing nothing, who suddenly burst into flames, leaving nothing but a stain of soot behind. It's witchcraft and very real, one of them says.

So much time passes. Time coalesces. When she's older

she's in a car with her father, driving. Or maybe they are riding a horse through a ravine. Maybe they are simply walking. These sort of memories are so far away, melding together, a barely sortable stream, and the people in them amorphous, interchangeable types. She has lived so many lives. Memories have merged.

She remembers the car. They're driving and it needs to stop for water. It's old and swaybacked and they stop and Violet unbuckles her seatbelt and turns on the radio while they wait for the traffic signal to turn green. The horse is sweltering. There is no air conditioning. They swat at flies.

She can't remember much about her father. She can't remember what they talk about there, sitting on the rocks by the creek while the horse drinks. She can't remember the pop song on the radio. She can't remember how the visuals mesh.

The light turns green and the car accelerates. The horse breaks into a canter. The wagon wheels shake. Trees pass by overhead as do streetlamps.

Then the pain flares. She remembers this.

Her head rings out like a gong. A tremor pulses under her ribs and slithers all the way underneath her fingernails. It stretches and fans its wings like a giant moth, tormenting her there in the passenger seat of the car. She closes her eyes and trains her thoughts, not ignoring the pain, but embracing it. She faces it with her inner eye, as they say.

A crackle inside her. The sound of a snare.

Her mind suddenly leaves her body. It lifts itself into the air and panics. It begins searching in urgency for the body, to get back down inside, communing with everything, checking and connecting automatically and rapidly, like a typewriter whacking away at a ream of paper. It jumps from one thing to the next, opening and unpeeling everything, seeing specificity inside of specificity. The car or the horse is broken down into individual segments, down to the screws and parts, down to the fleas, down to the liters of diesel water sloshing around its fuel tank stomach, which is rusted and cancerous and needs to be replaced, put down. Her mind flies further beyond the immediate, out of the ravine, out of the present. She sees a lark in a large empty field, a field mouse, then a line cut across, a dusty lane with a farmhouse at the end, infested with snakes, then more lines, an entire grid of houses there in that same field, not a single speck of dust left, just people.

She has to remember to breathe. She focuses her gaze, shifting her vision on its axis, terrified she will lose herself completely. The pain recedes the more she does this, as if she is stopping the spinning of an enormous, marble globe. She looks at her father and gasps. She sees a disease inside him. Something is wrong with his heart and he doesn't know. It thumps incorrectly – she hears it. She physically sees it. Da-dum, da-dum, da-dum. He's also afraid, worried about their constant moving around for his daughter's sake – for her sake. He struggles to find work after so much hopping around to protect her – such a strange daughter, a cursed daughter. She tries to stop looking, to stop the layers that unpeel themselves just for her, but they won't stop. She sees his entire lifespan – the beginning and end of it. She sees every individual hair on his head, spiraling across her field of vision, every fiber of dust in the air surrounding them. She doesn't know where to begin.

She remembers consoling her parents. She is older now and they are grieving for the severing of the connection they had once had with their daughter. She has slipped into a kind of semi-transparency, keeping them aware of where she is and what she is doing with her life, but never giving them anything tangible, never an emotional context, never a shape. When she comforts them, she is able to do so in exactly the right way because she sees the perfect, calming words just waiting to be said, the ones they want to hear her say, the ones at the forefront of their minds, and she grabs them and they satisfy like juicy golden pears, picked right at dawn.

She disappears for months, sometimes years on end, and writes letters home from far-off places – places that would have been next to impossible to reach, since traveling isn't something done just for the sake of traveling at this time. Her letters are vague, filled with words but essentially empty; yet adequate. Part of the coercive allure is physical. When she visits, she seems impervious to age. Her clothes are always spotless. When people see her, they note that her voice and demeanor are not cracked with signs of cynicism or vice. She is otherworldly optimistic, happy in a way that the rest of the world hasn't quite yet evolved to.

Her parents pass away and their deaths pass away like dreams. One day they are in the periphery and the next they are not. Suddenly she feels both as if there aren't as many people in the world as there used to be, but also, simultaneously, as if there are more than ever before. People, as more come and go, are like leaves blossoming and dropping from trees – there and gone. She marries one of them, as she assumes you are supposed to do. When he dies of old age as you do, she marries another, and then, for the last time, another.

Her wealth becomes immense by sheer length of existence. She becomes a maven. As the world blooms around her, her strange gift of discernment becomes a tool that reaps success. She has always acted on the whims she sees and yet, more and more frequently, these whims favor accumulation and monopoly, legal tyranny. Suddenly she isn't a mystic, she's a businesswoman; she isn't reading some hidden truth about a soul, she just knows her way around a contract. There's a shift in the world order. She watches it churn down below, suddenly fearful of falling, breaking down into pieces in the atmosphere.

'Don't worry,' a man says to her, unprompted, somehow reading her mind. She's sitting next to him on an airplane. 'A pilot friend of mine says turbulence is just bumps on a road. Imagine we're in a car.'

Violet says thanks. 'This is my first time on a plane.'

'I think that can be said for most of the people here,' the man says. He hands her a cigarette and lights it for her. She inhales and exhales, feels the smoke curl up inside her, and she tries not to pay attention to the earth out of the window, so far away; her own mortality, suddenly so close.

'You gotta relax,' says the man. He has a swagger about him – something Violet has been finding more often in the people she encounters. It's a trait that hasn't really needed to exist until recently. They are thousands of feet up in the air and he is telling her to relax.

She draws her mind away from the window and lets it focus on only the immediate, on the cigarette, on her seat, on her seatmate, but an odd thing happens.

He is sealed off.

Maybe it's the nature of the airplane. Her mind has been lifted off the globe like a needle off a record. She can't read his mind. He is completely closed off to her.

'You all right?' he asks.

Her mouth is agape. She laughs and shakes her head. 'I am. I'm – are you all right?' It is the first time she has ever had to genuinely ask the question.

'I'm fantastic.'

191

They talk for the rest of the flight. The man is captivated by this precocious woman with the strange name, and, more surprisingly, Violet is entranced as well, as if she has finally met her match. They share a birds-eye view of the world. They believe the same things. They both look at a thing and see its past, present, and future, its depreciation over time, its market value.

They land at their destination and begin a courtship. Violet makes a vow with herself to never read his mind. She wants to preserve the authenticity of the seclusion of the airplane. She doesn't want to be let down. She wants time, for the first time, to surprise her. She doesn't want to know when he is going to surprise her with flowers, with diamonds, with invitations to dance, to make love, to marry. She doesn't want to know when he will be happy or angry or mad or sad or drunk or unfaithful or unhealthy or riddled with contention towards her for no reason other than hatred of the fact that she has everything nailed down in her life with perfect, tiny little strings, all in a perfect little line, because after sixty years of marriage and millions of dollars it is suddenly, overwhelmingly ingratiating goddammit.

He resents her by the end of things and he practically says so. Their marriage is an enterprise. Together, they have grown into an economic powerhouse, a capitalist smorgasbord. More money than a small country, more money than a large country.

She rarely suffers bouts of pain any more. Only if she shrugs off her connection to the deeper rhythms of the world. Only if she gets too comfortable – really indulges herself in her riches, really cows around with her fellow investors with that snide, all-American, good-old-boy civility – then there is a wincing pain.

She sails in the Mediterranean in the summer, spends springs all over Europe, maintains permanent residences in New York, Tokyo, and Lisbon. There is a certain lovelessness in her marriage, especially towards the end – or at least, the end for her husband – but mostly they stay tolerant of each other. Until one day when Violet breaks her promise.

She does it during his seventy-fifth birthday party, at an opulent hunting lodge in Nairobi. She has flown out all their closest friends and business partners for the occasion, for a weeklong celebration, for a surprise. It is something outside the norm for her to do, this kind of showboating, but something tells her, almost subconsciously, that it might be the last chance to do something like this for her husband. And so they come – dumb, dunderheaded men past their prime, swarming on the lodge like flies. These men, like her husband, have been taught to respect women with a gentle, perverse, arms-length fascination – often from allegories involving roses or clear water or footprints in sand – and now, old and still unlearned, they talk down to Violet with crude, snide, two-handed gentlemanliness, masking just barely the things they truly insinuate. It is at the forefront of their minds when they speak to her, she doesn't even need to read them. They're just like all the others she has known.

'What's he doing to you to keep you looking so young?'

'You never thought to settle down and give your man a son?'

'Why's a girl like you got to hop around the world for him anyway?'

There is no proper deflection. Any bone she tosses to them only transforms their bullying into something more ravenous and this lasts for days.

She spends the majority of the week outside, sulking in

the sun, counting the molecules of dust in the air, waiting for time to continue its never-ending passage, watching it flow through her fingers. She wonders, almost subconsciously, how much longer this will last. Wait. Stop. Before she realizes what she's done, it's too late. Her mind springs into action, the muscle memory. In seconds it is inside her husband, retrieving an answer to her question, breaking her vow.

Everything changes. A cascade of information issues forth, as if it is physically flooding out of the hunting lodge with the strength of a tsunami. Violet sees everything – their courtship, their milestones, every second of their time spent together through his eyes. She finally sees herself for what he sees her as and it is everything that she has always feared. The backlog of information pummels her. It sweeps her across the plain and flings her beyond the present, beyond the future. She sees versions of herself she has never imagined. She balks and wrenches. Everything she thinks she has ever known suddenly inverts itself. The truth becomes intolerable. She can no longer pick her husband out of a crowd. Every single one of these men look exactly identical. He could be any one of them. All this time the only thing that has differentiated him from the swarm is simply the fact that she has held herself back from truly looking at him. And this, she realizes, is how it has been for her entire life.

Pain crimps itself across her skin. Her nerves pinch between bones, tendons, and muscle. A pulsing heat magnifies everything and her mind goes out of control, zooming in on everything – a fly in the air, the grain of the wood, an olive in a drink, the sounds of the city miles away, great heaps of people she has encountered over the years, a thin string of gold around her neck, tightening, choking her, never letting her go, the pull of it. Colors bleed into one another.

Memories from years ago – centuries ago – become tangible like rocks, unsteady and cracking under her feet. She screams in pain, enraptured.

She finds herself in an empty, mauve-colored room, decorated sparsely, utilitarian. Every surface has a corner or an edge that has been sanded down to be non-confrontational and painless. There are no windows and there is minimal light, which only comes from odd places – from behind a desk, from under a bed, from the immediate center of the ceiling – from no discernable source, fluorescent but dim. A bleachy smell hangs in the air, or, more accurately, it is the air completely, it is inescapable.

Violet wonders aloud where her husband is and he appears out of thin air, or, rather, the image of him as he relates to her appears. The span of their relationship enters the room as if wheeled out on a metal cart, not making a sound, not even a squeak. She picks it up, examines it, and sets it aside without feeling. She lets it fade away with all the other things that have been passed over. She's afraid to think about anything else. To think it is to invite it into this space, this small little room that can become overcrowded so quickly if she isn't careful.

She wakes up in a Nairobi hospital with her husband by her side. They go back home. The party is over. They spend time apart. They spend time together. She continues with her work – reading the structure of the world around her and unraveling it, weaving it back up in a way that feeds her. Her husband dies at the age of seventy-seven just as she had uncovered in his mind. There is a funeral, a period of regrouping, and she moves on, nomadic.

She continues to form relationships with people in the

sense that she makes associations: links between humans, crafting them, in a way, in her own image – and it is always as a means towards an end. She creates a network of wealth – a multilateral scheme that morphs over time into something that is so ill-defined that its power and influence become infinite, abstract, and organic. And it is all her own organ, omniscient. Once admirable millions become untraceable billions, flirting with trillions. An abomination. And she communes with it every day.

CHAPTER 20

Doreen proudly, defiantly thrust the key card for a room at a Best Western into Tom's hand when she returned, but there was no time to worry about that. No time at all.

'She needs you, quick,' he said and rushed her down to the conference room where Violet's meeting was taking place. Inside a glass-walled room, Violet sat alone, facing a herd of faceless, black-suited men. Tom gestured to her through the glass. 'I don't know what's wrong with her, but she needs you in there.'

'What's wrong?'

'I don't know. She's – she's not herself. She doesn't know things. She's not thinking straight. She can barely carry on the meeting.'

Violet caught sight of them through the glass wall and dashed out the door.

'You're here, thank goodness, come in, come in, come quick!' She grabbed Doreen by the arm and pulled.

Doreen leaned back and shook her head. 'What do you need me for? You can't be serious. I can't just go in there.'

'You can! Come! Just try to follow along. Here—' she thrust a messy bundle of papers into her arms. 'Paper. Documents. You're just like me! Just follow along. Help me seal the deal.'

The entire room was waiting. It was too late to resist any further. Violet pulled her through the glass door and she was plopped down at a chair at the table, which was cluttered with charts and graphs, laptops, coffee mugs, crumpled notes.

Finally here was the specificity that Doreen had wanted all along, the evidence of Violet Cascade – again she regretted ever having wanted it. Representatives of Kwon and Partners actually existed and here they were, ten or twenty or twenty-thousand of them sitting across the table, speaking to Violet and now to Doreen with reverence and extreme formality, but with a hint of apprehension that smelled too strongly of the incongruity the meeting had spiraled into.

Doreen was introduced as a Senior Executive Advisor – practically knighted by Violet on the spot – and brought up to speed in a cloud of jargon. There was no clear leader of the group and the men spoke over one another, sounding more like a chorus of rocks cracking into one another than a business meeting. They were negotiating a deal, that was apparent. Something to do with fracking. But whether Violet's objective was to engorge herself in a lucrative deal at the expense of the environment or to sacrifice something of her own to try to save it was obscured in the haze. Green technology or the lack thereof was irrelevant. Mostly, people spoke in numbers. They said simple figures like six or twenty-five or twelve but Doreen at least understood that a parade of zeroes followed each one. Legal arithmetic passed from mouth to mouth and she tried to follow along but lost sight of things for stretches of time. One thing, however, that was abundantly clear was that Violet was losing it. Something was wrong. She was still as scatterbrained and on the fritz as she had been earlier in the morning just out of bed and completely unprepared. She seemed to be coasting on the baseline intimidation she naturally imposed, but her maneuvering – her general sense of wheeling and dealing – was stilted and unrecognizable. She trailed off and blanked mid-sentence if she spoke at all. Mostly, she flipped through pages of documents not like an encyclopedic expert at her game, but like a failing student, all while the men spoke around her. She looked at Doreen for support and she gave it as best she could, which was a smile and a nod, then a befuddled shrug of the shoulders. Violet turned to her with more and more frequency until finally, she did the unthinkable and said, 'I'm not so sure on that one, gentlemen, but my partner here, Doreen, might be able to shine some light on that for us. She'll be able to answer any further questions from here, as well as finalize the transaction once an agreement is reached. Doreen?'

A shock of laughter broke Doreen's face. She stared back at Violet – she couldn't be serious. But she was. She stood up from the table, saying nothing else to neither Doreen, nor the businessmen, nor to Tom who had been standing by the door with his mouth agape. She turned and left the room and Doreen saw, for just a second as she turned away, a thin line of sweat along her brow.

The room was suddenly half its size and double its occupants. Doreen alone faced a team of businessmen who were already carrying the meeting right along. One of them cleared his throat and passed Doreen a sheet of paper.

'This will be for the land grant we were just discussing,' he said. 'You'll need to sign at the bottom.'

Another man was flipping rapidly through a slideshow presentation. Another was punching numbers into a computer program. Another was chewing gum and loudly proclaimed, seemingly unprompted, the word 'tungsten.'

Doreen looked to Tom but he could only shrug. He was looking nervously at the door, more occupied with following after his boss than staying here with her.

A pen was pressed into her hand. 'Just need your signature here and here.'

'Sorry, let me just get my head around this,' she said. She pushed the paper away. 'What's this you're having me sign?'

'Land grants.'

'Tungsten.'

'The exploratory committee will launch—'

'It's tungsten.'

'It's a shale survey before the drilling.'

'Doesn't get any better than this.'

Doreen leaned back in her chair away from them. Their nonsense jittering was the opposite of intimidation and the room didn't seem so claustrophobic any more. The men were almost shrinking, the more they clamored around her. They turned into termites, soothsaying, just needing a deeper scratch in the woodwork. Doreen marveled at how suddenly none of it mattered. She tested the waters.

'I won't sign it,' she said. 'No drilling.'

'This is for the land grant.'

'We shouldn't have said drilling. Drilling is digging and digging. This is pumping and sucking. It's fracking. It's cleaner.'

They pointed at a figure on a screen.

'Doesn't get any better.'

'No,' said Doreen again. As the men shrunk, she felt herself inflate. 'I'm sorry, but I won't sign it. This isn't the business Violet is interested in at the moment. You'll have to find backers elsewhere.'

She repeated herself upwards of fifty more times for the next three hours as the men threw more documents before her to consider. They took her noes but came back with more variations, more scenarios for her to consider. There was the risk that they might be able to go on like this forever. Tom left the room for a period of time to check on Violet and when he returned and they were all still going at it, he left again and brought back food and drinks. Now an altar for these men, Doreen realized that fracking was merely the physical manifestation they had chosen for their monster. This was about the exchanging of money and nothing else, like senselessness, like the circulation of blood, and as she rejected them, their advances transformed. It was no longer fracking now, no, not exactly, but a nature conservatory under which a natural gas study would be conducted – still a no, said Doreen. Then it was an off-shore wind farm, a solar cell factory, a 'clean' coal political pundit they could hawk – no, no, and no, said Doreen.

The men were flummoxed. 'We don't understand. It's as if you're severing your ties with us. We're hoping for a two-way exchange here. We're mutual beneficiaries.'

Emboldened, higher than she had ever been, Doreen said with as much finality as she could muster, 'That's exactly what I am not – what Violet is not. There will be no exchange, I'm afraid. For now, we'll be severing ties. There's nothing.'

And like a spell at midnight, the words made the men disappear. They vanished. Papers were folded. Briefcases were snapped shut. New phone calls with strangers were started to make up for lost time. They were gone. The room itself seemed to shudder with relief.

Tom was bemused and cautiously impressed. 'We'll have to see what Violet makes of this. I suppose it could have gone worse. There's technically no harm in coming out empty handed, but empty hands . . .' He pawed the air for words that would give some sense of finality, for an idiom or something, but gave up. Finally, silence overtook.

Violet was holed up in their new room at the Best Western like a wounded animal, hidden under frigid darkness. Doreen opened the door and yellow light cut a line across her body, tangled up among sheets and pillows. This was still Rome though, after all; still a nice, four star hotel – but with a quaint and familiar touch, like finding the Big Dipper in the sky. There was no need for anything else, no veneer. Reliability is what tourists wish for when they toss coins into a fountain, thought Doreen. You will return. Again and again. To any of our franchised establishments.

Doreen was decisively cheery. She switched on the too-bright lights and tossed a grocery bag on the bed. It was filled with chocolates and cheap sweets and a variety of potato chips and sodas. She sat next to the bundle of Violet and helped herself to an Italian brand of soda and puzzled over the label. Out of the corner of her eye, she saw one delicate eyeball watching her from under the covers.

'I've seen this kind of thing happen before,' said Violet, barely audible. 'After I tell people my story – about the gift I have – they eventually sober up and do these sort of ambivalent things to take back control.' She stuck her head out and gestured around the room. 'But I already told you, I'm in need of a recharge. I'm powerless right now. Your mind is your own. It's always been in the first place. It doesn't work how you think.' She sounded older, muttering almost, not exactly making sense. Doreen stuck a sour watermelon flavored marshmallow in her mouth to shut her up.

'Best Western isn't about control. I just like them,' said Doreen. 'They remind me of road trips.'

'And the candy?'

'Sure, yeah, the candy is about taking control. This is *my* meal that *I* have decided to eat. Finally I get to make the dinner decisions.' She leaned back against a pillow and laughed. 'I'm kidding, Vi.' She noticed her recoil at the name. 'I'm not worried about mind control, or whatever you're thinking I'm thinking. Of course, if you knew what I was thinking you wouldn't need me to tell you that. How come you don't like being called Vi?'

'It encourages inauthenticity. I need my environment to be as true and authentic as possible.'

'Well good thing we're at a Best Western. It's not trying to be anything but a Best Western. Everything is completely spelled out for you to read. Nothing hidden away.' Doreen felt her cheeks starting to flush. She was becoming impatient and her ability to tip-toe around the border of rudeness was becoming less and less. 'If everything is plainly spelled out for you and all you're doing is reading the truth, which is plain to see, is it still mind reading?' She unwrapped a chewy gob of chocolate. 'Why do you need authenticity? If something's inauthentic, isn't the whole point of a psychic to be able to see through all that? To see past the façade?'

Violet sat up and sighed. She slouched against the headboard and looked up at the ceiling. It was the worst posture Doreen had ever seen her in. 'This conversation won't go anywhere, I can see that,' she said. 'But what I can't see is what you're angry about.'

'What happened back there? Why did you leave me?'

'I told you, I need to recharge, I'm not myself. I forgot I had a meeting – *I forgot* – I've never forgotten anything before in my entire life, you have to believe me. I just need time. I need—'

'You deceived me!' Doreen couldn't hold it back any more. She knew it sounded irrational, but she found no other words to describe the feeling inside her. Violet looked hurt and taken aback. 'You deceived me in more ways than one and I went along with all of it. Do you remember what you told me? You told me there were things in this world I wouldn't believe existed and you could help me find them. You said that yourself. And I trusted you completely because that was all I had left, but now I've realized that you're just as calculating as the rest of the world. For a moment there, I thought I had broken free of that, or at least I gave it an honest try – sure I wound up having a breakdown, but at least I tried, I tried living free of calculation, free of agendas. Then I meet you, this woman who seems to have gamed the system, completely on her own terms, but no – that's not true at all. Psychic or not, you're actually operating completely in sync with the entire formula. You are the agenda! I thought we had found each other, Violet – no mind reading party tricks shit – I thought we had been brought together genuinely because we needed each other, because we both had no agenda. But now you're saying you looked me up in God's phonebook or answered the Batphone or whatever and picked me up like a labradoodle at a puppy mill. You're nothing but the agenda boiled down to a crisp. You can dress it up as much as you want, but it's just insider trading – that's what you do. There's nothing psychic about you, you're just a psycho.'

Doreen was on her feet now and shaking. She surprised herself with how much fury she had let boil over. She expected continued meekness from Violet, the wounded deer, and felt instant guilt. She breathed deeply and prepared herself to go right into a stumbling apology, but there was no more meekness. The room was suddenly sucked dry and void of comfort. Violet cracked her knuckles – another odd show of mortality – but when she got out of bed she looked suddenly more powerful and imposing than she had looked all week. She went to the mini fridge underneath a small TV and took out a can of Diet Coke, disregarding the snacks Doreen had brought. She cracked it open and drank most of it in one go – but not all of it. She threw the half-full can in the trash.

'Look, you want to know the truth, Doreen? It is insider trading, you're right. Actual insider trading? I've done that too. How do you think I've made my money? For me, things are spelled out – I am a psychic, I know you don't believe that, but I am, that's what I am. My intuition is able to have the complete, naked truth revealed to me and I act accordingly because what else am I supposed to do? Not be successful? My mode of operation isn't dishonest because it's laid out for me in plain sight. If you're driving a car and come to a stop sign, you stop. That's how it works. And I've learned that not acting in accordance with what I see is dangerous. With you, I told you – it was the strongest, furthest reaching insight I've ever felt, so I came and found you. It's an agenda, Doreen, sorry to break the news but all of human life is an agenda. Without an agenda a person would crumble to pieces. And as far as you feeling adrift and angry at the world, angry at the agenda, unsure of what to do, I'm right there with you. Really. Yes, my original intention was to find you, but why I even saw you in my mind in the first place I still have no idea. I'm just as lost as you. My business affairs, my meetings – those are null and void compared to what preoccupies my mind now.'

'I killed the deal,' said Doreen.

'Tom said you more than held your own.'

'I had no idea what they were talking about half the time and what I could figure out I didn't like the sound of so I didn't sign anything. I lost you a lot of money.'

'I have a lot more money I need you to lose for me.'

Doreen was the first to break. The smile was microscopic, but it was enough to set off a chain reaction across the rest of her face, infecting Violet as well. The two of them broke into a kind of laughter that punctuated the walls of each other's frustrations, like laughing upwards against a slope. Doreen flopped down onto the bed and Violet leaned back against the wall, slowly sliding down to the floor. They stared at each other in silence. Violet looked tired. She still possessed her alien beauty, but she was looser. Her hair had slightly more ruffle to it. Her skin was still porcelain, but dented slightly with stress and weariness. She looked like a wealthy vampire on vacation, which, to Doreen, felt more relatable than she had ever been before.

'I don't have any idea where to go from here,' said Doreen.

'Exactly.'

'Then what do we do?'

'We've got a statue to meet. And I've found just the spot for it.'

LAGOS

CHAPTER 21

It had been almost a whole year. Cara had been dating Solloway for almost a whole year now and she still struggled with what to call him. She was at odds with it. His first name was Dylan, and she had called him that at first – during their first date, actually (that odd first date where he had brought up his girlfriend, which should have been her cue to get up and leave) – until he mentioned that all his friends just called him Solloway.

'Are your friends a football team?' she had asked in response, coupling it with an eye roll. At this point she had been actively attempting to dismantle the date, but under the twisted mores of modern dating it had only come off as flirtation.

'No, they're mostly police officers,' Solloway had answered.

'Oh yeah. That's right.' She had forgotten. He was a police officer.

She was dating a police officer.

That was all she learned about him on that first day. About his cop life and about his girlfriend – how he was trying to track her down, like a psychopath, like the living embodiment of every unfair assumption she had ever had about police officers.

'Stop calling her my girlfriend, please,' he said now, one week away from their one year anniversary of dating, which wasn't a big deal to either of them, but here they were anyway, booking flights to Portugal, to a small town called

Lagos, in the Algarve region, on the southern coast. Solloway was adamant about it. 'It's got the best beaches. Locals love it. Cheap hotels.'

Cara was banking on it being a blowout. Here was a barely-a-step-above-casual couple planning an international trip to a place neither of them had ever heard of until now (though, Solloway seemed to have pulled it from somewhere, which was suspect), to celebrate only their one year together. Their one year of being a hardly-better-than-average couple that had come to fruition only after a series of escalating 'Sure, yeah I guess so' conversations and hookups.

'Is your girlfriend coming?' Cara had said.

'Please don't call her my girlfriend.'

Solloway said it in a panicked, blurt of a voice, as if she had caught him off guard, walking in on something in the corner of his mind. He added, 'But no, she's not coming,' and continued clicking through confirmation screens and seat selection charts. He bought the tickets quickly, as if he didn't want to leave opportunity for changing minds.

The girlfriend. It was a strange inside joke between them, but only sometimes and rarely funny. Most of the time it fluttered on strange wings into a realm of discomfort and jealousy – the sort of advanced emotions that weren't usually tampered with in a below-average relationship such as theirs. Maybe there was more to them as a couple than Cara knew of, or that she had invested in herself, which worried her. If there was more passion, if Cara was madly in love with him, sure maybe there would be cause for a flare up and absolutely no space for joking about Another Woman, but there wasn't, she was sure of it. They were nothing special. In fact, they spent most of their time together ensuring each other of how much they didn't care about being a couple. They had said 'I love you,' to each other a few times, sure, but usually by accident, in an appreciative, objective sense of the word, the way an electrician loves duct tape or a firefighter loves water, in a light, knowing tone that only ever required a kind of 'Then why don't you marry it?' joke in response.

But this joking about the girlfriend always seemed to make him uncomfortable.

They went to Lagos in the middle of the million-degree core of the summer. They traveled through a mind-bending procession of planes which acted as a sort of sieve to filter out the more basic American tourists going to London, the more basic European tourists going to Lisbon, down to jaded travel connoisseurs, weirdos with something to hide, and weirdos looking to find something – like Solloway – and Cara, tagging along.

Dylan? Solloway? Cara avoided saying his name entirely. They had adopted the generic terminology of 'Babe' and 'Baby' for one another and calling each other by any other name would feel like a foreign tongue or an epithet. Dylan would be an encroachment. Solloway would sound like football. Babe it was.

'Babe, can you tie my purse to your bag?' They were at an airport waiting for their millionth connection. Solloway the babe was twitching, fiddling with something that had fallen out of his wallet when he had pulled out his credit card to buy food. A pastel green little card fell out with nothing on it.

'What's that?' said Cara.

'Nothing. Piece of paper.'

'Can I put my gum in it?'

'No.'

'Why not? It's a piece of trash.'

'Because. You can put your gum in the trash.'

'Can you tie my purse to your bag?'

'No.'

'Why not?'

'Because you're just going to need it again when we get on the plane in a minute.'

'We've got a whole hour.'

'Fine. But go throw your gum away in the trash.'

This was every conversation they had ever had: coverups and uncoverings. Cara wasn't even chewing any gum. She got up and trudged over to the garbage bin and pretended to throw something away. Her flip-flops slapped the cold airport floor and she saw the rest of her life play out. She was going to be a baby. A babe. A beach vacation bikini-babe. Married, if she didn't do something soon, to a cop, and she'd have to post things on her social media pages about that kind of life. Police Appreciation Day. Blue Lives Matter. Kiss A Cop. Never Forget. The kind of mantras that were cosmetically harmless but seeped in a kind of warped web of double-thinking and not-thinking and, in essence, violence. Oppression. At one point on their vacation they would surely take a photo together on the beach with her gorgeous half-naked body wrapping around his gorgeous half-naked body and that would be it. Hot.

Solloway's gorgeous, objectively objectifiable body had been Cara's main stake in their relationship at the beginning and was increasingly her only stake now. She assumed it was the same for him. They would be like this for ten years, hopefully survive another ten years without divorce, and then another ten and another ten after that. She planned on dumbing herself down to not intimidate or shake up whatever cop-psyche disease he would surely develop or had developed already and not get herself killed. The ending she saw was laid out like baggage. Literally baggage, strewn about the terminal waiting area, and she realized it would be best to put a stop to it now.

She would break up with him. It was decided. They had talked about it before, actually, in a shockingly casual manner. They both knew it had been time, they had run each other's courses. Waiting any longer would cause a blowout. Lagos was going to be a blowout, she thought. But a good story. And if they had good beaches, she might as well wait until the end of the week.

There were planes, planes, and planes. Then there was a taxi and then a train still to come.

'Jesus Fucking Christ, Dylan. Why are we going here?' she said, halfway into their two-hour train ride, after a whole twenty-four hours of traveling. Her pores were oozing McDonald's and Diet Coke. Her hair was greased and matted like the tail on some breed of roadkill.

Solloway almost looked around for someone else. 'Who's Dylan?' his expression seemed to say. There was no one else on the train except for some desert rat tourists and a few locals with headphones blaring music too loud.

'Lagos, Nigeria makes more sense at this point,' said Cara.

A light in Solloway's face seemed to flicker. There was a track he knew he had to stay on, at least for now. 'C'mon babe, it's an adventure,' he said.

Cara cursed again. She swerved onto her own track of mind and let out a cartoonish whimper, the kind that she knew invalidated anything else she said, but signaled to Solloway, like a dog whistle, to put his arm around her and kiss her on the neck. She played a smile and cuddled into his bicep, which lay too heavy across her shoulders like a scarf of rocks. She caught a glimpse of herself in the window, in the setting sun, of her reflection. She vowed right then and there never to look like this again.

They made it to their hotel and Cara collapsed. She turned on the air conditioning and positioned a chair to where the cold air hit her exclusively and she fell asleep in it. When she woke up twenty minutes later, she slipped off her bra and unbuttoned her shorts and let the air hit her a while longer.

Solloway was outside on the balcony, standing with his back to her.

Soll as in Saul? Dylan? Babe? She hated every option and said no name instead. 'Can you close the door? You're letting out all the cold air.'

Without even turning around, Solloway reached behind and slid the glass door shut. His other hand was occupied. He was holding something. Cara leaned back in the chair to see. It was his wallet. He had something in his wallet.

With the door closed, the room became silent. Only the air conditioning hummed like a rectangular beehive, strung up in the corner of the room.

'This might be easier than I thought,' Cara said to herself. She watched Solloway through the glass. She could break up with him any time, she was ready. It would be a sprint through a couple of emotions and maybe some yelling, but she was ready. She knew he was ready too. He was so ready it seemed to Cara his mind was already somewhere else. She watched him consult with the something in his wallet and look up, off into the distance as if he was searching for something specific out in the scattered orange roofs, the line of ocean on the horizon. He took his phone out and thumbed through a few screens, looked up again. It seemed to Cara that even if she weren't here – even if they had broken up months ago – he would still be here in Lagos for some reason, that it was inevitable.

She got up and joined him out on the porch.

'What are you looking for?' Solloway jumped when she slid the door open. He stuffed his wallet in his pocket and turned around.

'There's a statue,' he said. He showed her the map on his phone. 'There's supposed to be some famous statue out somewhere beyond the town.'

If this were a relationship worth salvaging to Cara, she would have said something explosive now – blow things up to kill whatever weirdness was infecting her man and put it all back together again like normal. 'What do you mean a famous statue? Out here on the edge of the earth? What are you hiding? What was that in your wallet? Speak to me!' she would have yelled if she were committed to saving it – whatever it was that they had. Instead, she felt a pool open up between them. A hole in the ground where there used to be something normal – something normal like a beautiful couple in their prime taking a romantic beach vacation together on their anniversary. Instead of kicking and screaming, Cara said nothing. She wrapped her arms around Solloway from behind. She selfishly felt up his chest and tight stomach and turned him around to face her. In another reality they were a golden couple.

'What kind of statue is it?'

His face had slightly reddened with embarrassment. Cara tried her hardest to pull an expression that wasn't skeptical or ironic. She had a weeklong vacation to get through and she wanted to engage. She wanted to learn all she could in the twilight of their relationship and then be off. In one week she could talk about the 'blowout breakup on the vacation from hell' with her friends and hit all the right notes, but for now, she wanted to explore this new space they were in. Or, this space Solloway had always been in and she was only just now entering.

Solloway took out his wallet and carefully removed a folded piece of white paper, not the pale green one from before. He unfolded it and showed it to Cara. 'It looks like this,' he said. 'It's huge and bronze and was made by some British guy. It was bought by some rich woman and she put it out here somewhere.'

On the paper was a photo of the sculpture, all curving and imposing. Below it were a set of directions on how to find it. Cara read them out loud. They were specific to a point, then crude and bare-bones.

'...Then head south-east for fifteen paces. You'll see the sculpture over the hill in the next clearing.' That was it. Cara looked up from the paper and frowned. She thought for a moment and stopped herself a few times before she finally spoke again. 'Well then tomorrow, lets go find it.'

'Yes,' said Solloway, 'we will.' He leaned in and kissed Cara on the cheek. The peck was forceful, more like pushing her away with his lips than anything else. She took a step back and assessed him. Solloway could feel the energy of her trying to act involved, trying to connect. He squeezed his mouth into a smile for the first time all day and widened his eyes, stamping their plans with finality, leaving things there. They would find the statue tomorrow – the two of them together.

Solloway hadn't planned anything up to this point, content to glide along the waves of his obsession, too afraid to admit to the end goal, but drifting closer all the time. Everything he had done in the past year, whether consciously or not, had added up to him standing here in Portugal, on the hotel balcony, alone with his thoughts, his girlfriend hesitantly going back inside.

Like a dog chasing a car, he would never confess to the audacity of the act upfront. Like he had told Cara, he just really wanted to come to Portugal, to this obscure little beach town, you can read about it online, honest, it's not weird, it's a place people go. And this statue he had been researching – he was amazed at the red flags Cara was seemingly ignoring – there was nothing odd about it, nothing strange about wanting to find it. His vacation tendencies were austere – that was his quirk. He was more than just a heavy-handed cop. He liked art. Statues in the desert.

The truth was harder to handle. But he felt it coming – or better said, he felt the truth that had been there all long. He had studied the maps, memorized the address from the business card, learned about the statue, the nearby landmark. His handcuffs were in his backpack. He had thought about bringing his gun – even starting the paperwork for a license that might let him bring it along – but had relented to sanity in that regard, relented at the last minute, the last bit of relenting he ever did before throwing himself wholeheartedly, unstoppably into the truth.

CHAPTER 22

In the morning, Cara and Solloway ate breakfast, applied sunscreen, packed a backpack with food and water, and did nothing touristy from there. They kept their shoes and shirts on and all the tan lines Cara had hoped to get rid of were made even worse by the afternoon as they wandered the southern cliffs that hung high over the ocean. They scooted around narrow edges and climbed up makeshift staircases that had been carved into the rock face, all while crowds of tourists played and lounged on the beaches far below them. Cara's white shoes were stained red with dirt. Grains of sand mixed with sweat along her ankles, rubbing uncomfortably at her heels. She slipped a couple of times and tried to avoid looking down at the ocean waves crashing at the whittled and hollowed-out cliffs below. Solloway looked back every now and then, helping her when he could, but with a look of guilt on his face. She knew he hadn't expected her to tag along this far into his game and the reality of it was settling in.

'Are you all right?' he asked with more sensitivity than he had ever used in their entire worthless relationship. Cara said yes, yes, yes and waved him off, she could get up the rock on her own. Her arms wobbled and red dust swarmed up her nose, but she made it over the peak. Solloway would have smiled if he wasn't so unreachable.

Cara tried to get more out of him. 'What's so special about this statue? Where did you hear about it? I didn't know you were so into art.'

He said nothing, only turning away and continuing on the hike. She was growing frustrated and was having a harder time coming up with subtle ways to get him to tell her the real reason they were there.

Another hour passed and they reached a high plateau that looked out over the ocean, but there was nothing around, only the sun above them and a line of mansions in the distance, a man watering plants in his backyard watched them with his hand shielding the sun. Solloway spun around in frustration.

'I thought it would be here,' he said, wiping his sweaty face with his shirt. His confidence was nosediving. He looked like he could break down in tears. 'I'm sorry. I don't know what we're doing. This is so stupid.'

In what she knew was the worst twist of chemistry, Cara felt a rush of arousal. She sighed in frustration at herself and dipped into their 'Babe' and 'Baby' pool of vernacular – it was too sweet to resist. Any impending blowout threatened to teeter over the edge into the opposing realm of pure lust.

'It's OK, Babe. We'll find it.' She pressed her hand to his chest, feeling the sweat and muscle.

Solloway raised one eyebrow at her, but took the bait and let her kiss him. She kissed him again but he pulled away.

'What's your plan?' he asked. 'Why are you going along with this so easily? I know you think this is weird. You didn't come along because you thought it would be fun. We're not hikers.'

'I just want to be on the same page as you, Babe. You can trust me. I want to help you. I want to find this statue.'

'No, this is all wrong. Lets go to the beach, I can do this later. It's nothing.'

Cara touched his arm with her hand, but he pulled away again. She frowned. Blowout or not, she wanted to know what they were really here for. She reached out again, but this time he jerked away, twisting violently around.

'Stop!' he said.

It was right there, the blowout, so tantalizing and close. Cara saw the act play out in her mind as clear as day – the kind of fight a cop and his girlfriend have, the screaming, the tears, the last bit of sex, the parting of ways, going back to America as disillusioned separate entities. 'Babe.' It was so easy. The two of them, perched right on top of this rock. Give in and go, come on, Cara.

It took everything inside herself to reverse course. She shepherded her emotions into another place in her mind. She closed her eyes and pushed her mind to the very back of her skull and breathed. She needed to wait and for the first time she felt the stirring sensation that it wasn't for her sake. There was someone else. Somewhere.

'Solloway,' she said, opening her eyes. For the first time it didn't sound strange on her tongue. 'I want to help you find what you're looking for.'

For a minute, Solloway considered her tone. He searched her face with his eyes, but when he could have switched and let her in, he shut her out instead. His expression squirrelled itself away behind an expertly blank face.

'Don't call me that,' he said. 'We're going back and going to the beach.'

He readjusted his backpack and brushed past her, clipping her with his shoulder, nearly on purpose. Cara stumbled slightly and regained her footing, looking up to see him already begin to hike down. 'Wait,' she called out to him, but her voice rang hollow. She called out again but it seemed futile, calling after the figure she had seen inside him for a split second, the answer to why he was here, but it had gone away, hidden.

Cara caught up with him at the beach, where things went horrifically back to normal. Hike, what hike? Those two desperate, dusty people? That wasn't them. This Cara and Solloway staked out a swath of empty sand among the hordes of beachgoers and laid out towels. Cara stripped to her bikini and went in the water and washed off the red dirt and dust. When she came out, Solloway had turned into a sweetheart and had bought her an ice cream cone. She positioned herself at a perfect angle towards the sun and let it blast away her tan lines, and soon, it was as if their hike – their strange wanderings along unmarked trails – had never even happened.

It's a difficult swing to ride, this back-and-forth between what you think you should be, what you are, and where you fall in line as a consequence of being neither one nor the other of those things. It was right there – the need to end things. Resolve these mysteries of life and move on from each other. But there was also the ecstasy of reconciliation – 'No, not reconciliation,' thought Cara. Sweeping under the rug. Tricking the emotions. Waving a flag in front of a bull and convincing it to run the other way. This is a fuel to get you through your twenties, but Cara was turning thirty-two.

She asked Solloway, Babe, for her phone. 'I've got sand all over my hands,' she said. She poured water over them and patted them dry on her towel, then took the phone from him.

She opened her list of reminders for the day: pill time, SPF, pastel de nata, get water. She added a new one: breakup. She set the timer for seven o'clock that evening.

They fought again in the meantime. But this time about normal, petty things. The kind of things Cara would be able to joke about later with friends, things that made sense superficially. 'You broke up with him over ice cream?' they might ask, and she could say yeah, it was about ice cream but it wasn't really *about* ice cream, and she wouldn't be expected to delve any further into the multitudes their relationship contained.

Were there multitudes? In a relationship that she had thought was barely a step above casual?

Yes.

She had seen them up on the cliffs and back at the hotel, in the way he looked out over Lagos, searching. Maybe it wasn't anything to do with their relationship, but a depth had revealed itself to her and as for the time being, she felt connected to it as well, or at least she could wedge herself between Solloway and the thing and see the vague vision of it. This wasn't something she could convey to her friends over coffee and so she was sure to make ice cream the tangible blame.

'You don't have to snap at me like that over every little thing.'

'I wasn't snapping. I just asked why you got strawberry, that's all.'

'What's wrong with strawberry.'

'It's not my favorite, but that's – hey! look at me, don't turn away – that's not a big deal. It's still ice cream. Any ice cream is better than no ice cream.'

'Then why did you have to say anything in the first place?'

'Literally all I said was "Oh, you got strawberry."'

'You said it with a weird tone.'

'A weird tone?'

'Like you were mad. You scowled.'

'What do you want me to do about it then, Solloway? I'm sorry I gave off a bitchy vibe over ice cream. Did you want it? Why didn't you get yourself anything?'

'I didn't have any more coins and they didn't have any change for a twenty.'

'What happened to the coins?'

'What do you mean?'

'We had like, ten bucks in coins. There were at least five one-Euro coins and a few two-Euro coins. What happened to them, Solloway?'

'Will you stop calling me that? I don't know what happened to them, you were the one that put them in your bag.'

'And you were the one who took them out to go get ice cream for some reason.'

'I got ice cream for you because it's hot as hell outside and I just made you climb up a cliff for no reason. Jesus.'

'We needed those coins for the shuttle bus to get back to the hotel.'

'They'll take the twenty.'

'The ice cream stand didn't have change for a twenty and you think the shuttle bus will?'

'Fine then.' Solloway stood up, boiled over. He brushed sand off his bare back, which flew into Cara's face, forcing her to look away and grimace. He grabbed the backpack and unzipped it, then he held it in the air directly over her, turned it upside down, and emptied everything out onto her. The water bottle, the sunscreen, and an extra towel dropped on her head. She yelled and swung her arm at Solloway's leg but he jumped away. A woman lying only a few feet away from them sat up, mad at the sand that was kicking up. Other beachgoers pretended to be distracted by anything besides this very distracting scene.

Solloway stuffed the empty backpack with his shoes and shirt and zipped it up. He took out his wallet from the back pocket of his swim trunks and threw a wad of Euros in Cara's face.

'Take a taxi back. Take all the twenties you need.' He threw the backpack over his shoulders. 'I'll walk.'

Tears of embarrassment welled up behind Cara's eyes. She

thought she had been ready for a blowout at any moment, but suddenly not here, not now. Pressure pounded behind her ears and she felt a pain in the center of her forehead where the water bottle had hit her. The eyes of everyone around her were darting back and forth between her and Solloway, who was walking away, leaving the beach.

She wanted to chase after him, tackle him and demand to know what was going on, what kind of animal he was. Shake him by the shoulders until she was able to rattle awake whatever she had seen behind his eyes for that spare second on the cliffs, but he was gone. And there were practical matters now, physical things she had to react to instead – the sand in her eyes, the things he had thrown all over the place, the money, which was picking up in the breeze and twitching in the sand, threatening to blow away. She crawled all over her towel, gathering it all together. Her phone was jammed with sand. The Euros were wet from Solloway's sweat.

'I should have ended things right after that first date,' Cara thought, cursing out loud. She counted eighty Euros in total – more than enough for a taxi – but there was something else. She found another piece of paper among the bills. She flattened out the money and took out the piece of paper that didn't belong. It was the paper from the airport, smaller than cash and thicker, like cardstock. It was a greenish, sun-stained color, practically yellow. There was nothing printed on the card but the texture was off. She ran her thumb over it and held it up to the sun so she could just barely make out the two words that were stamped in the center.

Cara had never been abused. She had never hit anyone and no one had ever hit her. She didn't think that kind of thing would ever happen to her and she still wanted to tell herself that that wasn't what had just happened. She didn't want to *think* about that kind of thing. But what was that? What kind of man was that who would hold a backpack over her body and drop everything on top of her. The water bottle had hurt. The sunscreen would have hurt too if she hadn't held up her hands and blocked it. It wasn't the kind of breakup story she'd be able to tell her friends. It wasn't just about ice cream.

She stayed on the beach a long time. Over the hours, the cycle of beachgoers sitting near her filtered out until there was no one left who had witnessed their fight and she was able to regain a feeling of dignity. She was able to lie out again and look as if everything was in order and nothing had happened, but she could only trick herself for so long.

The sun began to set right in front of her and she felt she was looking at a perfect black circle. A hole in the universe that Solloway had opened up.

The breeze picked up and the beach emptied even more. She dug her feet into the sand and looked down at the cheap ankle bracelet she had bought with the coins – that was where all the coins had gone. She had bought a dumb fake-leather, beaded thing she was sure hadn't been made in Portugal. But she looked at it and smiled. She saw the potential for guilt – to trick herself into thinking she had brought this on herself, this was her fault, if she had just not bought this dumb thing they wouldn't have fought – but she steered clear of it. In fact, she took pride in it. She took off the anklet, not in shame, but in admiration of herself. She took it off and threw it far away into the sand and forgot about it. That was how much she valued Solloway.

She got up and waded into the ocean. She wanted to take everything with her – the towels, the money, her clothes, her phone – and watch them all sink to the bottom of the sea, but she thought better of it. Instead, she swam out as far as she could, far enough that someone watching from the shore would never see her, and let the plush, expanding might of the ocean move her up and down.

The water pressed every one of her limbs in accordance with its own will, making her acutely aware of her body – her bones and the muscles that were taped to them like notes in music, like fruits in trees; and the electricity soaring up and down her spine and her head, guiding everything into motion – and how easily the ocean could decide in one second and in one breath to pulverize her.

It took her nearly half an hour to swim back to shore. She was caught in the riptide and had to move slowly, timing the strength she exerted with the current. When she finally stumbled back on land, the beach was dark and empty. She was exhausted and tasted nothing but salt. She walked slowly back to her things and gathered them up without a care and left. The taxi ride back to the hotel only cost fifteen euros but she told the driver to keep the twenty. In fact, she gave him two more.

Back at the hotel, Solloway wasn't there.

Cara examined the green business card under the desk lamp, tilting it slowly back and forth. Small warbles of shadows traced the outline of the words that had been embossed into the paper and were nearly rubbed away. She took out a pen and transcribed what she was able to read: Violet Cascade, an address in Lagos and a phone number. Was this what Solloway had come here for? She shuddered at the thought of what he was doing now – he wasn't at the hotel and there was no sign that he had ever come back after the beach. She felt like she was on the cusp of discovery, but also real danger.

She went downstairs and used the computer in the lobby for hotel guests. She tried searching Violet Cascade and found nothing. The phone number was listed nowhere and, when she called it, it rang and went to an answering machine with no greeting message. She looked up the address – a house out in the middle of nowhere, only a couple miles away. She printed out a set of directions.

It was a last resort, she told herself. 'I should just get out of here.' She went back to the hotel room and paced around, debating what to do. She tried to remember Solloway's 'girl-friend'. There had been one from a long time ago – a Sophia that he had known from work. Then there was the witness. The girl who had seen a car crash or something and fled. She had an alliteration of a name, something like Duran Duran. Doris Day. She had turned into such a charade, not even real, just 'your girlfriend.' Cara had pestered him every time he brought her up. He rarely said her name, usually only calling her the witness or, when he was going along with Cara's pestering, the girlfriend.

Cara shook her head. Why had she done that? This was why their relationship was nothing. Anything human and discoverable had been paved over with these deflective jokes and spins. She couldn't even remember the girl's name. She had let Solloway get away with something and now he was so far gone with it he was gone. He wasn't coming back to the hotel. There would be no blowout breakup besides what had already happened at the beach. He had planned all of this for a year.

CHAPTER 23

Doreen Durand didn't drop off the face of the earth. She had to remind her parents of that every couple of weeks when she called them. She called from blocked numbers and never used the same calling card more than once, but she wasn't secretive in conversation. She was open about where she was and where she had been – Atlanta and Rome, then Lagos and Lisbon, Tokyo, Porto, Lima, Hamburg, and Paris, then Lagos again. Lagos was home base, she told them, but no, they couldn't come and visit because she had to fly to Dublin or Dubai or Shanghai next week, and no, she couldn't meet them there because she would be busy in meetings all day.

'All of that just for your internship?' her mother would say.

Yes, all of that.

Calling what she did an internship was a lighter way of putting things. It felt indefinite – something she could stretch and contort like a putty to fill any empty excuse. Saying 'my job' or 'work' felt permanent, like saying 'Yes, I am going to be doing this vague, wishy-washy business and bouncing around forever.' She wanted to maintain an illusion, at least for her parents, that she was still relatively a child who could back out of whatever she had gotten herself signed up for. But she wasn't a child any more and she had no intentions of backing out, and she hesitated to wonder if she even could.

She was waiting for Tom outside the airport in Faro, a speedy two hours away from Lagos. She stood out on the curb and watched sunlight lick around her nude patent leather heels. A breeze lifted the hem of her skirt into modest waves, but the fabric and construction of it were of such a refined craft that it fell perfectly back into place. A tiny dew of sweat had formed along her forehead but her hair was tied back into an elaborate bundle so there were no stray hairs at risk of getting stuck to her face. The temperature was ninety degrees, but the white silk jacket she wore had an inexplicable cooling effect. She looked down and marveled at it – the jacket, the subtle embroidery of it, and the life she had wandered into that afforded such an extravagant purchase – and when she looked up, Tom was there in a black Audi.

'How was it?' he asked as he drove them through winding hills along the coast. The roads were empty but even if they weren't, it would still feel like they had the whole world to themselves.

'Not bad.' Doreen sighed and patted at her forehead. She slouched back in her seat and let the tone of her voice switch from the elegant business-professional tone she had used for the past week to something more normal. 'It was very stuffy. Rich and pretty, but very stuffy, which is, I guess, the point. I can see why Violet did business with them. They offered this insane counter-offer to keep us on – it involved an aircraft carrier, if you can believe it – so that made my whole...' she paused to search for a word for what she did, '*performance* all the more difficult, but I think I got us out cleanly without much loss.'

'That's good,' said Tom. He was stoic. Even though there was no inherent risk that could affect his livelihood – he was guaranteed wealth beyond what was normal for a driver – there was still an air of tension surrounding the downsizing. Cutting back prompted a natural aversion in humans who have been conditioned to believe that more was more and less was less and growth and accumulation were actually not as good as extreme growth and extreme accumulation. But that was just what Doreen was doing: downsizing. Gathering all the bits of wealth Violet had scattered around the world, cutting them down, and weaving what little bits were left (those bits representing billions) into a sizeable nest that was clean and immovable. Soon there would be no more need for a full-time Tom.

The *performance* Doreen mentioned was exactly what it sounded like. As Violet's representative, she was tasked with putting on the last dog and pony show for whatever board of directors, investors, mob bosses, state department heads, and CEOs that were tied up in Violet's assets, securing a not-sizeable but at least modest exit deal and saying, 'We appreciate you for your business, but Ms. Cascade is just no longer interested in continuing the relationship any further. She's retiring.' Oftentimes this ended with one last, extravagant effort on the part of the organization to keep Violet's investment. In Morocco, from where Doreen had just returned, the head of a media conglomerate had bought (not rented) a fifteenth-century palace out in the middle of the desert, flooded it with several hundred-thousand gallons of spring water flown in from Colorado, and staged a ball complete with naval battle reenactments and mermaids. The water alone cost the GDP of a small country. There was enough caviar to feed a small army (and there was one – a small army for the naval battles). Doreen had been given one diamond for each of her fingers.

Her instinct early on, during her meetings with relatively smaller businesses (private universities, car manufacturers, social media companies), was to be blunt: 'Thanks but no thanks, bye, see ya.' But those interactions had been unsuccessful. She learned that there was an art to unpeeling yourself from an 'entity.'

'Think of an entity as a childhood memory,' Violet would say, coaching Doreen. 'Think of how hard it would be to expel a memory from your brain. Not cover it up or hide it away with therapy, but physically remove the memory from your brain tissue. That is how you need to go about these meetings. Just saying no means nothing to these people. There's a type of incantation that needs to be recited in order to undo what has been wound up.'

Doreen rolled her eyes at this. She considered her hatred of this kind of capitalist sex-fest a hallmark of her own moral code (never mind her stint at Mario's), and with every deal she closed she felt an accompanying sickness inside her. After all, this was what she had fought Violet on, claiming she was just as bad as the kind of economy she claimed to be superior to. They had never really reached a true compromise on that fight.

'You're just thinking about it wrong,' Violet would say. She would dive into metaphors and abstract ideas to justify the dealings. 'Think of a bee and how it enters a flower. Think of the dance it has to do. Think of how it gets to gobble down as much nectar as it can but in the end the flower still wins, the pollen gets spread. Think of that.'

The most important thing Violet had given Doreen was space. Doreen had a task at hand, yes, proper employment, but she suddenly had a sort of freedom that was inconceivable to most her age. The money at her disposal was limitless and Violet let her, almost encouraged her, to dispose of it at her discretion, almost as a way of exploration, of testing out her own relationship to money.

She paid off her student loans, she paid off her parents' mortgage, she bought houses and cars and sometimes forgot about them and left them empty for no reason. She sent money to old friends. She went to hospitals and paid off the medical expenses of strangers. She once gave a homeless man a briefcase filled with one-million dollars in cash, just to see what would happen. She gave one billion dollars to an underfunded school in America, just to see what would happen. She bought an entire skyscraper in New York City and tore it down. She paid her way into dinners with celebrities, politicians, religious leaders, and criminals and would just sit there, saying nothing to them. She bought a popular television station and turned it off. Just to see what would happen. But nothing ever did. The fact that in many of these instances she was playing with other people's livelihoods was not lost on her. She knew that she could very easily have been one of those low-level office workers falling casualty to her movement of funds. She felt it all. She experienced both a sanctimonious high from her uber-charity work and a nihilistic curmudgeonry when she did the exact opposite; both feelings battling for dominance, ending most often in a tie, cancelling each other out.

It was a currency of emptiness. And the more she used it, the more she began to believe that Violet had had it all wrong.

The house that Violet and Doreen lived in was at the end of a long stretch of gravel road a few miles away from the ocean but still close enough to have a view of the gradient of blue on the horizon. They were away from the tourist beaches, the Lagos old town, the highway, the cliffs, away from everything. The house had a difficult address to find, but if you managed to be in the general vicinity, you would see it right away. The house stood out from the surrounding green vegetation and red dirt like a garish white whale that had washed ashore. It was a modern, skeletal type of compound, with large sheets of glass taking up entire walls, so you could see in and then out the other side like a translucent fish. The inside was more of the same: glass, white walls, stone slabs, sleek furniture – but aged, as if the surface of everything had a coarse, grainy texture.

Tom helped Doreen out of the car, took her bags, and disappeared, as he did. Doreen took a deep breath of salt-water air and smiled, glad to be home. The deal with the moguls in Morocco had been the last big tango of Violet's business deals. There were a few other tasks to be handled, but they were minor and most could be done over the phone. Doreen now had a few days at home to rest and study the remainder of Violet's assets before setting out for somewhere else. She called this place home and still startled herself every time she did.

She went inside and to her bedroom, showered, and changed into more comfortable clothes. By the time she wandered out into the living room, the sun had fallen in the sky and bathed the whole house in a heavy purple blushing with orange. In the center of a white overstuffed couch, Violet was curled up, not asleep, but dazed enough to not register Doreen entering the room. She stirred slightly, trying to mask how much she really hadn't noticed her.

'Sorry. I didn't mean to startle you,' said Doreen. She flopped on the couch opposite her and put her bare legs up on the coffee table.

'How did it go?'

'Done and done,' said Doreen. 'The money will be wired over tonight, the bonds will be cashed out over the next year minus interest – and not too bad of a rate either – and the rest is in my suitcase in cash, which Tom can deposit tomorrow or you can keep here, your choice.'

'Either way. Doesn't matter,' said Violet. She waved her hand. Her voice was hollow and far off. She was staring out the large windows at the feather of ocean on the horizon. This was Violet's most common response when Doreen returned. Doreen told herself the dismissive tone was just a result of high emotions – losing and breaking off investments that had taken years of hard work and sacrifice to make had to be emotional for her – but it was steadily becoming more frustrating. She once questioned her on it, but she would never explain herself. Violet was becoming more and more silent, aloof, a cipher. Whether she was making any progress in her own wellbeing – in her special abilities, her psychic powers – it went unnoticed, and Doreen never asked.

'Then I'll just keep the cash here for now, if you're really OK with it,' said Doreen. 'It's a lot of money. I have to tell you how they tried to woo me back. They flooded this giant castle out in the middle of the desert and put together this whole flotilla parade thing.'

'I don't care,' said Violet. She fidgeted slightly, as if she had surprised herself with her abruptness. 'About the money, I don't care. You can keep it wherever you want.'

Doreen tried to measure her tone in response, but it was difficult. 'The thing is, I don't *want* to do anything with it. I'm doing all of this for you. It's your money we're tying up, so I'm doing what I think is best for you, or what I think you would want.'

'We can keep the cash here. That's fine, I don't care. The only other option I can think of is throwing it away.'

'If you don't care then why are you having me do this for you?' asked Doreen. 'Why not just leave everything as it is. Let the money depreciate and disappear in the ledgers. Your investments are practically anonymous anyway.' She tried to get Violet to look at her, to make eye contact. 'Isn't this what you wanted? Look how much we've gotten done. All your trusts are closed and emptied. Most of your accounts are squared away. All cash, no debt. Doesn't it feel good?'

She knew it didn't feel good or bad – Violet hadn't been feeling much of anything. She spent most of her time holed up in the house now, with never-ending unstructured days. She had accompanied Doreen on the first couple of business trips to show her the ropes, but had largely placed the task in her lap and trusted her – with an uncomfortably extreme degree of trust – that she could handle everything. She no longer asked Doreen about the specifics of the deals. Doreen often gave her a loose report like this one, out here in the living room, but it fell on deaf ears.

'Sorry,' said Violet. 'It does feel good. You're right. You're very perceptive.'

Doreen shrugged her off and stood up. 'I'm going into town for dinner,' she said. She stated this more as a fact. Months ago it would have taken the form of an invitation, or an insistence that Violet join her, but now it hung neutered in the air, unanswered. Both women faded away from each other into their separate corners of the house, into the separate silences that they each had sown.

CHAPTER 24

Tom drove Doreen into Lagos and dropped her off in the center of the old town. She liked to wander the streets in the evening, right as the tourists were descending on the town after their long days at the beach, plump, red, and tired. It was a way for her to check the pulse on the rest of the world – a world she was increasingly finding herself outside of. The narrow alleyways quickly filled with heat and loud voices that clamored for drinks, menus, English. She wandered through them, even though she already had her slew of favorite restaurants where she knew she could get a table right away. She wandered more to assess her reality, recalibrate. She walked slowly, much to the annoyance of people behind her, one foot in front of the other like a high-wire act, thinking, and listening to the voices all around her.

A British family argued outside a burger joint over where to go next. A gang of Spanish girls were manhandling a carousel of sunglasses, trying on different pairs and squeezing into the mirror. A pale husband and wife were lost, looking down at a map. They noticed Doreen walking by, walking aimlessly but at the same time looking like she knew where she was going.

'Excuse me?' The wife called over to Doreen when they made eye contact. 'Hi. Hello. English? Do you speak English? Can you help us?'

Doreen stopped reluctantly. 'Yeah,' she said.

The husband and wife were American in a shrill sense of the word. Overdressed and yet, underdressed at the same time. They wore hiking boots that were also sandals. Shorts that were also pants. Purses and backpacks that looked like camping bags. Doreen tried her hardest to avoid direct interaction with these types of tourists – she would rather just float amongst them – because they made her hate herself for how much she hated them. They were too earnest, too doe-eyed. They would get her going on a horrible unending cycle of cynicism.

'Do you have any idea where we can find the for-tay da ponta da bander-ah?' the man asked, leaving Doreen with two choices: say the actual name correctly – Forte da Ponta da Bandeira – with maybe an extra flourish in the accent. Or charge straight ahead into plain English.

'Oh, the fortress?' she said, opting for the latter. 'It's all pretty close. Just keep wandering down this way,' she pointed over her shoulder, 'and you'll end up on the main avenue, then you can follow that down to the point. You'll see the fortress when you're there. You can't miss it.'

The woman wasn't satisfied with this. 'How far away is it?' she asked.

Doreen laughed. 'Like, two minutes.'

'Less than a mile?' The woman was serious.

'Less than like, a football field. You can't get lost here, trust me, you'll see it.' She turned and started to walk, but the husband spoke again.

'Hey, where are you from? You from the States? We're from Washington.'

'Oh, that's cool,' said Doreen with disdain. She could have sworn she was already walking away but the couple appeared to be walking along with her. There were only two directions – forward or backward – in this alleyway that was beginning to narrow itself even more. The crush of people squeezed in on itself and the Americans were right up on her.

'Where are you from?'

'I'm from the States too.'

'Right, but where?'

'All of them.'

'What brings you here to Lagos?'

'Work.'

'Wow, what kind of work brings someone out here? It's pretty cool here isn't it? You seen the cliffs?'

Doreen blurted out another set of half-formed words to unchain herself from the couple. She tried to walk faster than them to get away, but in a strange sort of limbo, the three of them spun around each other to let the other pass and Doreen's shirt got caught in one of the woman's straps on her backpack. The woman spun back around and yanked Doreen forward at the same time.

'Hey!'

'Get off of me!'

The women spun around again. Doreen almost fell forward. She pulled her shirt free and in a startled, reactive maneuver, pushed the woman in the chest with enough force that she fell backwards. She landed on the ground on her backpack like a turtle and looked up at Doreen with a face of shock and disgust. The husband danced all over the place, scrambling to help his wife.

'What's your problem?' he said.

Doreen said she was sorry, but she was still stabilizing herself and just wanted to disappear. The crowd of passersby had all stopped around this scene. The cobblestones felt looser than normal. She backed away, but into the sunglass carousel, almost knocking it over.

'I didn't – I'm not—' she couldn't finish a sentence. A

sudden fear she hadn't felt in ages flashed over her. A sudden sickness.

She turned on her heel and ran, pushing her way through the crowd. She ran far enough away at first, then slowed to a fast walk. When she was away from the crowds, she stopped and leaned against a wall to catch her breath.

She shook her head and tried to laugh at herself, but she was scared.

The two tourists had brought something out in her. A kind of disdain that revealed what was still inside her – a kind of venom she thought she had expunged. She had put up a wall so quickly when they spoke to her – she didn't think she was still the kind of person who would do something like that. She pushed her hair back around her ears and tried to justify her haughty recoil from the husband and wife. They had been so in-her-face, earnest, and gleeful – but they were on vacation, of course they were those things. Doreen had put on a new face immediately, assuming herself to be on a higher level of living than them. She had crafted an air of inauthenticity and it had stung.

'But I wasn't being inauthentic,' Doreen thought. 'This is me now. I'm a serious businessperson and can't just walk around like this.' But that didn't feel true either. She felt another flash of disassociation, another sting. She wasn't that. But whatever she was, was extremely sensitive, down-right closed-off, at risk of shattering.

And still, there was something else.

Doreen's line of work, or rather, Violet's line of work that Doreen was inhabiting, had infected her with a kind of muteness. Not necessarily a numbness, but a sense of stoic observance. She couldn't point to exactly how it had happened, but she became fully aware of it during her first business trip on her own. She had flown to Virginia to meet with a defense contractor to pull out Violet's stake in a venture. Right away Doreen was inundated with a barrage of papers meant to intimidate and threaten with maximum financial fallout. There were thick stacks of memorandums of understanding. Safe harbor statements. Power of attorney. Projected dividends.

It made her head spin. She tried to remember the training Violet had given her. She tried to remember the way Violet seemed to float above a conversation, choosing to reply to questions with only a few keywords that always seemed to be enough. If Violet was ever given papers to sign, she didn't sign them, and, if she absolutely had to sign them, she did so with the most minimal, curving black line. Doreen crumbled under the pressure. With every minute she let slip by without control of the conversation, the cost of the negotiation trickled away by the millions.

She closed her eyes and left the room. She left Virginia completely. She left the country. She kept her eyes closed the entire sporadic flight to Israel and when she landed in Tel Aviv, she had Tom drive her straight to the offices of the arms dealers who had been in business with the defense contractor. She didn't have time to even change her clothes or sleep, but after only two full trading days, she returned to Virginia with the entire defense and aerospace industry landscape turned upside down, just as she knew Violet would have done. She handed the defense contractor a single piece of paper. There were a few words on it, but mostly numbers and a single black mark at the bottom. A thick inky slash of a signature that represented the closure of Violet's relationship with the company.

The man agreed to it. He had no other option. It was as if she had read his mind.

Doreen developed a new sort of sensitivity to others. She wasn't a psychic like Violet (though, her skepticism of what Violet actually was was still an ever-widening divide), but it was more like she could tap into the *world* of others. She flew to all these different countries, yes, but what was more important, she realized, was that every person she encountered inhabited their own individual world, and, if she placed her mind at the right frequency, she could enter inside it.

She couldn't always do it successfully – the mermaids and sailors at the Moroccan palace had been too distracting to get the exact outcome she had wanted – but when she did, she tapped into a vein she had never imagined for herself. The barons, the stars, the CEOs, the wunderkinds, the sheiks, the moguls, the frauds, the czars inhabited worlds of ecstasy at its most potent. They were unrelenting, beyond good and evil. Wealth and power were givens and thus, irrelevant, creating a space for something else

Doreen could never get over it. 'This is what Violet has been doing for so long? She's been inside this thing?'

She would try to remember Violet's reassurances that she was not, despite appearances, at all in that world, that she had risen above it. She only engaged with it because the course of psychic truth that she was tapped into ran through it. She wasn't a slimeball like the others, not at all. Sure.

'Doreen, the greatest disaster you can create for yourself is oversimplification,' Violet would tell her in a tone of voice that was almost a plea, becoming this beggar while Doreen would be raiding her closet, wearing her shoes because what need did she have for them? She never left the house any more. She had become a recluse.

'I'm becoming you and I'm realizing that what you are isn't right.'

That was Doreen's line. She practiced it in her head. She never said it to Violet, but she came close when they argued. She thought it to herself, loud and proud, keeping it front and center in her brain, dangling it in front of Violet, who, mysteriously enough, couldn't sense anything any more, couldn't read people, even blatant, obvious things. Something had turned off. She had become almost feeble.

Doreen calmed down and regained her breath. She took out her phone to check for any calls or messages from Violet, but there were none. She knew there would be at least one before she headed back home – this was how it worked now. For a woman who had once psychically picked up on someone living in Beaverton, Oregon from the other side of the world, Violet was obsessed with checking in on Doreen. She would call or text at least once daily to confirm her whereabouts even though she had access to Doreen's calendar of appointments and trips. It was hardly an annoyance – she never sent a flurry of messages demanding to know specifics, nor would she ever follow up Doreen's reply with another message – it was a simple call and response.

Doreen scrolled through the messages.

'Where are you?'

'Faro airport.'

'Where are you?'

'Couple miles outside Marrakesh.'

There was never anything more to them. It was like a daily itch Violet would get. She just needed to know, she didn't need to know anything else. And the fact that she didn't already know was the biggest sign that her powers, if she had ever had them at all, had faded.

One morning, after Doreen had returned from another trip, she confronted her about it. She asked her in a light, extremely sensitive manner, the way a family member would ask another about something delicate, a concern for their health. Violet didn't take it well and after a war of words, she had convinced Doreen that everything was fine, that things had just '...shifted,' she said. 'That's the only way I can explain it. Everything is there, but things have just shifted. My mind can still bound into the future and tap into the unknown, but what it finds is darkness, what it hits is a wall. I experience the sensation of knowing what's ahead of me still, but it's as if what's there has been inverted. I don't have the words for it. I know it's revelation, but it's unknowable. Like trying to see past yourself in a mirror.'

Doreen had left it at that. Discussing things any further only led to anger on her part. Here she was bending over backwards to tidy up all of Violet's assets, and for what? So she could hole up in Lagos and do nothing? She still had the sense, after all this time, that she was flirting with only an enormous charade.

'Trust me,' was all she would say. 'We're uncovering this together. There's a reason for all of this, I know it. I really do know it.'

On days where she was feeling particularly angry Doreen considered Violet the biggest fraud: a witch doctor who had pulled the wool over her eyes at best, a con artist handing over the deed to her wretched finances at worst. The connection between the two women – the two sisters, as they had both once felt they were – became filled with the static of unsaid words. There was a silence between them on most days, a silence that sometimes lasted weeks, months, even, with big, thundering clouds of doubt and regret stifling both of them. Doreen found herself in the same old position she had been in at Mario's: working her life away for a morally ambiguous monolith, fantasizing ways to escape and flee. The temptation

was there. She could slice off a cool one million for herself –
that was all she would need, she told herself – and run away.
She could go create a new life for herself somewhere else and
never have Violet in her thoughts again – in any sense.

CHAPTER 25

The last of the Moroccan accounts closed up exactly as they were supposed to, all while Doreen ate a dinner of grilled sea bass and potatoes. The notification appeared on her phone and with one push of a greasy finger, the biggest remaining chunk of Violet's wealth was solidified. Her assets were completely hers. A chunk of emulsified amber. Off the market. Sole proprietor. Cash only. It provoked a feeling in Doreen that was identical to the sensation of completeness that comes from finishing an addictive cell phone game – as sensational as it was, it was trivial.

'Well that's that,' she said aloud. The nearest waiter heard her and came over to her lonely table.

'Yeah, OK?' he said. His eyelashes were abundant and he gave her a questioning thumbs up.

She smiled and nodded her head until he smiled and went away. She finished her dinner and felt full, but having not yet received the usual call or text from Violet made the night seem unfinished. She ordered a baked cinnamon apple for dessert and a cup of coffee. She ate and drank slowly and tried to lean back in her chair in a relaxed, I'm-a-local manner, but she couldn't help but still feel unsettled. There was an extra sense of electricity in the air, caused by the embarrassing run-in with the American tourists and Violet's radio silence.

She finished and paid and texted Tom, telling him she'd walk home and wouldn't need to be picked up. She left the restaurant and wove her way out of the city. The sky was black above the yellow streetlights and the streets themselves were clearing out, making way for the booming bass lines of bars and clubs just beginning to fill up. Doreen took the quickest street out of the old town, passing neon green lights and girls in pastel pink dresses. The people in the streets were either one-hundred-percent ready to party or completely spent, late for bedtime, trudging back to their hotels.

Doreen passed through the walls surrounding the old town and entered the more suburban stretch of city. Here were the cheaper hotels and blocks of apartments and bulk grocery stores with imports from France and the UK. She walked along the main road, which connected onto another main road, in a never-ending chain that cut up into the hills, into wealthier neighborhoods.

The houses in these stretches were almost always dark. There was no pattern to the ones that were lit up. Their lights were scattered around like an old switchboard, while others sat vacant behind black hedges, hidden away. Doreen had a fantasy – a familiar one for her – of sneaking into one and squatting there for a few days. She would stop in front of the ones she liked best and imagine how she would do it. What she would do if an alarm went off. How she would break in. How she could be sure no one else would walk in while she slept in a stranger's bed. Even now, at the height of summer, there were empty houses. The neighborhoods she passed were silent, save for the occasional voice, in Portuguese or sometimes English, usually a parent scolding a child for tracking sand in the house, echoing for miles.

The houses became grander and then smaller and fewer and far between. The road grew wider and less defined and more strewn with gravel and sand. Wind from the sea picked up and found its place, pooling together the smells of sage and agave, wild leek and bougainvillea, trading with the occasional gust of diesel from a passing truck.

A mile before she reached the house, Doreen walked off the road onto a pathless stretch of tall grass and brush as if she were a coyote with its own side streets and waypoints. She walked for some time through dirt and dust until she came to a clearing. Brambles opened up and the terrain evened out to form a spacious, singular plateau. And in the center of this flat, empty space, was the statue. Its giant black head peered over at Doreen as she came up onto the plateau. If the homeowners in the nearest houses were ever home, they would certainly have vetoed Violet's decision to put it here, in the middle of nowhere. It was audacious, too modern, they would say, and sure, pretty, but belonged somewhere else – a tech campus or a hospital lobby or nowhere, really, as there were plenty of these out in the world.

The statue depicted the figure of a woman reclining on the ground, propped up on her elbows, or maybe her hands – it was hard to tell as her limbs merged one into the other. There were no hard angles, just sweeping, rounded curves that denoted a head, a torso, two legs that folded and connected into one foot. She looked like a woman pulling herself into two people, or one woman, folding herself into something less. If it were white and found on the beach, it could be mistaken for the bone of a blue whale, but it was black and bronze and up here in the middle of nowhere. There was a hole in the center of it – several holes, where the different body parts spread and bent, but one large, central hole – right beneath the woman's chest, formed by her looping, connected arms. The void was big enough for a person to stand inside and have the statue envelop them, which was what Doreen did now. She ducked under the statue's bent knees and climbed up through the empty ring, resting on the statue's arm like a tiny child, a human puppy.

She took out her phone. Still no message from Violet. One new message about the Moroccan accounts – just a final confirmation receipt. The dollar amount was listed. A nine-figure number had changed to only seven figures, which was fine. The fact that the assets were secured was what mattered most. Maybe Violet had received the notification as well, and, as this was the last of her major financial ties, she didn't have use for Doreen any more. It was a strange feeling of completeness. Like a coat of thick paint over a porous surface. This arbitrary task.

Doreen has forgotten about something.

Suddenly more worried than she had been all night, she drummed the statue and listened to the brassy echo ring inside. She got down from the inner circle and ran her hand over the gently curving surface, rubbing the spot where it had been split in half in order to be transported across the ocean and then welded back together. She walked all the way around, slowly, running her hand. Sand trickled off the bronze surface, barely making a sound.

A twig broke. There was a loud snap.

It came from below the plateau, from the embankment along the road. It wasn't a gentle sound, nothing the wind could have rustled up, it was an unnatural break, unpredictable and not a passing car. Doreen froze for a moment. Her shoulders tensed. Her eyes widened as she willed them to try to see better in the dark. A few minutes of silence passed and she stepped away from the statue. She crept slowly in the opposite direction of where the noise had come from and when she was far enough away, she cut around the hill and moved briskly through the tall grass, down the slope, out into the road. She looked back at the spot, but there was nothing in the embankment, nor in the road, nor was there anything up on the plateau, just the black head of the statue barely peeking into view as if it was saying hello, as if it was trying to tell Doreen something, as if she had forgotten something vital and it needed to tell her.

Back at the house, Violet was sitting in her usual spot on the couch, curled up in a robe and looking despondent, empty. She looked up at Doreen when she entered the house the way you looked up at telephone lines in a passing car. She asked her how was dinner and Doreen said she had the usual, fish and potatoes; it's swamped with tourists; it's hot outside; the usual.

'You didn't text,' said Doreen as an afterthought, although she couldn't say it in a way that was convincing enough to sound spontaneous. She blocked the sound of her voice with the closet door, which she opened to put away her shoes. 'I was surprised. You usually text.'

'There was someone here,' said Violet.

Doreen went quiet and stopped what she was doing. She closed the closet and turned around.

'Someone was here? At the house?'

'Yes.'

'Who?'

'A woman,' said Violet. 'About your age. She was a tourist, I think. A little sunburnt.'

'You *think* she was a tourist?' Another daily tell. The Violet she used to know never needed to say 'I think.'

'What did she want?' asked Doreen.

'Nothing, I think,' said Violet, drawing a scoff from Doreen again.

'Well did you say anything? You're telling me someone came to the house and you didn't know who they were? What, did she ring the doorbell and not say anything? Did you say anything?'

'I think she just had the wrong house. She rang the doorbell and when I opened it she seemed embarrassed, like she was second-guessing herself, so she apologized and left. I tried to talk to her, but I couldn't think of anything to say. I sort of froze and she walked away before I could say anything.'

Frustration showed on Doreen's face but changed to pity as Violet began to cry. She leaned forward in the couch and hid her face, weeping into her knees.

'Hey, come on,' said Doreen. 'It's all right.'

She went to Violet's side and wrapped her arms around her slender frame. The woman's spine shook and trembled and her hair, which she had grown longer over the course of the year, covered her in blonde, nearly white and gray lines. Doreen slowly brought her upright by the shoulders and leaned her back against the couch, letting her sink into the cushions, eyes closed. She moved hair out of her face and wiped away the woman's tears. Her face was marvelously pale. While Doreen had been permanently kissed by the Portuguese sun, Violet remained pale and blue like fine china, still seamless and without wrinkles like a doll, but ancient at the same time. She was beautiful, but in a fantastical sense, as if her beauty had been derived from the zodiac, commanded by the stars. But silent tears fell now and betrayed every single one of those enigmas, washing her self away.

Still frustrated and afraid of what she might say if she opened her mouth, Doreen got up and went to the kitchen. She made a cup of tea for Violet, slowly, and when she brought it to her, she had stopped crying and her eyes were open. Both of them stayed silent for a long time.

A parade of unsaid words stampeded through the room. A fight could have played out – one that had played out before – about Violet's complete zapping of power, how her abilities were gone, how a stranger had shown up at the house and had remained a stranger, how maybe this – all of this, the whole past year – had all been for naught. But they both remained silent. Doreen paced slowly around the room, anticipating confrontation, but knowing it would never come because what could it possibly amount to? What had been mystical and inexplicable had been just that – barren and empty, drifting away into the nothingness it had always been.

There were covers for these types of feelings – acceptable skins in which larger truths could dwell. Table manners. Doreen structured her distress with the tangible. 'The Moroccan accounts closed.'

Violet silently nodded her head.

'It must feel good to have everything all tidied up now. You should be proud.'

Violet let a chuckle escape. 'Proud of what? Of you?'

'No.' Doreen smiled. 'Proud of yourself, proud of all you accomplished. Or at least, proud of the sheer magnitude of it. You impacted a lot of people's lives, for better or for worse.'

Violet nodded her head again in recognition. 'Yes, you're right. I am proud. I've done a lot. Maybe for better. Maybe for worse.'

'Or for neither,' said Doreen. 'It doesn't have to be categorized. It can be just *for*. I think we've reached a point that's beyond category. So much of your life has been this push and pull between the authentic and the inauthentic, digging your way around the guards people put up – it's like you can finally breathe. We're at a point where everything is letting you go, where everything is . . .'

'Over.'

It was the clearest word Violet had spoken in months. The silence that followed was so wide and open they could almost hear the moon passing by overhead.

'Thank you, Doreen. For everything. It's a strange feeling. When I first met you, my mind was a swarm of commotion. I knew exactly what was going on everywhere – you, me, the world, where it all began, continued, ended, where things fit, how they worked, what they meant. And now, almost very suddenly, in this exact moment, I don't know a single, absolute thing. Doreen, I don't even know my own name.'

She said all this with a calm, wide smile. Her eyes were glazed with tears. She stared at Doreen through a haze of gratitude, and, almost as if to bookend these more abstract feelings with the more immediate finite, she blinked and stood up, then went and kissed Doreen on the forehead.

'Goodnight,' they said to each other.

Violet disappeared down a hallway into her bedroom, leaving Doreen standing inert in the living room, wondering if it was only her that had felt the sudden rush of wind and then nothing, as if when Violet had left, there was something else there in her place, an expanse.

CHAPTER 26

There was a void in the center of the room where Violet had turned on her heel and left for bed, and it grew to encompass Doreen inside it. Perhaps it was a trick of the lights – they had a tendency to flicker from white to yellow sometimes. In fact, the whole room looked dimmer, taking on a sort of mauve color, as if the moon outside was an alternate sun, filling the house with its not-light, casting shadows of ultraviolet.

It had been a long day.

Doreen closed her eyes and drifted to sleep on the couch.

She slept for only a few minutes and opened her eyes with the sheer shock of having sunk like a stone so quickly, so deeply asleep. She woke up exhausted, or at least she thought she had woken up, and the room was even more colored mauve, a deep mauve, almost completely purple. The whites and grays of the furniture and the walls were bathed in the purple light, mixing with it and becoming nearly pink, one solid mass like balloon animals. She pushed on the couch cushion as if it would pop or squeak, watching the light bounce off the leather. It flashed across her face. The light was in the air. The air was thick with it. There was a tightness in her throat. She struggled to breathe. The air was so thick it was chewable – the entire room a chewable, noxious, pink foam and tasting salty and wet and feverish.

Doreen woke up again and bolted upright, shaking her head viciously to make sure for good she was awake. She put her head in her hands and felt tears. Her entire face was wet.

She licked her lips and wiped her eyes and when she looked up, she saw a light outside in the yard.

She peered over the back of the couch, through the giant pane of glass, at a sharp yellow rectangle of light on the lawn.

She got up and pulled herself together. She blew her nose and drank a full glass of water in the kitchen, then she considered the backyard again. The rectangle of light was still there, but it was just that – a light coming from Violet's bedroom. Her bedroom had a glass sliding door that gave her direct access to the surrounding property, and curiously, the door was open. The yellow rectangle of light from the bedroom spilled out onto the grass. Curtains that had been drawn back rippled in the night breeze.

Puzzled, Doreen watched. There was no sign of a presence. She moved further along the living room window to get a better view into the open bedroom, but saw no trace of Violet inside. There was no movement, shadow, or noise that hinted of anyone in the room. She frowned. She left the living room and walked slowly down the long hallway to Violet's side of the house, lightly clearing her throat to announce her arrival.

'Violet?'

She knocked on the door with one knuckle.

There was no answer, only the draft of wind on the other side making a tapping and scuttling sound back to her. She opened the door wide and scanned the room.

There was no one there.

Violet's bed was still made, her things – her keys, her phone, her office equipment, her purse, her books – were all in their usual places, untouched. The silk robe she had been wearing was on the floor in the middle of the room, as if she had just stepped out of it – stepped out of it and walked outside? The sounds of the night overwhelmed the room:

crickets, flies, and the hum of the air conditioner. It was a warm night. Doreen checked the bathroom, the closet, under the bed, then, more urgently, the entire rest of the house. There was no sign of her.

Annoyed more than worried, she ran back to the bedroom and went outside through the open sliding door, barefoot onto brick, then grass. This lawn was Violet's greatest extravagance during these summer months, but even with all the water that was wasted on it, the grass never changed its rough, bristly texture, competing with weeds, and showed no sign of anyone's footprints. Doreen raised her arms in wonder and shook her head. She looked up at the sky and smirked, unsettled, as if the moon was someone she could share a knowing look with, as if it were an old friend, as if it were someone like—

'Whitney.' Doreen said the name out loud.

That was the name of her old roommate. That was who she could have shared a knowing look with. It had been so long. Huh. It felt strange rolling off her tongue, stirring her memories. It was like remembering a phone number from childhood. Whitney. A name that felt so far away. An old life suddenly remembered.

But there were others. Doreen couldn't stop her mind before it went to them as well.

'Leo and Harry.'

The names spilled out. She said them aloud with a grievous staccato, only aware of their incantation before it was too late, spitting them out. The muscle of her tongue broke down over the words. Fever spread throughout her body. She shook and fell to the ground – hands and knees hitting dry grass and she coughed up a kind of wail. A gasp at what she had done and what she hadn't – the action of her inaction. She shrieked.

The little boys smashed out of their bodies. Doreen saw it. Turtles ripped from their shells. Shells ground to dust. The car, a boulder. She trembled.

She pulled herself up from the ground and brushed off blades of grass, trying to keep herself together, trying not to stumble. She walked away from the lawn and walked all the way around the house, panicked.

'Violet!' she called out.

She walked faster, sniffing and wiping tears away. After a distance, the grass turned to gravel and dirt under her bare feet as she walked all the way down the long driveway onto the main road.

'Violet!'

She broke into a run. She cut across the road and went out into the open bush. Rocks and thistles pinched her bare feet. She yelled her name again but the night was impenetrable.

The statue. It was one of the last places Violet had gone, back when she used to leave the house, back when they first arrived, back before all these disenchantments and ruins. Meeting the statue – that had been the beginning of the end. It had been just the two of them, instead of what Doreen had expected would be a grand unveiling, a ribbon-cutting ceremony, champagne, it was just them. Just her and the baroness, the soothsayer, the mystic, the peddler.

Her instinct was to head to the statue. Out there on the nothingness plateau.

She ran until she got to the hill. Straggly bushes nicked her bare ankles. Her feet were so filled with slivers and brambles that they hurt and stung everywhere, cancelling each other out with a deafening pain. The ground evened out and on top of the plateau, the statue greeted Doreen again with its grape-shaped head, forever tilted at an angle that provoked only an inquisitive trance, no resolution. Below its head and shoulders and chest was the round void and in the void, framed by the void, one hundred feet away in the distance, was Violet, standing with her back to Doreen.

Doreen called her name again and stumbled out to her. She almost leapt through the hole in the statue as if that felt most logical, but ran around it instead, grazing her hip on the cold surface.

Violet was completely nude and wasn't standing still but was walking forward in a slow, steady line as if in a trance. Doreen slowed to a jog and stopped when she reached her, but Violet didn't stop, so she had to shuffle alongside with her. 'Violet please stop. What's going on, what are you doing?'

She had seen Violet naked before but there was something new and alien about how the night wrapped her body in a brilliant pale blue. Her skin was smooth and flawless, without a single unwarranted ripple or fold from her neck to the backs of her legs. Doreen had stopped thinking about the mystery of the woman's age until moments like this where her youthfulness took her aback with how much it seemed ancient, intangible, and otherworldly and—

'Violet stop!' Doreen grabbed hold of her by the arm and pulled, keeping her from walking any further, forcing her to stop. And she did. She turned around and looked at Doreen in the eyes.

'Please,' said Doreen, crying, pleading.

Violet's face had been blank and expressionless until now when she turned her mouth into a small smile. The corners of her mouth indented and turned upwards and seemed to smudge the rest of her face in a strange way. The usual perfection of her face had somehow shifted, like a charcoal drawing rubbed over by a careless hand. The sudden change startled Doreen enough that she lost her grip and Violet was able to break free. She shook her arm away and looked at Doreen one last time with that startled, blown-away expression, then turned and broke into a run.

'Wait!'

She ran straight ahead, continuing in the direct line she had been walking in, now running fast, gaining speed, unburdened by her surroundings.

Doreen called out again and again and ran after her – two women running out into the wild night. They tore through thickets and under low-hanging trees. Leaves and blades of grass cut into Doreen's arms and legs, stones pierced the soles of her feet. She sprinted. Violet was still ahead of her, just out of reach, like a slippery white seal, darting through the world. Doreen pushed hard, using everything she had left in her thighs to power her legs over and over and over the earth, ignoring the stabbing pain in her side and in her lungs, and then, when she was just a few feet behind her, she reached out her arm like a relay sprinter and reached and grabbed hold of her by the arm and the arm – and the arm – 'Oh my God!' Doreen screamed, horrified.

The arm came off.

Violet's arm became unhinged and broke off of her body. It didn't snap or break or tear. There was no cut and there was no blood and no bone or ripped skin. But her entire left arm came clean off, right at the shoulder, and stayed with Doreen. Without the arm, Violet stumbled slightly, then rebalanced and continued running on.

'No, no, no, no,' Doreen said over and over. She felt the arm in her hands. She felt sick. The skin was Violet's perfect, smooth skin, even at the top where it had been attached to her body. There was weight to it. The hand was attached, with Violet's perfect, almond-shaped fingernails, painted with a nude lacquer. Absurd as it was, Doreen's instinct was to hold onto the arm and she did, but the arm had other plans as it was moving – *the arm was still moving* – its muscles were flexing, bending back and forth at the elbow. It was moving around like a fish out of water, trying to free itself from Doreen's grasp. Its fingers splayed and opened its palm and pushed Doreen away by her head. She screamed and tried to hold onto it but it broke free. The arm soared through the air like the arm of a freestyle swimmer and when it landed on the ground it broke at the wrist. Now the hand separated from the arm – again, bloodless and without any sign of a cut or a rip. Then the hand opened and the fingers popped off, each one of them like little worms, which then split at each joint, multiplying, becoming smaller. The nails popped off. Everything divided itself in seconds. The larger parts of the arm – the forearm and the bicep – each broke off from each other as well, breaking down into smaller parts, which broke down into even smaller parts and in less than a minute, all the bits of Violet's arm were indecipherable from the pebbles and rocks on the ground.

Doreen felt a thundering beyond nausea inside her. She steadied herself but found the only way to keep from throwing up or passing out was to keep running, and so she ran. She ran right over the tiny bits of Violet's arm that were still splitting themselves into infinitely smaller pieces. She broke into another sprint, catching a second wind of energy, and caught back up with Violet. She didn't grab her again this time, but slowed her pace and stayed close behind her.

No sooner had she decided to do that than Violet's right arm broke off as well. Doreen shrieked again but didn't stop this time. She stayed on course, following Violet, and so did the arm. As soon as it hit the ground, it flopped and wiggled forward as if to chase after its owner but after only a few paces, it began to break down just like the left arm had. It split at the forearm and wrist, then at the fingers and joints, dividing itself and disappearing into the earth.

Violet kept trotting along, her pace much slower than before. She moved onward with the same military precision. Animalistic dedication to an invisible line in the sand. An armless creature. A body, no longer human, decommissioning itself. Doreen stayed running close behind and watching, feeling more helpless than she had ever been.

'Violet . . .' Doreen whispered it through breathless tears.

The left leg detached itself. It broke off slowly, like a road diverging, and Violet's pace slowed to a wobbling series of jumps. The freed leg hopped alongside her for a few minutes, then broke at the knee, then at the ankle. The foot broke apart at each toe. Big slabs of skin and muscle divided into smaller and smaller portions like soapsuds popping away into nothingness.

Doreen ran ahead now. She ran around in front of Violet to cut her off. Violet's face was wild with the determination to stay empty and vacant of expression and to keep moving. She strained and twisted to get away, but Doreen grabbed her, hugged her body to hers and they fell to the ground together. Violet withered and flopped around. Her other leg broke off and divided itself away. With just a torso and a head, she still wrenched back and forth and tried to wiggle away from Doreen.

'Please, Violet, please,' Doreen cried. She held onto her and buried her face against what remained of her body, crying and pleading for all of this to stop. Violet's face was emotionless still. Her eyes looked only ahead at something far away and her mouth was immobile. She was also bald, her hair having slowly broken off and blown away like loose straw. She was missing an ear.

After a struggle, what was left of Violet's body folded and split at the hip. The abdomen broke away, as did the chest, and then the shoulders. What Doreen had been holding onto crumbled apart and fell through her fingers. She gasped and cried aloud. It was impossible to contain anything as it broke down and disappeared into the earth. A round, expressionless bald head broke away and rolled along the ground on its own. Doreen crawled after it and grabbed it. She held it against her body, not bearing to look at it, but refusing to let it go. She wept into the top of Violet's bald head and held it as tight as she could. But she was powerless. She felt the round shape change as she clutched the head with her arms and legs wrapped around it. The head and everything in it began to break down and divide itself up. The other ear broke free and fell onto the ground. Two eyeballs dropped into Doreen's lap, then rolled away. Everything went away.

Without thinking, or perhaps, with only one thought, Doreen grabbed whatever last bit of Violet she could find to hold onto. She grabbed a rounded ball of flesh the size of a baseball and cupped it in her hands. When that too broke apart, she clenched a tiny ball of Violet the size of a marble between her fingers and before it could break down any further, before she could think of anything else, she popped it in her mouth. Without chewing or even feeling the fleshy sphere with her tongue, she swallowed it whole. It slipped down her throat like a small boiled egg.

CHAPTER 27

Doreen moved dirt around with her hands but there was no other material there – no other matter – besides dirt, sand and rock. If there was anything there, it was microscopic now and what could possibly be done with that.

She sat there for some time. She passed out and came to several times. Waves of shock came and went. She lay back on her elbows and let her legs rest, let her muscles flare and harden. Dirt and vegetation surrounded her, the smell of dry pine, and the rest of the landscape slowly revealing itself as the sky lightened. The sun didn't rise, but the sky – distorted by a gray, cataract lens – lightened. There was no more moon, no sun, no shadows, just an overall lightening. Whole hours could have passed by and Doreen would have had no way of telling.

She thought about Leo and Harry – nothing substantial or groundbreaking. There was no epiphany or momentous curtain of grief as had happened when she had said their magical names out loud. She simply ungated her mind and let them in. She watched them skip around and laugh and giggle. They raced around on their scooter, still without helmets, scaring one another. Leo stopped for a moment and took out his cell phone – he brandished it in front of his younger brother as a kind of triumph. Ha-ha-ha-ha, look what I have, he said. Harry shrieked and laughed, circling him. Leo dialed Doreen's phone number and this time, she answered. She said hello and he was stupefied with giggles.

He said hello back. He told her about the little bird outside her apartment. 'It's a big old pigeon,' he said. 'It's gonna have a baby inside the lamp and live there.' He warned her it was too late to shoo the bird away – she couldn't touch the nest or the eggs or else the bird would fly away and never come back for its baby. Doreen smiled and almost said, 'Well that's exactly what I want to happen,' but she resisted the dry sensibility and simply acted surprised at this wildlife lesson. She felt the boy's earnestness over the phone. She felt the ingenuity of the universe.

She watched the car come barreling around the blind corner and she watched Leo and Harry disappear, as if they were last minute passengers getting picked up. It ran into them, it ran through them, it ran over them – any way you put it, that was what happened. It was Harry that flew up into the sky like a ballet dancer. Leo dove into the earth like a deep sea explorer. She watched this happen over and over and every time it happened, she stayed on the phone with Leo, listening to the percussion.

There was the sound of gravel crunching and twigs snapping, coming from behind. They were the same clumsy rustling sounds Doreen had heard last night at the statue, when she thought she was being followed.

She stood up and there was silence. She looked all around. In the distance there were rocky hills and plains awash with dull green. There were a few houses lining a suburban boundary. And there, less than a hundred feet away, was Officer Solloway.

He stood there like a lost tourist in a dirty tank top and shorts and an anguished, bewildered glaze over his face.

Even without his police uniform, Doreen recognized him immediately and she knew exactly why he was there. She didn't bother to ask him what he was doing, or if he was out of his mind, or how he could have possibly found her, because she turned around immediately and ran.

Her legs had turned to jelly after chasing Violet, but this gave them an unexpected bouncing numbness as she ran. She was able to sprint without much effort, just let her joints flip back and forth and propel her legs forward. Her feet were bloodied and beyond feeling pain. Her hair was wild and long and just out of reach of Officer Solloway, who was faster, but less agile over the bushes and rocks.

Like tandem bicyclists, the two of them ran through the bush, back in the direction of Lagos. The massive barrier of ocean appeared – a blurred line on the horizon. Signs of life appeared. They crossed paved roads and cut through neighborhoods. Doreen sprinted and cut dramatically in different directions, she ran down a side road, cut through a backyard, but nothing was able to shake him. Her lungs burned and her vision became fuzzy. Her head pounded. She felt a lump in her throat and remembered Violet – how she had burst into a million pieces and how Doreen had taken one little bit of her and swallowed her whole – *what in the world* – and she felt a bizarre but stabilizing sense of peace that granted her one last push. Her legs kicked into high gear. She climbed a fence, ran, then climbed another, and crossed an empty lot, then another. She heard Solloway behind her, breathing heavily and further behind, and in front of her now, the roar of the ocean came splendidly into view.

She reached the edge of the earth and a barren maze of cliffs stretched out in front of her. Seagulls cawed in the air, but they were flying well below where she was standing – the sea was far, far below, a permanent white froth, crashing against the side of the cliffs.

She slid down an embankment and hiked halfway down

the length of a rock face, then ducked into a gully that wrapped around, facing the sea. She tiptoed along the side of this, then reached a ridge that jutted out over the water some hundred feet below. She steadied herself and mapped out her next move – she could climb down either side of the ridge and wind her way back to the shoreline, or try to climb back up to higher ground. She looked up to see if she had lost Solloway and she nearly had. He was far away from her – just beginning to climb down the cliffs, but choosing a more difficult way than she had gone. He hadn't seen the route she had taken and the one he was on wouldn't reach her. Rocks and pebbles skidded out from under his feet as he slid down the side, crossing a narrow gap, losing his footing at times. His face was flushed and determined, completely focused on the path in front of him and it wasn't clear he had any idea where he was going. His only intent seemed to be relentlessness.

His backpack got caught on a rock and he clumsily yanked it free. The rocks crashed to the sea and almost took him with them. He wobbled to one side and leaned into the rock face. He didn't know what he was doing.

Doreen climbed back up to the top of her ridge and put herself and the path she had taken in plain view of him.

'Hey!' she shouted up to him. 'Stop! You can't get down that way. You have to go up and around.' She pointed at the path he was on and how the cliff petered out into an eroded slope. There was nothing stable for him to hold onto. Doreen called out again, but he continued to ignore her, seemingly intent on on this one thing.

He skidded down a few more feet onto the lip of another ridge, which curved around and connected, just barely, to the ridge Doreen was on. But there was a gap that was too wide. The rocks were too loose.

'Stop! Go back the other way.' Doreen waved her arms

frantically. She was powerless to do anything but watch.

Solloway jumped and climbed over the connecting boulder with surprising speed and for a moment, Doreen thought he would make it, but then there was a loud crash. The ground slid out from under him. He dropped ten feet and crashed against the slope of the cliff. His legs flew up and over, flinging him down. His hands flailed about for anything but they were useless. His backpack dragged against the cliff wall, pinching together his shoulders and neck unnaturally. He went over another drop and fell ten more feet, head first, and crashed down onto the rocks right on the lip of the ocean.

Doreen held a hand over her mouth but didn't make a sound. Everything had happened in silence – the chase, the climb, the fall – only her unanswered calls to Solloway had interrupted this orchestra of sliding rock, whistling wind, and crashing waves. She peered over the edge at his body and where it lay. He had landed in a wedge between two boulders, surrounded by other jagged, black rocks. He was already soaking wet from the sea spray.

There was suddenly an array of chances before Doreen – as many and as far-flung as the gulls that called around her, interlacing each other's paths. Luck. Chance. Choice. She laid them out in her mind like cards. But whether she heeded one over the other or let each one pepper her movements with its influence was indeterminable as she made her way down the cliffs. She was slow and methodical with how she climbed and it wasn't clear she was doing this be safe or to give Solloway enough unattended time to die. She dug her bare toes into the earth and steeled her focus with an expression that was both hope and fear. She could throw a rock and crush his head and it would be just as believable an action as tending to his wounds. She shuddered to think of all the different things she could be.

She slid down the rest of the way and stumbled over to his immobile body, wedged between the rocks. The sea wasn't cold and wasn't warm – it was simply there, adding more weight to everything, even the air, which was thick with salt. Doreen wiped hair from her face and knelt down. She snaked one leg down and then the other, into the wedge next to Solloway. Everything was twisted – his neck and his torso especially. A few thin lines of blood trickled over his forehead and arm, mixing with water and washing away. His eyes were closed but his mouth was open. Somehow, despite his twisted body and his broken, crushed appendages, he was breathing. His chest rose and fell against his own twisted muscles.

Doreen said his name and there was no response. She crouched over him and pressed gently against his chest and his arm. She wrapped her hand around him and felt the weight of his head, trying to see if there was anything she could do to move him into a better position, but everything was firmly nestled against the rocks as if it were a stony bed fitted perfectly for him.

His backpack had broken free and was tangled in his legs. Doreen removed it carefully and opened it. There was nothing inside the main compartment. In the smaller compartment was a phone and a wallet with Solloway's police badge, and underneath that, a pair of handcuffs. Doreen looked up at him and shook her head.

There was a stir and Solloway moaned. He turned his arm an inch and opened his eyes.

'Relax,' said Doreen. She took out the phone and handcuffs and looked the officer in the eyes. 'Was it worth it?'

He gave no response, but he kept his eyes open, blinking and looking around. He coughed and winced in pain. Then he cleared his throat and said, 'I could ask the same of you.'

'Then ask me.'

He said nothing.

Doreen opened his phone and dialed 1-1-2 for the police. They took some convincing as her voice was monotone and nonplussed – steamrolled by the adrenaline that had passed. She named the closest beach. 'Yes, down by the rocks on the other side of the cliffs. He's bleeding badly. Right below the ridge. Yes, he's alive.' They gave her some instructions and told her how to check for ruptured arteries or a broken neck.

'No on the arteries but yes on the neck. Yes, as in I think it's broken. Yes, he's still alive.' It was like she was ordering a meal. She waited on the line with the operator until the coast guard was able to spot her. She waved her hands and guided them to the wedge in the rock. Two men in orange deployed a raft and motored it across the treacherous water. Doreen put away the phone and zipped up the bag. She sat down next to Solloway, who widened his eyes and tried to move again.

'Stop, don't move,' she said. 'Just give me your hand, can you do that?'

He looked at his arm as if it were a mile away and slowly tested its movement. It was clearly broken, but with a few agonizing movements, he was able to move his wrist slightly and open his hand to her.

Doreen took his bloodied hand in hers. Carefully, she opened the handcuffs and placed one cuff around Solloway's wrist, then the other around her own, then locked them tight, together.

'Go on then,' she said. 'Ask the same of me.'

But Solloway was unconscious.

DIAMOND LAKE

CHAPTER 28

The year that has been, up until now, tightly wound up inside itself, bursts forth in rivers of satin, embalming everything that has been, up until now, scurrying beneath its shadow in fear. People who have been, up until now, walking in and out of one another's lives, now walk through one another's lives – inhabiting them for a while, peering through as if spying through the windows of an empty new house, seeing the inside, seeing the other side, moving in, sharing space. Moving forward.

You feel, in the pit of your stomach, a pinprick of heat. You worry it might be an aneurism or some exotic breed of flu or terrible heartburn – anything grand enough to distract you from what unbelievable thing it might actually be.

You replay Violet's disassemblage over and over in your mind. You go back and reread it. Is that really what happened? you ask yourself. You count the minutes it took to happen, the number of pages, rehearing the plunking sound her body parts made as each one hit the ground. You think about metaphors and symbols which place it in a dimmer light, something easier, anything to lessen its shocking reality. You distract yourself with menial things for days and months to get away from that sound. You starve for what feels like an entire year, sitting nervously through meetings and interviews and phone calls and negotiations as the administrative mandates inseparable from traumatic events work themselves out.

But what about how her arm had come off? What about how you had picked it up and held it – felt the actual human flesh – and it had sprung awake as if it had a mind of its own?

You move around a lot. You go back home and you land, as they say, on your feet. Your parents are relieved. Your friends are in awe, incredulous. You flirt, for a few days, with waking up in your parents' house, suddenly younger, suddenly starting over – not a fairytale ending but a fairytale ended, over. You know you have to leave and so you do.

You take long flights and sit in economy class even though you have the money – you have lots of money now – to sit in first class. The people smooshed around you are nice, are rude and pushy, are completely silent, and they all emit a kind of buzz; a tiny copper wire from one head to the next, reconnecting you to them, keeping you safe, calibrated, back in the world. You take long flights across the world like this. The plane goes up and goes down. It curves around the top of the globe, short-cutting across Greenland and Canada as if the Atlantic Ocean is an open pit, something magnetic, even, with the same strength as whatever pulled Violet apart. You cling to the people surrounding you. Some you speak with, barely, but most you simply exist with.

You take your time.

You go to Oregon and go to Diamond Lake in the winter. You think of flying from San Francisco to Eugene and hopscotching from regional airport to regional airport until you wind up there, like playing Battleship, but you decide at the last minute to drive the whole way instead. You have to drive yourself as there's no more Tom. You like to think he's off enjoying his generous severance, or perhaps he's already in some luxurious new employment, but another part of you wonders if he was simply another appendage that broke off, broke down, and vanished. You rent a car on your own. You swing purposefully off course during the journey, into the majesty of the Cascades, up to Mount McLoughlin and then Crater Lake. Snow inflates their majesty even more. You take naps in your car and wake up to see your breath in the sunny frost. You drive through the night on meticulously icy roads. You stay inside for all-day snowstorms, sleeping in A-frame motels, eating thick-cut fries, sloppy burgers, and other mountain fodder. You keep your eyes trained on something always in the distance, letting the gradients of white to blue and brilliant green to brown keep you at ease as you become, on more than one occasion, helplessly lost.

When you find the town, you find an almost Scottish land-scape that has been spoiled by winter, engorged with freezing water. It is endlessly trees, snow, and muddy grass, blending seamlessly into the Diamond Lake itself. It shimmers with a cold sheen. There's an old mountain glaring charcoal in the distance.

You understand why this place appeals to someone who wants to hide from the world. Its forests shroud its people, who live quiet lives. They drive pickup trucks and four by fours but somehow seem to float along the roads, in almost complete silence, their comings and goings swallowed up by pine and snow. But on the day you arrive in town, one of the locals has chosen to walk, carrying a bag of groceries along the road. You nearly miss her, driving past her. You stop just up ahead. You roll down your window. Snowflakes saunter lazily into the car, melt on the dashboard.

Need a ride? you ask the woman. You speak in a reasonable way – not too sing-songy. You don't want to sound self-serving or pompous and maybe that's part of the reason why April turns you down.

Yes, that's her, it's April. You're certain now.

You've trusted your instincts up to this point – listened to the flow of things, or what have you – and let yourself be led to her. But she turns you down with a wave of her hand, hardly making a sound. You can lead a horse to water but you can't convince the water to force itself down her throat, or something like that, you think.

You're embarrassed. You think of leaving. This is silly. This is intrusive. But there is something new inside you, planted firmly, embedded, that tethers you to where you are. You know you don't want to run away any more.

You follow April for a few more days. She lives at an even rhythm, walking every day to a sleepy restaurant lodge for work, then back home to her modular, simple house. She talks to her neighbors every once in a while and has one close friend, a coworker. She grocery shops at a store in a strip mall at the far end of town and walks back home through the snow. She reminds you of yourself. You think about how everyone in the world does these basic tasks in some form or another, and you swell with a sense of fulfillment, of connection. You feel insulated and snug like the banks of snow that hug the trees. People need people – it's as clear and loud as the supermarket tabloids.

You think you're brave enough now.

April comes to your table to take your order. You feel a throbbing in the back of your throat and you're suddenly unprepared, completely out of words to say.

You order just a coffee and maybe it's the sound of your voice or the nervous look in your face but April recognizes you.

Have I seen you before? she asks. She doesn't really need to ask. Her face is suddenly zoomed too far out. She's blurry. She freezes. You wish she's only remembering the other day when you offered her a ride but you know she's remembering something further away. Something else. This is already not going how you wanted it to go.

What are you doing here? she demands. You followed me here? You can do nothing but stutter over your words. You have practiced what you want to say – you rehearsed it in the car, over and over, on the ride up here – but everything you say sounds esoteric, spacey, and untenable. April wants you out of her restaurant, how dare you show up at her work of all places. You say you're sorry.

Sorry? she says. Sorry for what? It's been years. I don't even remember your name any more.

A chill runs up your spine. You shudder as you suddenly realize just how much of a role you didn't play in the final narrative, how irrelevant you were in the end to these people. You've been scrubbed away from this thing that has become the centerpiece of your own life. And if not this, then what?

April shakes her head and walks away. You get up from your table and follow her. It feels futile and empty but you say more of your rehearsed words anyway – something about guilt and atonement, inaction and action, the disenchantment and thievery of life. You feel the words bounce off April's back and come right back to you in silence. You exhale. You turn to leave and you notice she's still standing there, still not facing you, but no longer walking away.

Come back at eight o'clock, she says.

The inside of your car is freezing. You drive aimlessly for a few hours and keep the heater off. It's a disservice – a cheat – to rehearse words now, so you turn the radio on loud. You go back to your motel and turn on the TV. You eat a pastry wrapped in plastic you bought from the gas station.

The restaurant is warm and lively now. Massive stacked logs form the walls and ceiling. Everything is wooden and sturdy, bathed in an orange light. Steam from warm meals forms a fog around every table, shrouding the booth you share with April in privacy. Everything feels suddenly much better than before. You're able to smile a greeting and April is able to smile in return.

You apologize for earlier.

No, no, I apologize, April insists. I guess I was shocked more than anything. It's funny, I still can't remember your name, and I can barely remember what you looked like, but somehow I knew who you were. It hit me hard.

She continues talking. Justice – or whatever they call it – was served pretty quickly, she says. They caught that reality star and threw her in jail and after about a year, everything was done. But I didn't want it to be done. Everyone had moved on and it made me angry. Then I remembered you – this key witness the policeman kept trying to find – and I found myself blaming you for everything, not that it made much sense in the bigger picture, but it was my way of holding on. The car hit them at seventy miles-an-hour – a five year-old can't live a second longer after something like that, but still, there you were. This mystery woman.

Her eyes flicker with the memory and she remembers one final question. She asks you how you knew her boys. Why were they calling you?

Her eyes close – a form of satisfaction – when you tell her you didn't know them. You don't know why they called you. You don't even know how they got hold of your number in the first place – kids will find a way to get their hands on anything, you say, and you were just the luck of the draw.

You apologize. You apologize for everything.

It doesn't feel the way you want it to feel. There's no massive upheaval, no catharsis. In fact, you feel, for a moment, further outside of yourself than you ever have felt in your life, and maybe that's the point. You see yourself objectively. Your burdens are not lifted off your shoulders, but pushed around, like a bulldozer moving dirt from one place to another, finding a better fit. April watches you struggle with this behind your eyes and she smiles. She reaches across the table and forgives you – it sounds as flippant and as much of a dearth as your apology and you both smile crooked smiles at this, but this is how it goes.

The two of you talk all night. You tell April about every interaction you had with the boys – every prank call, every sight of them through your window. You owe her these memories. You tell her about the haze of days you had that summer. The bird trying to build a nest. Your escape from reality and your stumble into a strange new world.

April nods along with everything, seeing herself in your story. She recognizes the same beats, the same rhythms that she herself went through, almost simultaneously, in her own story, which was resolved without you, just as yours was nearly resolved without her – which reminds her – sorry, after all this time talking to one another, after all this connection, you still haven't told her your name. She still can't remember it. So come on, tell me your name, stop shaking your head ...

And so you finally reply.

Violet Cascade.

www.sandstonepress.com

Subscribe to our weekly newsletter for events information,
author news, paperback and e-book deals, and the occasional
photo of authors' pets!
bit.ly/SandstonePress

 facebook.com/SandstonePress/

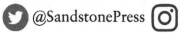 @SandstonePress